HAVE YOU SEEN HIM

HAVE YOU SEEN HIM

A NOVEL

KIMBERLY LEE

For Timothy, whose confidence in me surpassed my own.
You see me. I love you.

Sic Parvis Magna:
Thus great things from small things come.

BEFORE

Any dead bank employee could tell you this simple fact—bullet-proof glass only works if you're standing behind it. So if you were like Olivia, just promoted to loan officer with a lovely desk out on the floor, you were well on your way to essentially becoming a sitting duck.

Olivia's aunt brushed off her reservations as they sat in the orderly kitchen that night. Aunt Bernice was a no-nonsense woman; the shiny fixtures and appliances gleamed. "That's got to be one of the best opportunities you're gonna get without a college degree. Don't you dare tell me you're thinking about turning it down. You better accept that position like the smart girl I raised you to be."

"I know, Aunt Bernice," Olivia said, moving to the sink to rinse her teacup. "And you're right. I already accepted the spot." She wiped the sink with a yellow kitchen towel and folded it into a tight square, then placed it onto the counter.

"Well, good. You worked hard enough to get it." The dilemma resolved, Olivia's aunt returned her rhinestoned cat-eye glasses to her face, her attention back to her ledger.

Despite the increased paycheck and enviable benefits, Olivia's initial anxiety about her new position never waned. She'd watched too many movies and was highly suggestible, easily spooked by the images she'd seen. She was drawn to crime thrillers, often involving banks, a morbid pull she knew wasn't good for her. And the little measures she developed to soothe her fears—entering and exiting the establishment only in the company of other workers, fingering the panic button under her desk—didn't have much of an effect. She tried to be as thrilled as Aunt Bernice was about the new position, but she would have done better to follow the older woman's more relevant, oft-repeated advice: "Always follow your gut."

Olivia's final transaction was a simple one—to close the accounts of a nice-looking family who was moving out of state. They'd arrived at her desk with pointed looks, their identification documents at the ready, their slips filled out. She worked more efficiently than usual, wondering about their backstory. A $75,000 withdrawal—that was a lot to take in cash.

As she handled their transaction, Olivia snuck long glances at the family. The mother had a soft, understated beauty. Something about her was fragile, almost sickly. The teen daughter was pretty, yet solemn. But it was the father's face, the last one Olivia was to see in this life, that would have haunted her, had she lived.

The robbers approached her desk with small guns in their outstretched arms. Some patrons gasped and others screamed, clutching the nearest stranger. The mother and daughter froze, but the father simply looked at Olivia with bemused resignation, recognition that this was the end. As if he'd been expecting it.

The handsome man had taken a visible and audible deep breath, slowly closing his eyes, then opening them as a handgun was pushed into his neck. Olivia's ears registered the shots as if they'd taken place far away, on another planet, and she felt the muscles in her own neck clench while blood spurted out of the man. Frozen, she watched the client's body lean toward her and slump over, his eyes locked on a small, worn photo in his hand. The picture slipped onto Olivia's desk and she studied the boy's face, his gleaming eyes. But then the gun turned to Olivia, commanding her attention. The barrel's diameter was smaller than the ones she'd seen on TV. But just as effective.

PART I

25 YEARS LATER

ONE

David placed his stack of files on counsel table, then glanced around the small courtroom. He surveyed the sullen faces of the other workers, their mouths in straight lines, their dull eyes. The prevailing sentiment was obvious—none of them really wanted to be there. Not the bailiff, the court reporter, the probation officer, and certainly not the minors seated with their parents just outside the tiny room. Even Commissioner Wong was checking her watch, as if she had more pressing things to do. David shook his head slightly. Sometimes he felt this whole thing was a huge waste of time and money, a misuse of precious resources. Truth and justice were rarely excavated here; it was all performative. The general public, duped by its addiction to the ever-present legal fare on TV, was under the mistaken impression that courtrooms were dramatic, exciting places. Those employed in the field knew that on most days, a job at the dry cleaners—sending racks of clothes around a never-ending steel track—would be more thrilling.

David was once again covering for a sick office mate. This time it was Todd in Department 51, out with the flu. Calling in sick and taking the day off was a luxury reserved for either the truly afflicted or the dishonest. David was neither. His secretary had practically salivated when she saw how much sick time he'd accrued—and how much he'd get if he cashed it out.

The case he was subbing in for was uncomplicated. Todd had gone over it with him on the phone—a quick win on a technical issue. The minor had shoplifted a bottle of Jack Daniel's from the

Ralph's in Ladera Heights. Fortunately for the kid, the city fathers of Los Angeles and Inglewood had drawn the boundaries such that half the store was in Los Angeles proper; the other half was in Inglewood. The wine-and-spirits aisle was on the LA side, as was the door the kid had dashed out of. The case had been filed in Inglewood, so David would argue improper venue. The Inglewood court had no jurisdiction to hear a case about an alleged crime that had taken place in LA, so it was a sure dismissal. The prosecutor would promptly transfer and refile the matter in the proper court. But it would be a win for the public defenders' books, regardless. And the kid, clearly in need of some supervision, would eventually get just that.

The other items on David's calendar for the morning were non-descript, requiring little effort on his part. Kids on probation had to appear before the commissioner at regular intervals to show they'd performed community service, attended anti-bullying workshops, or otherwise followed through on some order given in lieu of more severe punishment. These matters were simple—the kids had either completed the prescribed tasks or not. If proof was shown, they'd get to go home; if not, off they'd go, into custody and on their way to boot camp in the mountains.

The courtroom's side door opened and David glanced over. A scrawny kid entered with the bailiff and took a seat. The boy sat at counsel table in a gray jumpsuit, looking around the courtroom with jerky, anxious movements. No lawyer joined him, making David wonder if the court would assign the matter to his office. He caught the eye of the probation officer, who just shrugged. Though he knew nothing about the child, David felt sympathy for the boy, a strange kinship.

He opened one of his files and dipped his head into a police report, then raised it when the boy at the table popped up, his chair falling backward to the ground. The bailiff leaped over his desk and went at the boy, who was brandishing a small weapon. A full-fledged struggle started; the kid was stronger than he looked.

"Call the other bailiffs!" Commissioner Wong yelled, then retreated to her chambers.

The probation officer and court reporter both cocked their heads, then looked at each other for a beat. *She's just going to leave us here?* Both stood and hightailed it to the far side of the courtroom. David backed away from the altercation as well, his eyes bouncing from side to side. The women looked at him expectantly. David knew what the look meant. As the only other man in the room, he was supposed to do something. But he'd never been a fighter; he wasn't the type to jump into the middle of a brawl. What could he do? He turned, grabbed the nearest chair, and threw it in the direction of the ruckus, which had become a living, breathing, two-person creature, with twists and turns and rotations as each party alternately got the upper hand, then lost it. The chair landed squarely on the bailiff's back. As the bailiff faltered under David's "contribution," two other deputy sheriffs rushed into the courtroom. They took the boy down swiftly, smashing his face into the courtroom's dingy carpet. One of the deputies wrestled the weapon from the boy's grip—a toothbrush that had been whittled and burned into a shank. The bailiff stumbled to his feet as the boy was dragged from the courtroom. He started to follow the motley group through the side door but glanced back at David, his eyes narrowed, before continuing on.

David's gaze dropped to the floor and he started to back out of the courtroom. The court reporter and probation officer stared at him, their eyes wide, scathing. David turned and scurried away, both his files and his ego abandoned at counsel table.

———

Home, much earlier than usual. The courtroom had gone into recess for the rest of the day while the Sheriff's Department regrouped, figured out what had gone wrong. David looked around his apartment for a chore, a task, something to keep himself from thinking about facing his coworkers the next day. It was a tall order; he was a minimalist, freakishly neat. Everything was "in its place." Sifting through junk mail was the thing he resented the most, so David forced himself to do it as penance for his milquetoast behavior in court.

Even though he knew recycling was the right thing to do—for the melting polar ice caps, the coral reef, all that—he hated the monotony of sorting through everything. He suppressed the urge to chuck it all into the same bin. Trash, like pretty much everything else these days, was unnecessarily complicated. Who knew for sure if the carefully categorized items ever even made it to the place where things could be salvaged and revived and turned into handbags made of candy wrappers, seatbelts, and pull tabs? A documentary he'd watched had uncovered the fact that in at least one town, and probably many others, every single throwaway went to the landfill, whether it was put in the blue, black, or green bin.

But he felt guilty when he didn't do it, and he had enough things to feel guilty about. The incident at work, his useless behavior. Not picking Gayle up from the airport. He'd wanted to see her, especially after the upsetting day. On the brief phone call before her flight took off, he'd promised to meet her at LAX. But he knew he'd conjure up a reason not to be there. Airports were overripe with too much—too many people, too much movement, too many unknowns.

He rifled through the papers and envelopes. Deals on mattresses, La-Z-Boy recliners, chimney cleaning, and toward the bottom of one of the leaflets, the words "¿Me Has Visto?" He had taken Spanish from the voluptuous Mrs. Boyette in tenth grade, so the translation was easy. "Have You Seen Me?"

The pictures accompanying the plea were obscured by something from the Red Cross. He crushed all of the pages into a pointy, misshapen ball, then felt shame for not even glancing at the photo of the poor lost child. He opened the bundle back up, laid the paper on the table, and smoothed the crinkled paper with his hands.

David focused in on the ad and saw his own face gazing back at him. He shook his head as if to shake the foolishness out.

"What the . . . ?" His eyes locked on the image. "This. Can't be real." He leaned further in and squinted. The technology had somehow managed to match his skin's exact shade of brown. Although the nose in the picture was a bit too narrow, it was close enough. David had a full, close-cropped beard; the man in the picture barely had a mustache. Regardless, it was him in the "computer-generated image of subject at thirty-six years old," as stated by the printed words below the man's—well, his—picture.

What the hell?

The photo on the left was a picture he'd never actually seen, but it was how he remembered himself at eleven years old, refusing to smile for the goofy school photographer. "Wha's happ'nin," the photographer had said as David approached the stool, centered in front of a faded blue background. David frowned. The only people who spoke like that were characters on the old reruns his parents watched. But the photographer had kind eyes. After the photo, David smiled and held out his hand as he exited the band room–turned–photo studio. "Gimme five," he offered, the way he'd seen it done on TV. It made the man's day; he'd slapped David's hand with enthusiasm. David was glad he had done it, this grand gesture. The photographer was married to Mrs. Dalton, the hard-faced third grade teacher. He deserved a break.

But David was at a new school, living with his new family, by the time the batch of photos was developed and sent home in cellophane envelopes with his classmates. He'd never seen the pictures.

Until now. He looked at the childhood photo more closely and noticed something. The name printed under his pictures, his images, was not his own. It was "Leonard." Where had that come from? What was that about? His felt his stomach turn, a symbolic protest. It was too much to digest.

Forgetting he'd failed to pick Gayle up from the airport, David grabbed the phone and tapped her name. When she didn't pick up, he remembered this neglect and blamed the geniuses in Silicon Valley for alerting her that it was him. He hung up and tried again, hoping the second call would convey some urgency. It did, and she picked up but didn't speak.

"I'm . . . missing." He choked out the words.

Gayle was calm. He could hear her inhale deeply and then slowly exhale. "I know. I don't even want to hear whatever lame excuse you have right now, I had a car bring me home, I'm gonna take a shower and go to bed, I'll talk to you tomorrow." Her words were a continuous string of thoughts, as if David wasn't worth the effort it took to make separate sentences.

"No, I mean, I'm a missing person. I—" David looked around the room, eyes wary, as if someone might hear this and cart him away.

"Wow." She paused for a beat. "Creative." Another beat. "So that's how you've decided to play this? What is that, a metaphor?" Great, David thought. Gayle resorted to sarcasm when she was agitated. He'd started the conversation knowing it'd be an uphill battle; he now realized that was an understatement. He was climbing Mount Everest.

"Gayle, please, if you would just listen, somebody's looking for me. I'm on a missing-child ad. They have a picture of me when I was eleven, you know, when my parents and my sister left. Somebody's been looking for me. They have my picture here, what I look like now, but it's not my name." It was all coming off like gibberish, but David didn't care. He had to get it out in one big heap.

"What, are you on a milk carton or something? Like they used to do when we were kids? I thought . . . ? Well, who would be—"

"Look, I have to show you this. You have to see it. Can you meet me at Lola's? Apple crisp with a scoop of vanilla—your favorite. My treat." Talk of dessert seemed surreal under these circumstances.

"Well, what did Hersh have to say about it? You called him?" It was a logical question, and also Gayle's way of delaying an agreement to meet. She was still pissed about the airport.

"Yeah, well . . . I mean, no, I'll talk to him later. I just, I need . . . you. Please. Please."

She agreed to meet him. Some things became truth only after he talked to Gayle. Until then, they were just distant clouds that could easily change shape.

TWO

Gayle picked up her spoon as the waiter set the dessert in front of her. She was hungry, and David was late ninety percent of the time, so she'd ordered within minutes of being seated. She'd foregone the apple crisp he'd suggested, opting instead for Lola's superb crème brûlée.

Gayle tapped the firm sugar shell with the side of her spoon. The spoon obliterated the crust and penetrated the pudding below, hitting the bottom of the white ramekin and causing a loud ting. Gayle looked around, embarrassed, but no one even blinked an eye in her direction. Were the patrons zombies? For fun, she tapped the dish a few more times to see if she could get someone to look her way. An older man at a table across the way glanced over and smiled. *Finally.* Gayle grinned, then dipped her chin and lifted her right hand. *Guilty*, she mouthed. The man smiled again, one eyebrow raised, an invitation. Gayle's eyes widened and she dropped her head back toward her dessert, took a big bite. *Does he think I'm flirting with him?* Probably not. His eyes were kind; he was just being friendly. But then, all people looked benign, almost vulnerable, when they were eating. Watching someone chew food stripped them down to their humanity.

Where was David? The muscles in her neck tightened. She tried to focus on something else—the crème brûlée, tomorrow's lesson plan—but these things only caused her to get more wound up. An old boyfriend had once pronounced she spent too much energy fighting against her feelings, a fight that only made things worse.

"Stop feeling bad about your bad feelings. Accept them. Feel them all the way through. Simply let things be." Gayle had dismissed this psychobabble; she wasn't going to be analyzed by someone whose expertise was based on a long-standing subscription to *Psychology Today*.

"Anything else, miss?" The waiter, smelling faintly of weed, picked up her empty dish, Gayle's check at the ready.

"Well, I'm still waiting for someone. Um—"

"Alright." The waiter looked off into the distance at nothing, then turned back to Gayle. "Did you want to get anything else?"

Gayle worked to come up with something. "An apple martini?" she said, her eyes wide, a plea for both permission and approval. The waiter didn't soften as she had anticipated. Instead, he sucked the meat on the inside of the left part of his face and simultaneously rolled his eyes. Probably anxious to get home and light up, Gayle thought.

"Coming up."

Gayle couldn't pretend anymore. David had stood her up twice in the measly three hours since she'd arrived back in LA. With no call, no text, no message of any kind. He'd essentially begged her to come, and now this disappearing act. She should pay her check and go. *Apple crisp and vanilla, my ass.* His call had been strange and nonsensical; his dramatics and dysfunctions were beyond exhausting. *Shit, I get enough of that on my job.*

But thinking about her classroom of unruly fifth graders reminded Gayle of how sweet David could be. He took off work whenever she took the kids on a field trip and helped keep the rowdier boys in check. He stood in the back of her classroom at every back-to-school night, giving her a soft smile as she explained the curriculum to scrutinizing parents, their arms locked and folded. He was always game for her silly ideas, once dressing up as a bottle of mustard to complement her hot dog costume for the school's Halloween parade.

Gayle shook her head back and forth, then raised a finger to catch the attention of the sleepy-eyed waiter. "Could I see the menu? I, um . . . I'm gonna order dinner, after all."

THREE

The door was almost closed when David realized he hadn't turned off his computer. He had a bad habit of leaving the bulky components of his ancient setup on when he left, so he could easily jump on without the two-minute boot-up when he returned. He hated waiting for the internet to connect and for the clunky computer to warm up, painstakingly watching each icon appear. But he'd read about the dangers of hacking, and only fools dismissed these types of warnings. Cookies were blocked on his web browser and all available privacy settings were enabled; the opportunities for some nut to track him were pretty much nonexistent. Still, there was no reason to take chances. He trudged back in.

He looked at the missing-person ad in his hand, now limp from perspiration. He'd torn it from the larger page, disregarding the tiny pair of printed scissors and the dotted line that ran directly above the head shots of his eleven-year-old and grown selves. Were there people who actually cut these things out of the coupon mailer when it came twice a week? Or was this simply a courtesy for those like himself who happened to see an age-progressed version of themselves and needed the encouragement to cut, not tear, before going in search of the truth of their lives?

In his haste, he had ripped the ad, and as a result there was now a rupture that invaded the computer-generated picture of his thirty-six-year-old self. It started at the top of the mottled blue-gray background, passed through his hair, and ended just above his eyebrows, like he was being struck by lightning.

Drawn once again to the pictures, he read the caption for the umpteenth time:

Name: Leonard Goodwin From: Chicago, IL
DOB:9/21/82 Sex: Male Hair: Black Eyes: Brown
Height: 5 ft. (at age 11) Weight: 92 lbs. (at age 11)

He was again jolted by the name "Leonard" assigned to his picture. His eyes kept wandering back to it as he scanned the facts. The Goodwin part was accurate—he had been a Goodwin, his biological mother and father were Goodwins. He had been David Goodwin up until shortly before his twelfth birthday. But the Goodwins—as he now referred to them—had left him to languish in the child services system for weeks, shuffling from place to place with a dirty blue duffle bag. When Hersh and Regina Byrdsong had gotten clearance to adopt him, he'd accepted their offer to change his last name to theirs, hoping that stripping himself of the Goodwin name would also strip away the pain.

It hadn't worked. The traumatic ordeal was a recurring plague, descending into his thoughts at regular intervals, like the locusts, frogs, and whatnot in the stories of old.

Were the Goodwins looking for him? Had they placed this ad? And if not them, who? Why would they or anyone else be calling him "Leonard"?

David continued to scour the clipping, searching for answers, rhyme, reason, something. Anything. He looked below the profile and read through the organization's info:

National Center for Missing & Exploited Children
Toll-Free Hotline: 1-800-THE-LOST
24 hours a day missingkids.com

David knew he'd be late to Lola's and Gayle would be upset, but he couldn't help himself. He typed the web address, and an official home page appeared with the typical list of categories across the top—About Us, Contact Us, Find a Location. Most prominent in the body of the page was a red button with the command "Report a Sighting." He clicked on it and a pop-up box appeared, repeating the organization's phone number. Not ready to set the whole thing in motion, he quickly closed the box.

The home page also offered the option to do a Quick Search, a glib phrase under the circumstances. This wasn't like checking to see if Lands' End had the latest insulated jacket in your preferred size and color. At least they hadn't spelled it QuikSearch or called it iSearch, David thought, as some sites did to look trendy.

He sat for a few minutes, pressing his palm to his forehead. He realized he was holding his breath and felt ashamed. "You're either a man of action or a man in traction," Hersh always said. It wasn't a quote you'd ever see on a refrigerator magnet, but there was something to it. Mulling this over wouldn't change the situation.

He typed "Leonard Goodwin" and the page changed to one with his image. Clicking the picture caused it to enlarge to dimensions that were close to the actual size of his face, making him feel like he was looking at a mirror instead of a computer screen. He scrolled down and saw the requisite height and weight information, but with one addition—a very matter-of-fact sentence about what had happened to him, the last time he had been seen.

> **Leonard Goodwin disappeared from Chicago's O'Hare Airport while on vacation with his family.**

The inaccuracy of the statement made David shake his head. The part about O'Hare was true, but he wasn't the one who'd disappeared.

He turned his attention back to the picture. Looking at it up close was eerie. It was a plasticized, robotic version of himself, the skin waxy, the eyes dead. David as android.

He switched back to his eleven-year-old photo. Even though he hadn't really smiled for the photographer—some silly attempt to be cool—there was something real behind the eyes. Life. Living. Blood and spirit running through the flesh.

It got to be too much, and David clicked to the profiles of other missing children. All of the age-progressed portraits, regardless of age or ethnicity, had the soulless quality he'd seen in his own picture. The photos of kids in their youth, on the other hand, carried a tenor of sorrow, of pleading, for rest, for peace, for their stories to be told so they could be released from the curse that had frozen them in this stage of development.

David scanned the photos and read some of the descriptions. Most, if not all, of these stories would never be told, the cases left unresolved until the people looking for these kids were dead themselves. He said the names out loud: "Josiah Flores. Keira Maubry." Some were runaways, some abducted by a parent and whisked out of the country. Most were dead and would remain suspended here in the fraternity of the missing, until removed from the website after the average American lifespan had passed.

David's story was different. He was alive. He'd had the chance to grow up. Nothing had happened to him—at least, nothing he hadn't been able to survive physically. But now he knew someone had been looking for him for most of his life. And that someone just might still be out there. His chest felt like too many organs were stuffed into it; there was a painful stinging around his eyes. He looked up at the far corner of the room, where wall and ceiling met, inspecting it as if the answer to this madness might lie there.

FOUR

The little girl walking a few yards ahead of David was doing her best to avoid stepping on the cracks and seams in the sidewalk. The mother, holding the child's hand, was looking down at her, smiling as her arm was yanked back and forth.

Step on a crack, break your mother's back. David watched this, his mouth a straight line. As a young boy, he'd followed these types of juvenile superstitions to the letter, right up until the last day he had seen his mother. After that, he'd made a point to step directly on the cracks.

He'd decided to walk to Lola's instead of driving—he could think better that way. His mind couldn't stop turning everything over; brand-new neural pathways had already formed to accommodate this bolus of information. It would be impossible to focus behind the wheel.

He passed a women's clothing store, the mannequins staring through him. The facial features, especially the eyes, were unnatural even for mannequins, reminding him of the age-progressed photos he'd just viewed. David had seen more realistic mannequins at higher-end stores; this boutique was cheap. Shopkeepers needed to be careful with their displays. There was a fine line between effective marketing and just plain creepy. But it didn't really matter in the end, he thought. The mannequins weren't supposed to look real; their job was to give an illusion, a replica, of human life. A life, a story, that you might just buy into.

————

They'd celebrated David's eleventh-and-a-half birthday on that last night. It had been his mother's grand idea, a suggestion he thought was goofy. He wasn't one of those kids who kept track of his age in fractional terms. Even he knew that referring to oneself as ten and three-quarters was absurd.

But his mother had some type of illness, one he couldn't name or comprehend because the family didn't talk much about it. She was often painfully sick, and during these spells she'd confine herself and her misery to the quiet, empty room at the end of the hall. When she was up and out, enthusiastic about some cockamamie plan, the unspoken rule in the family was to go along.

David pretended to be excited about the half-birthday affair, which had involved, among other things, eating half of a piece of champagne cake and blowing out the flame of a blue-striped candle that had been cut at its midpoint. His sister, Deanna, had blown up green balloons just halfway and tied the limp objects to each chair. Braised short ribs and fettuccini Alfredo, David's favorites, were restricted to just one side of each person's plate; each water glass was only half full.

Had David remained indifferent about the party, he might have noticed the anxious glances passing between his family members. But as he sat among the festivities, he'd gotten drawn up into it and had started to enjoy himself. At bedtime he'd easily fallen asleep, half of a new Lego set spread out on his bed, anticipating the family's trip to DC.

————

Depart Monterey. Layover in Phoenix. Layover in Chicago. Arrive at Dulles International. The adventurous vision David had attached to traveling through the various cities and airports was nothing but a series of "hurry up and wait" situations. At least they were on the final leg of the journey. He looked around. Chicago's airport, the largest of the trip so far, was a maze with all its terminals and wings and offshoots. It had taken nearly twenty minutes, an overstuffed people mover, plus many twists, turns, and dead ends, to get from the last flight's gate to the next one.

He sat in the blue bucket seats and remembered the afternoon he'd gotten lost backstage at his sister's play. He'd wandered back holding a bouquet of gerbera daisies in noisy cellophane his mother had given him to present to Deanna. The unused props were gargantuan and distorted; the dim lighting cast odd, frightening shadows. He felt like a kid lost in Willy Wonka's chocolate factory, waiting for some kooky calamity. Stumbling over the thick cords, he'd run face first into countless heavy, dark curtains as he went from corridor to corridor. He felt he'd never find Deanna's dressing room and would roam the theater indefinitely, like the phantom he'd read about in English class.

But he wasn't alone this time, and he wasn't in the dark. They were all here together, and this next flight would be the last. Soon he'd be standing amidst the stone landmarks he'd studied, where the great speeches he'd memorized had been given.

"Who needs to use the restroom?" David's mother didn't like airplane bathrooms—the stalls were too tiny, too full of chances to brush up against the toilet and other unclean surfaces. "Let's have everybody try. David?"

David got up and looked down at his father, who remained seated. "Dad, you coming?"

"I'm good, little man. You go on ahead."

David ambled in the direction that his mother and sister had gone, but before he got too far, his father spoke. "Hey, little man." David looked back to see his father motioning for him to return. "Shake hands."

Shake hands? Now? What? His dad could be so strange. He was a devoted scientist, with a host of eccentricities that might lead some to call him a "mad scientist." They allowed him some leeway, but this was silly.

David grasped his father's hand with the tight grip he'd been taught. His father squeezed his hand, holding it a beat longer than usual, then let go. "Alright, get going, little man."

David took off toward the restrooms. As he got to the men's room, he spotted his mother and sister emerging from the women's room a few yards away. They looked his way and both gave a little wave. Their lips were turned up into toothless smiles, their eyes blank. Everybody was acting weird, he thought. Or maybe it was his imagination. Nothing was wrong. Sleep was just calling, making itself known, its reflection pooling at the edges of their tired forms.

———

And that had been it. The final time they had been together as a family; those images of them, his last. He'd come out of the restroom and wound his way through a large group of kids wearing Kelly green T-shirts, the accompanying adults harried and hoarse. He'd returned to the seats where his family had originally been camped out and sat waiting there for ten minutes before he realized all of the carry-on luggage, except his, was gone. He'd wandered through the airport grill, then paused to look into a bookstore and craned his neck to see into a perfumery. His heart started to clench; he told himself to stop. He told himself not to get nervous. You must have missed something, he told himself. He often tuned his mother out because she tended to ramble, belaboring whatever point she was trying to make. She must have said to head directly onto the plane after the bathroom. He ran toward the plane's gate but was stopped short by a man in dark blue. After showing them his pass, a flight attendant accompanied him onto the aircraft to locate his parents, then politely escorted him off when they couldn't be found on board. After some time, he heard a muffled announcement: "Attention, airport patrons, we have a lost child, David Goodwin, missing his parents. Repeating, David Goodwin, a lost child. Please report to terminal security to be reunited."

He was taken to a dingy office where a beefy, uniformed woman offered him chalky, flavorless hot cocoa with tiny marshmallows. When no family came to claim David, a tired social worker arrived and took him to her office, where he sat for hours, then eventually returned with him to the airport for a nonstop flight back to Monterey. At his family's home, sheriff's deputies had knocked at the door, first softly and then aggressively, pounding as if criminals were inside. When their patience had worn thin, they broke the door down. It had been then—the alarm shrieking, the completely vacant, freshly-scoured house—that David's certainty this was all a big mistake turned to a bitter conviction that it wasn't a mistake at all. His family was gone from him. Forever.

———

Gayle waved to David as he entered the warmth of Lola's, its earth-toned interiors a comforting balm. His eyes connected with hers, causing him to smile despite the events he'd just relived. He loved the way she greeted him. When she waved, she put her entire arm into the air, fully extended with fingertips reaching toward the ceiling, then tilted her forearm enthusiastically from angle to angle, bending at the elbow. The gesture involved her whole torso, but despite all the movement, it had a stability to it, a solidness—as if she, for one, was here to stay.

FIVE

Gayle was weary of lines. She'd been in several at the airport, and now she was on her way to the grocery store to stand in yet another one. Although she kind of liked those—they offered the chance to browse through silly magazines she was ashamed to buy. But did lines have to be part and parcel of every human activity in this city? She'd just been relieved of her place in line by the valet at Lola's who'd retrieved her blue Fiat Spider, only to find herself in a line mid-intersection, waiting to make a left turn. Within seconds, she'd be lined up on an on-ramp to enter the I-10. People lined up in this city to get hot dogs from Pink's, a diner named after a man named after a color. They lined up to see the latest movie when it opened at midnight on Thursdays. South of here, they lined up and followed the line, back and forth, kept in line by steel gray bars and placated by the music of Scott Joplin, to bear witness to what a small world it was, after all. They lined up where there were no lines, silently wondering what was wrong with a particular place if it had none. Instead of the City of Angels, LA could rightfully be called the City of Lines. But Los Lineas wasn't as pleasing to the ear.

Stop the rant. Right now. Recognizing she was under the influence—not of alcohol, but a combination of overstimulation and fatigue—Gayle decided she wasn't up to the forty-five minutes it would take to drive five miles. She pulled off the road, drove into the lot of a closed auto body shop, and cut the engine. She sat in the dark for a moment, watching shadows move across the building's exterior, letting her mind turn over her conversation with David. It was some strange shit. She kept seeing the empty, dead eyes in David's computer-progressed photo, staring back at her. Spooked, she reached up, clicked on the car's overhead lights. Sitting in a vacant, unlit parking lot at 8 p.m. was a no-no, according to the safety guidelines that women were supposed to follow, rules designed to make a person fearful of the world. She pushed away the anxiety, replaced it with resolve. She'd sit here until she was good and ready. She looked out beyond the overpass to the freeway below and saw a multitude of red lights, the look-alike cars at a standstill. Another fifteen minutes and she'd get back on the road. Her phone would be a good distraction—that was the purpose they served for humanity, wasn't it, to take your attention away from what was right in front of you. She gave her email a moment to load, then glanced at it. Something from her school's principal about parent-teacher conferences; something from the school district reiterating the new field trip regulations. *Forget that.* She was off work. Bureaucratic school board mess could wait until later.

The more agreeable choice was browsing through the offerings of a popular athleisure store—it was expensive, but she was a pro at finding promo codes. She began typing the web address with her thumbs, but her thoughts kept going to David. She pressed the backspace key, went to the missing-child website, and quickly clicked the "Accept all cookies" button so she could do her search. She reached David's page and gazed at it, frowning, trying to conjure up a reasonable explanation that would put the little mystery to bed. Was this for real? Or was it the latest thing David was using to avoid dealing with their relationship, their issues? Gayle stared at the frozen faces on the web page, imploring them to reanimate and reveal the truth.

Thwump! Gayle jumped and looked toward the noise, the pounding of flesh on metal. A grizzly face was pressed up against her window, a cap obscuring the eyes. "You can't park here!" the man yelled. He held up his arm, revealing a wrench. *I know this man doesn't think he's gonna hit my brand-new baby with that.* Gayle felt tempted to get out and tear him a new one, as her mother used to say, then thought better of it.

She fired up her car and peeled out of the parking lot, straight off the curb, the axle hitting the ground like its own little explosion. After driving for a bit, she started to calm down and thought back to the encounter, wondering if she'd run over the man's toes. She huffed. *If I did, he deserved it. Coming up to me like that, hitting my car. There better not be a dent, or I'll be going back for the rest of his ass.* She steadied the steering wheel with her left hand and patted the passenger seat with her right, feeling for her phone. She glanced over at the light coming from the floor. Her phone lay there, with David's computerized face staring up at her.

SIX

ersh pulled on the thin white ropes holding up his sweatpants and tied them in a neat knot. He'd lost six pounds since starting his walking routine at the local park. Nineteen more and the doctor would be off his back about his weight and on to some other bad habit he needed to get rid of. Extra girth or not, Hersh was a good-looking seventy-two. His dark skin had few wrinkles, only smile lines and a couple of creases traversing his forehead. Although the days of high school girls mumbling to each other about getting a "Hershey's Kiss" were long gone, he still got plenty of smiles from women in the senior set.

Sometimes he enjoyed talking to the ladies during his walk; it made the time go by more quickly, appeased his ego, infused his lower parts with some excitement. Other days, he didn't feel like being bothered. On those occasions, he'd wear sunglasses and try to cruise by the other walkers without making eye contact. His Mississippi home training prevented him from passing without speaking, though, so he would utter a listless, pro forma "How're you doing" to fellow walkers and proceed on, hoping there wouldn't be a response.

Besides, observing people was much more entertaining than actually talking to them. He liked to come up with names for the regulars, based on some distinct or irritating feature. The woman who wore rollers in her hair and was obsessed with impending epidemics was "CDC." A new virus had been detected, according to the headlines; she'd be hyped today. "The Dogcatcher" was a bald, gravelly-voiced man who made sure people picked up after their pets, always at the ready with a roll of green bags for the occasion. "Who Wore It Best" was the lady who donned outfits in the same color scheme as her twin poodles' homemade dresses.

The park had undergone a fine upgrade, making it popular with the retired folks of Windsor Hills. Along with lush landscaping featuring native plants, the county had installed a rubbery ergonomic surface that a seven-year-old Hersh, with his many falls from the monkey bars, could have made good use of.

But Hersh's walk—and the accompanying flirtations and mental gymnastics—would be cut short today. David had called at first light and said he was coming by to talk. Hersh hadn't bothered to ask what the topic was. It was always one of three things: whether he should get more serious with Gayle, possibly propose to her; whether he should allow himself to be promoted to a lucrative position he would hate; and the big, never-ending subject—his abandonment by his biological parents.

At least the first two issues were current and had actual bearing on David's life. These items had been hashed and rehashed, deliberated and redeliberated, yet Hersh could tolerate them. But he was sick of talking about the abandonment. Twenty-five years had passed. David needed to get over it.

He and his late wife, Regina, had adopted David with their whole hearts, determined to give him all the love he could stand. Back then, Regina had insisted, "The boy needs somebody to talk to about all this." Instead, Hersh had sent David to see Pastor Douglas, a short, loud-talking man who had two degrees in divinity but had never set foot in Psychology 101.

So now, when David called to talk, there was nothing to do but sit and listen, like an actor doomed to play a recurring, nonspeaking part in a bad drama. No understudy was available; the role was his until further notice. Hersh finished his final lap around the track, then headed home.

SEVEN

Address. City, state, zip. Emergency contacts. Alejandro zipped through the forms on the laptop the HR woman had given him, as if the slightest delay might result in the job offer being revoked. He typed out his full name more than a dozen times, over and over, reminding him of the standards he'd often had to write after getting caught in elementary school mischief. "I will make better choices. I will make better choices." He'd had to write it two hundred times, but didn't remember what bad decision had led to the punishment.

"Are you ready to get started." Alejandro's new employer, Angus, was back, his words more a command than a question.

Alejandro popped up from his seat. "Yes, sir." He hadn't really come up saying "sir" and "ma'am" to people, but he could tell Angus was the kind who'd like that type of thing.

And he was right. For the first time that morning, Alejandro caught a glimpse of Angus's pointy, off-white teeth as they flashed a brief half-smile. "All right, let's go."

Alejandro smirked. This Angus dude wasn't about to spout any empty niceties, like "Welcome to the family!" or "You're gonna love it here!" No bullshit, which was a good thing, because Alejandro wasn't in the mood. He was anxious to get started, to get his mind off Shelly.

Alejandro had gone out for this job because it didn't involve any-thing too taxing. He'd been hired by Angus's assistant, a nervous lit-tle man named Cyril, and his main task would be to watch various websites each day, monitoring consumer traffic. Programs existed that could do this type of tracking accurately and efficiently, without any human interference, but if he suggested that, Alejandro's face would need to go next to the word *idiot* in the dictionary.

He'd done this type of observation while he was an undergrad, at a TV station. It had been a night job, and his responsibility had been to watch the screens, make sure there were no interruptions in the programming, no technical malfunctions. He had played this experience up in the interview, acting as if these were highly fulfilling duties, ones he had enthusiastically carried out. It had worked, and here he was, choosing between HMO and PPO.

He followed Angus down a hall that ended in thick double doors made of steel. Angus placed his thumb on a black sensor pad on the wall, and the heavy doors swung open without a whisper, as if they weighed less than a sack of feathers.

Angus gestured toward the sensor pad. "Alli down in HR will get your fingerprint, set you up with this later today."

Alejandro barely heard this. Compared to the little gray room they'd just come from, the work area he now found himself in was an architect's dream. It was a huge workspace, about half the length of a football field, and it went five stories up, topped with a beautiful dome that operated as both a ceiling and a massive skylight. Unlike the metal doors that had ushered him into the area, the walls were made of an unusual combination of brown brick and decorated terra-cotta tiling, with polished cherrywood elements. The deep-red marble floors complemented the decor, and black wrought iron wove its way through in the form of floor railings and the staircase banister.

About fifty desks were situated on the ground floor, spaced perfectly apart in rows. The occupants worked silently, their heads bowed. Those with offices on the upper floors could be seen almost panoramically if one did a 360-degree turn, as all the doors and windows were made of glass. Alejandro could see a man talking on the phone in one of the offices, his face turning red. In another office, two women sat across a desk from each other, flipping through paperwork.

Alejandro continued behind Angus as he climbed up the grand staircase, a centerpiece that could have passed for a large-scale sculptural installation. At the first landing, they made a U-turn and walked along the collection of offices, each transparent glass door marked with a short alphanumeric sequence. They stopped at the last door on the right, and Angus tapped a code to unlock it, then pushed it open and motioned for Alejandro to enter.

Angus pointed to a black ergonomic chair that faced a wall with two huge flat-screen televisions embedded within it. Alejandro sat in front of the screens and took the printout Angus handed to him.

"You're going to let me know if the system registers hits to any of the thirty-two web pages listed here." He pointed at the paper. "Any questions?"

"That's it?" Alejandro slowly turned his head from side to side, then looked closely at the two screens. Each unit broadcast two pictures—a photo of a kid and, right beside it, a photo of an adult who looked like the kid. After a twenty-second interval, both screens would change to a different pair of photos, cycling the people through. The bottom of each screen listed a full name with a birth date and, below that, the words "Zero Inquiries." This was going to be even more tedious than the TV station job. Boredom was its own form of exhaustion.

"Yeah, genius, that's it. Find me if you see anything. I'm on the third floor."

Alejandro looked up and across to where Angus was pointing, on the other side of the building. Great. The location of Angus's office—combined with the transparent doors and windows throughout the place—would allow Angus to watch every move Alejandro made. He wouldn't be able to scratch his ass without Angus witnessing it.

As his new boss moved toward the door, something on one of the screens changed.

Alejandro looked at the yellow paper balanced on his left knee. The people were listed in alphabetical order, last names first. This sheet had names from *Gi-* to *Gy-*.

"Wait, Angus . . . uh, sir, there's something right now." Alejandro squinted and leaned in. "Yeah, right now, it shows that somebody's looked at—"

Angus hightailed it back to the room to stand behind Alejandro's chair, eyes staring at the screen, eyebrows furrowed. "Somebody looked at who? When?"

"Sometime last night, according to the time stamp." The two men studied the pair of pictures, the sullen middle schooler on the left, the expressionless thirty-something figure on the right, then said the name of the web page in unison.

"Leonard Goodwin."

EIGHT

Margaret scanned the display of wigs on her dresser, then grimaced and looked away, shaking her head. Her assortment of perfume bottles was a more welcome sight—an array of palm-sized sculptures sparkling on a mirrored tray, each hoping to be the day's chosen one. The wigs just sat there, emitting the dim energy of small, wounded animals. She detested the way they made her feel—not old, as one might think, but lacking. A reminder of the things she no longer had.

The detection of a few thinning areas on her scalp had sent Margaret flying to the beauty supply shop she drove past daily, its insides obscured by oversized pictures of sultry-eyed models with pixie haircuts. She'd gone overboard, buying five distinct and expensive styles, all endorsed by a B-list actress who starred in a low-budget series of thrillers involving cruise ships and reptiles. It wasn't one of her duties, but Amandine, the cleaning lady, washed the wigs every two weeks and placed them haphazardly around the sunroom that overlooked Margaret's backyard. While the wigs were drying, the foam heads where they usually took up residence stood empty on her dresser. When Margaret awakened during the middle of the night, she'd be startled by a posse of bald, disembodied aliens in tight formation, coming for her.

Not that she would mind being taken away from here. Margaret's home, a two-story colonial built in the late 1930s, was symmetrically perfect, its formal dining room to the right of the roomy foyer, its airy living room to the left. The second level was similar—the master bedroom to the left of the staircase, two smaller bedrooms to the right. Everything orderly, balanced. Leonard Sr. had added the sunroom and a guest house when their son was a baby, often working into the night after a long day on a construction site. Now that she was alone, Margaret occupied just two rooms of the spacious home—the kitchen and the master. The contents of the house were dusted weekly by Amandine, who used an entire can of Pledge for the job, but most of the home's carefully selected items and artifacts went otherwise untouched. As Margaret moved through the house, passing by the thresholds of unoccupied space or popping into a room to retrieve something buried in a closet, she often felt like a squatter in a stately museum, a memorial to a fuller, happier era.

At least she no longer had to spend as much time in doctors' offices and laboratories as in her younger days. The university hospital had pretty much left her alone for the past twenty years. During those decades of treatment, they'd never fully explained—at least not in a way she could comprehend—what illness she had that required this inordinate amount of attention. She felt fine, she'd always felt fine. "Trust us," Dr. Gaylord had said, "you're in good hands." He'd laughed and said something about an insurance company's supposedly well-known slogan. The joke had been lost on Margaret. But with their recommendation, she'd undergone more pokes and prods, transfusions and biopsies. Whatever it was, she guessed she was cured. Or they'd moved on to something, or someone, else.

Enough with the melancholy act. Buck up. She closed her eyes, waved her hand over the wigs, and randomly snatched the one named Cyndi off its base. Her Bible study group was scheduled to celebrate the September birthdays at lunch after discussing "How to Be a Drum Major for God." Did the master of the universe really need fragile, unreliable, sad-sack mortals as drum majors? She doubted it. Margaret needed someone to cheer her on much more than God ever would.

She wasn't in the mood for lunch at one of the down-market restaurants that Sandra, the group leader, was bound to choose. Things had to be just right for a dining experience to work for Margaret, or she'd just as soon stay home. Maybe Sandra would choose Chinese—Margaret liked fortune cookies, the thin, sweet wafers, the fulfilling crunch. She wasn't superstitious, that would go against the Good Book, but she still read the fortune and some-times stuffed it into her purse for further reflection at home. The red block writing on the little slips of paper often spoke directly to her, providing the exact morsel of wisdom, right when she needed it. "Accept something you cannot change," one message had read. You couldn't argue with that. Tucked in between the bills in her wallet was this one: "A short pencil is usually better than a long memory." She was still working out what it meant.

Yes, Chinese would be the ticket. If she got to Bible study early, she could grab a seat next to Sandra and convince her. Maybe the place with the lanterns hung throughout the restaurant, glowing like giant fireflies. As long as she avoided entrées with shrimp. Margaret remembered an article in *Better Homes & Gardens* cau-tioning that the tiny black line on the back of a shrimp meant it had not been properly deveined; one was therefore consuming both the poor creature and its poop. Her throat practically closed up at the thought.

She glanced in the mirror at Cyndi, perched dutifully on her head, the synthetic bangs grazing her forehead. She adjusted it a bit in the back, tugging it down around the nape of her neck, dissatis-fied. She didn't feel alluring, as the ads promised. Margaret was 5'2" and small-boned, with dainty Cicely Tyson features; the wig was overpowering. She looked like a teenager in a school play, wearing a wig dragged out from the drama department's coffers.

A thought occurred: What if she showed up at the church sporting her own hair? She'd just made sixty-eight years; the opportunities to break out of character were slowly diminishing. A look of satisfaction took over her face as she imagined the church ladies' reactions. But she knew she'd never do it. She remembered another fortune, this one from a cookie that upon opening had shattered into too many pieces to eat: "The fortune you seek is in another cookie." She pulled on the sides of the wig to straighten it, ran her hands down the front of her jacket, pressing down its lapels, and walked out the door.

NINE

The lawn needs reseeding. The security signs should be displayed more prominently. Doesn't anyone around here believe in raking up leaves? No, just let them get mushy and rot. Obscured behind the screen door, Hersh watched David come up the walkway, predicting his son's laundry list–style critique of the front yard. Hersh didn't know how David had become so particular about things, so critical. And there wasn't any realm of possibility in which David would keep his views to himself. Hersh girded himself for the comments and opened the door.

"Hey, Dad, you could pick up a new doormat for $15.99 at—"

Hersh cut him off. He knew where doormats were sold. David could be like those snotty-nosed, know-it-all kids you couldn't escape. Just without the snot. "So how is the beautiful Gayle Holland?"

"She's good." David brushed past him.

"And the job?"

"Same." The clipped answers made Hersh feel like he was talking to an adolescent, the boy David had been when he and Regina took him in. A fair amount of time had passed before David became comfortable enough with them to extend his vocabulary beyond "yeah" and "fine." During those first few months, Hersh entertained more than a few doubts regarding the success of the situation. But his wife was so sure, so confident, that David would one day feel they were his people, that their home was his own.

As usual, Regina was right on point. Hersh became convinced of it on a Friday night at Dodger Stadium, two years after the boy moved in. David was thirteen. He and Hersh took a rain check on Regina's spaghetti and meatballs, saving their appetites for nachos and Dodger dogs. They were on their way down to their seats, their arms filled with junk disguised as food, when Hersh tripped and fell onto the cement. He landed flat on his face, blood seeping from his nose, his legs awkwardly bent in areas where there were no joints.

A vendor screamed into her headset for an ambulance. Hersh felt the soothing hands of strangers on his back and shoulders, their voices a mix of panic and concern. Surrounded by the shifting feet and knees of people standing and squatting around him, Hersh closed his eyes to escape from the chaos and his increasing anxiety. He opened them when he heard David's voice.

"Hey, Dad, I'm right here. You gotta stay awake." David had lain down on the filthy steps next to Hersh, remaining there until the paramedics arrived. They were nose to nose, eye to eye, their faces inches apart. "Dad. Just stay awake. Please. Don't try to move. Just talk to me." Despite the pain in every cell of his body, this gesture made Hersh sigh with relief. He and the boy were finally linked.

"So did you go up to the track today?" Hersh felt nostalgic for that younger David. This adult one behaved as if he were the parent. "You've gotta walk at least three times a week if you're gonna keep the weight off. And I brought you some really good juice—try it."

Hersh took the bottle and looked at the label. Cranberry-grape. He sniffed with disdain. He was old school and didn't believe in these hybrid juice affairs. A drink should pick one fruit and stay true to it.

He decided to sample it anyway, to appease David. Hersh could tell his son was building up to something; he wanted this visit to at least begin smoothly. He took a sip. It tasted exactly like the beverage the church used for communion, which was actually pretty good. He raised the bottle again and took a big gulp, even though it felt sacrilegious to drink it in his sweats, without so much as an "Amen."

As Hersh brought the bottle down from his lips, David handed him a narrow slip of newspaper. "This was in my mail."

Hersh took a close look at the paper. It was a missing-child notice with a picture of David as the boy he'd first met, then one of David as the man he was today. The swallow of juice that had just gone down made its way back up, causing him to gag. David didn't seem to notice.

"This came to you in the mail? From who?"

"No, Dad. It was in the junk mail, with the coupons and ads. I just happened to see it. It's gotta be a mistake, right?"

Hersh turned to the sink, facing away from his son.

"Dad. You know what this is about, why this is out there? Is somebody looking for me? Do you think it has to do with my real family?"

My real family. It was like a kick in the stomach.

"Naw, man, I'm not sure what it's about. Must be a mistake, like you said. Has to be. I'll have a look into it, though. I'll check it out, let you know if there's anything to it. Or maybe I'll ask Uncle Ricky." As Hersh said this, he knew he wouldn't "look into it," nor would he mention it to Rick. He would immediately set out to bury it. He took a long sip of the communion juice, swished it around, fully coating the inside of his mouth, before swallowing. He sighed and poured the rest down the drain.

TEN

Alejandro pulled his phone halfway out of his pocket to check the time, then released it, hearing the metal clank as the phone dropped back down on top of his keys. He grabbed a protein bar from the kitchen cupboard and carefully studied the nutrition label as if it were crucial, lifesaving information. It was time to head into the office, which meant behaving as if he hadn't overheard confidential information on his first day there. His experience in subterfuge was . . . well, subzero, he thought, opening the refrigerator. He scanned the array of food, scrutinized the contents of the shelves, then closed the door. Looking at a tray of cupcakes wouldn't make his problems go away. He wished he could travel back to the day he'd met Shelly at Sprinkles. She'd smiled at him in a way that made his face hot, prompting him to say, "What, real men don't eat cupcakes?"

Yesterday had been a bizarro mess. After being on the job for all of two minutes and reporting a change on the monitors, Angus told Alejandro to take a little break, explore the rest of the building. He put Alejandro's cell number into his phone, then recommended the small, overpriced café on the building's ground floor as a good place to grab a snack. The gourmet donuts were outstanding, Angus said. "To die for." A short, chunky man, Cyril, appeared at Angus's side, bobbing his head in agreement.

Alejandro wondered what critical, transformative thing he'd discovered. He wasn't a complete fool; they wanted him out of the office so they could look into it, away from his newbie, uninitiated eyes. Nobody cared whether he tried any award-winning donuts. Even though Alejandro had just met Angus, he knew enough to know the man wasn't the type to describe anything as "to die for." Something was up. But as long as he was getting paid, he'd sample donuts, fritters, hell, even some dry-ass scones. He headed to the café.

Fifteen minutes later, Alejandro's phone rang, interrupting his conversation with a cute mail carrier named Deborah. She was probably a good ten years older than him, but she was working those blue shorts. Alejandro reluctantly answered the call.

"Come back up in an hour," Angus ordered.

"Yes, sir," Alejandro agreed, anxious to get back to Deborah. After a brief moment, his phone had rung one more time. Angus again. What the hell? The man hadn't been able to get Alejandro out of the office fast enough, and now he couldn't stop calling. Angus could wait.

He let the call go to voicemail and made plans to meet up with Deborah the next afternoon. Alejandro had earned extra points for pronouncing her name correctly; she placed the emphasis on the middle syllable instead of the first one: "de-BORE-uh." It had been worth the effort. She also seemed pleased, even impressed, that he'd kept talking to her instead of answering his phone. She'd left the café with her bundle of undelivered mail, looking back with a wicked smile.

The rest of the workday had been uneventful. Alejandro went back down to personnel to fill out some additional paperwork, then spent the remainder of the afternoon looking at the faces on the monitors. Angus peeked in from time to time to check in, irritating him. *Just let me do my work.*

Back at home, Alejandro's mother was waiting in the foyer and had actually pulled a chair up to a round table that held a massive white orchid arrangement.

"So how was it?" she asked, leaning forward. Alejandro glanced at the orchid, its curved shoots oriented toward his mother's ear, as if they, too, were listening, ready to express disapproval. He wasn't going to give her a chance to pick at his choice the way she plucked olives out of salads.

"All good. Exactly what I need right now," he said, moving toward the kitchen with a wave. He grabbed a cupcake and headed to his room.

He threw his phone on the bed and began undressing, anticipating the warmth of a long shower. The phone landed face up and he saw the notification. There was a new voicemail. *Angus. Shit.* It was the second call, the one he hadn't answered when he was talking to de-Bore-uh. Well, he'd been at the office all afternoon, and Angus had looked in on him approximately three hundred times. If it was important, there had been plenty of opportunities to discuss it, right?

It was probably nothing, he told himself, moving toward the bathroom. As he got to the door, he stopped, sighed, shook his head, and returned to the bed. He would listen to the message and get it out of the way so he could relax. He pressed play and heard a gurgling noise and other indistinguishable sounds. Two voices emerged, in a conversation that was slightly muffled. It quickly became clear to Alejandro that Angus hadn't actually called him a second time; it was a classic "butt dial," unlike any other butt dial he'd received.

Alejandro assumed the other voice on the call was Cyril, Angus's nervous wingman. The conversation had been short but dense. Alejandro listened to it once and then played it a second time to convince himself the whole thing was real:

CYRIL: ... new kid saw it?

ANGUS: ... sharp kid ... good pick ... So what do you have on this?

CYRIL: ... hit on the Leonard Goodwin ... traced back ... cell phone ... Gayle Holland. Thirty-seven-year-old fifth-grade teacher at Spikes Elementary ... South LA. Single ... fluent in Spanish. Chicago-born. UCLA grad. Lives Mid-Wilshire, near the museums.

ANGUS: Alright ... She must know him ... lead us to him. I want two people on this ... one to follow her and the other to become her new best friend.

CYRIL: I can put a tail on her ... easy. But what are you suggesting ...

ANGUS: She's a schoolteacher ... Let's get someone at the school, like in the classroom next to hers. One of our women. She's gonna do some lunches with her, some hot yoga ... whatever this babe is into ... find out what she knows ... Leonard Goodwin.

CYRIL: Alright ... the current teacher ... class next to Gayle Holland ... a little ... accident ... absent indefinitely. Without ... attention. But ... school district. They'll automatically assign a substitute ... strict union protocol. People pay ... dues ... jobs ... hard for us to get one of our people in there.

ANGUS: Cyril ... you ever heard me voice any concern about ... and ... union ... protocols?

CYRIL: Uh, no. Sir.

ANGUS: Look...looking for him forever. Computer progression...updating the ads all this time. This is it. Our chance...need one of ours in there. Any glitches, any hiccups, any holdups, by anything . . . anyone . . . deal with it. Alright? Deal with it.

It was clearly stuff Alejandro wasn't supposed to know, back-alley information that prompted characters in movies to spout that overused, cliched phrase: "I could tell you, but I'd have to kill you." And Angus seemed like one of those goons who would shoot you dead with the gun in his left hand while munching on a gourmet donut with his right.

ELEVEN

For the first time in weeks, Roger Bailey felt happy. It was an odd emotion for someone who was behind on both his rent and his spousal support payments. Especially the latter of the two. Candy was a stickler when it came to her checks, and she would sic her bloodthirsty attorney on him without hesitation.

The school district had called right before dinner, offering a long-term substitute position at Spikes Elementary. A fifth-grade teacher had been in a big traffic accident on the I-210, and she'd be in the hospital recovering and undergoing physical therapy for the next six months. He felt bad for the woman, whoever she was, but not that bad. With a steady assignment, he could finally get some relief from the accusatory stack of bills glaring out at him from the worn credenza.

Choosing clothes for the next day was easy. Tweed jacket, to let the kids know he was serious; jeans to show that, despite his age, he was hip. He laid these items and a white button-down shirt over the chair at his computer, then placed a clean pair of running pants and a T-shirt on top of it all. He'd start his first day off right.

On Roger's way to the bathroom to charge his shaving gear, the phone rang. It was the school district, once again. He answered before the second ring.

"Hello?"

"Roger Bailey, please." A gravelly-voiced man spoke, not the curt, no-nonsense woman who'd phoned earlier.

"You got him. Is this about the long-term sub position? I'm on it."

"Yes, sir. We're calling about the position. You're no longer needed for it."

No longer needed? What? This gig was his meal ticket. "What do you mean, no longer needed? Mrs. . . . uh, Ms. . . . well, uh, the teacher. She can't go in, can she? Don't they still need somebody for that class? She didn't just up and get better after a seven-car mashup!"

"No, uh, sir, she's still incapacitated. Very much so. Unfortunately it was a mistake that you were called. The position had already been assigned to someone else."

"Someone else? Who else? Look, this is my job, I got the call four hours ago and I've been preparing all afternoon." It was a lie. He barely knew the state standards for fifth grade.

"Sir—"

"Don't 'sir' me. This is my gig. I'm all paid up on my ridiculously high union dues. Call the other guy or gal. You tell *them* it's a mistake. I'm showing up tomorrow. And if anybody else comes, I'll be sending 'em home."

"Sir, I'm very sorry we can't accommodate you this time, and I'm truly sorry for the mix-up. Next time, the position's yours. I personally guarantee that you will be next up."

"As I just said, I'm showing up. *This* time. I'm teaching tomorrow, and I'm getting paid tomorrow. I'll send this other person packing. So you might as well handle it with them tonight."

Roger hung up the phone. He'd be damned, in innumerable and multifaceted ways, if he lost this opportunity. The district would just have to work it out with the other sucker—and get a better system while they were at it. The left hand didn't know what the right hand was doing down there at admin, but their inefficiency wasn't his problem.

Roger had been pacing around his tiny apartment during the phone call, further distressing the scruffy carpet. At one point his toe caught on a bare thread and he practically tripped. But he'd maintained composure, told the potential job snatcher where to go. Now that it was over, he stopped at the computer chair, fingered the tweed jacket. This time tomorrow, he'd be in a classroom wearing it, with money on the way to his—and Candy's—account.

Roger did wear the jacket one more time. News reports the next night declared that Los Angeles native Roger Bailey had been mauled to death by a pit bull while on his morning jog. The pit bull had been promptly put down, its owner unidentified. Candy had given the tweed jacket to the mortuary to clothe Roger's remains, despite the fact that his extensive injuries necessitated a closed casket.

TWELVE

Gayle had to give herself kudos for coming up with the social studies project she'd assigned. In lieu of the age-old book report on a historical figure, she'd had the kids cover cereal boxes with construction paper, and instructed them to study the public figure of their choice and create a cereal that represented the person. "The front, sides, and back of the label should tell me all I need to know about your hero," she'd told them, "and the ingredients list should include their character traits, like honesty and courage. Put a drawing of them on the front." It was a break from tradition, and the principal frowned slightly when she heard it, but after five years at Spikes Elementary, she'd gotten used to it. Gayle got students to use their imagination by repurposing mundane household items into useful and interesting things. Some people expressed their creativity as floral designers, others as writers, and so on. Teaching was her way. And who could complain? The kids loved it—wasn't that the point? Plus, the boxes would be much more entertaining for her to grade than a batch of written reports.

Nala, the most promising student in the class, finished her presentation of Harriet Tubman's Freedom Flakes, receiving light, distracted applause from the other students. Gayle's thoughts turned to Violet, her good friend who taught the class next door. Gayle had gone online and chosen a floral masterpiece featuring deep purple alstroemeria, black magic hollyhocks, green carnations, and lavender chrysanthemums. The bouquet had been over the top in its extravagance, with unusually dark blooms and spiky leaves, but it was the only thing that would match Violet's epic personality and hopefully bring that signature smirk to her face.

If she was able to smirk. The accident had been covered on the news, with helicopters swirling noisily above the scene and radio personalities warning drivers of delays. The crash had resulted in two fatalities, and three motorists, one of whom was her dear friend, were in critical condition. A long-term substitute would be finishing out the school year in Violet's place.

Gayle was exiting the copy room the first time she saw Violet and had immediately assumed she was some student's older sister. Her heavy black eyeliner contrasted starkly with her pale skin; her expression was a warning to stay far away. The layers of dark-colored clothing, bulky yet stylish, paired with a huge black bag stuffed to the gills, made Violet seem like a fashion-conscious vagrant. When the principal later introduced her as one of the school's new teachers, the entire staff had gotten a jolt. But they'd remained silent. Although the principal often made unexpected decisions, nobody could question that she knew how to pick 'em.

The kids adored Violet, and she and Gayle became tight, brought together as allies in their crusade for troubled students with uninvolved parents. They vented to each other about silly edicts the school district issued on a regular basis, gave each other heads-ups on other teachers, and shared details of what was happening in their lives in the areas of love and lust.

Gayle had even bravely ventured with Violet one night to the odd Malediction Society, a goth club close to LAX. Sitting on a round black-velveteen ottoman in the darkened warehouse, holding a goblet adorned with wrought iron, Violet leaned in and encouraged Gayle to release herself from the grip of David's ambivalence. "It's way too much to deal with. Do you really have the energy to sort through all that angst? How long have you been with him?"

"Three years."

"Three years." Violet dipped her chin and observed Gayle with a dubious look. "Three years," she repeated, "and just . . . nothing. No sign of anything solid on the horizon. Just long-term bullshit." Violet brightened and raised her eyebrows, giving Gayle a sly look. "What about that Geoffrey guy, the one the district sends out to do teacher training? Didn't he call you about going out?"

Gayle thought about Geoffrey as she checked to make sure Violet's floral arrangement had been delivered. He'd been hounding her to meet up, texting her every few days. When David had failed to pick her up at the airport, she'd texted Geoffrey back. Their dinner was tonight, and even though David had redeemed himself—somewhat—she hadn't canceled.

If she had been the type of woman who kept a lofty list of the qualities she wanted in a partner, she would have been able to check off each and every one with Geoffrey. He had his act together; he knew all the right lines. He was smart, entrepreneurial, and had recently published his own line of educational materials. He'd even offered to take her on board as a consultant. Gayle imagined flying off with him to teachers' conferences, getting a nice big dose of vitamin D before and after the keynote address. Oh, what she would do with his tight body, the deep bronze skin that glowed from the inside. But she didn't know if she trusted, or even wanted, that level of perfection. It would mean she'd need to be perfect; he'd probably expect that, even demand it.

Maybe, as Violet suggested, it would be worth it to at least *try* to want it. "It" meaning something more than what David was capable of.

The lunch bell rang, drawing Gayle's attention back to the class-room. She watched her students file out to the cafeteria, toting a colorful array of lunch bags and boxes. Nala waved as she left. She was a sweet girl; Gayle had high hopes for her, despite the girl's uncouth parents. Nala's mother had once showed up at school sporting a T-shirt that said "I Need A Drink, Dammit." Gayle had given Nala even more attention after that.

"Hello! Hi there!"

Gayle looked up sharply. The voice interrupting her musings was unnaturally cheerful. Its owner was a tall, horsey-faced woman with brown hair, someone she'd never seen. Who was this? A parent?

As if she'd heard Gayle's silent question, the woman answered, "I'm Isabella Rincon and I'm gonna be next door for the rest of the year. I meant to pop in earlier but the morning was like a whirl-wind!" She flung her hand toward Violet's classroom. "They said the teacher in there practically got wiped out in some accident. Were you close with her?" Gayle didn't appreciate how the woman spoke about Violet, so cavalierly. This was her friend in the ICU they were talking about, not some random celebrity.

"Oh, okay, hello. What can I do for you?" Gayle stood at the classroom's threshold, purposely not inviting Isabella inside.

"Well, I was hoping maybe we could grab some lunch at that Cuban place across the street. I told a friend I was gonna be here, and she said they have the best plantains in the city. Plus I wanted to get your ideas for changing around the classroom a little bit, some redecorating, and you know, what the deal is on the principal, what to look out for, who the players are, stuff like that."

As the woman droned on, Gayle's feelings solidified—she would most certainly not be going to lunch. It would feel traitorous to just pop out to lunch on Violet's first day out, as if she could easily be replaced. Plus, after four measly hours, Isabella was already plan-ning an overhaul of Violet's classroom. Gayle felt the urge to give Isabella a firm reminder: She was just a visitor here.

But courtesy won out, and Gayle suggested they round up a few of the other teachers to go as a group. "That way you can meet everyone, get a bunch of different takes on what's happening at the school." And it would lessen the pressure and burden on her, Gayle thought, to entertain this interloper.

"Well, you know, I was hoping it would be just the two of us. I'm not really that great with groups. It might be a little uncomfortable." Isabella tilted her head and adopted a pity-seeking smile.

Not good with groups? Gayle wondered what kind of teacher this woman was. Teaching elementary school, uh, by definition, involved groups. A different *group* every year. She didn't have time for this person. "You know, I have some things to do while the kids are outside, so maybe next time."

"Oh. Well, I-I'd just appreciate it so much if we could go today. I really want to get off on a good foot here." Isabella looked away and sighed, then glanced back at Gayle. "We're the only two teachers that have the little fifth-grade monsters, ugh. Feeling a little nervous."

The little fifth-grade monsters, ugh. See, this was the result of the recklessly lenient emergency substitute program. Who knew what underqualified, uncaring fools might be unleashed on poor, unsuspecting children. Gayle was suddenly thrilled she had put her hair in an updo today. She had David to thank for that. She'd driven straight to his house after the incident in the mechanic's lot, spooked by the crazed man with a wrench and the thoughts swirling around in her head about missing boys. They'd made the unspoken decision not to discuss any of that, finding other more pleasant topics, like old movies and where to get the best peach cobbler. She'd slept over, wrapped in his arms, safe for the night from whatever calamity was just around the corner. In the morning, David had woken her up, already wearing his suit, ready for a day in court. She'd quickly showered and he'd brought her chamomile tea and sat on the bed as she dressed and maneuvered her locs into position. He liked them up, he'd said. It brought out her eyes. It was a tough style to pull off and took several tries to get it right, but it was worth the effort. It made her feel regal, like a Nubian princess, giving her a sense of power that would enable her, right now, to say no to this person.

Gayle forced herself to say the woman's name. "Isabella. So sorry. Not going to be able to go to lunch with you today." She spoke cheerfully, with an upbeat smile, but began to close the door. Isabella tried to maneuver her body to maintain eye contact in the narrowing space, but Gayle continued aiding the door on its path until it clicked and locked shut. *Welcome to Spikes Elementary, lady! Now step off.*

THIRTEEN

Stone cut into the perfect filet mignon the waiter had set in front of him and quickly discovered it wasn't quite as flawless as he'd hoped. There was too much pink on the inside, much more than one should see in a cut prepared "medium well." He put his utensils down, sighed, then picked them back up and resumed cutting. He refused to call the waiter over. He'd watched a silly movie with Charlie back in August, the night before his son left for college. An obnoxious character in the film had complained to a waiter that the bread on his plate was not toasted dark enough. The waiter had taken the bread into the back and toasted it further, bringing it back out only after placing the bread between the hairy cheeks of his butt. The next morning, Stone had shaken Charlie's hand, surreptitiously giving him $5,000 in cash from his last gig. He'd patted his son on the back and said, "Remember. Never send anything back."

He took a bloody bite and looked around the restaurant, making sure to get a good look at the evening's targets as he chewed. The Gayle woman wasn't his type, but she was still pretty good-looking, making her an easy one to watch. The guy she was with didn't really look like the man in the photo he'd been given by that asshole Cyril, although Cyril had been quick to point out that the photo was a computer progression. The man they were trying to find might look a bit different. Gayle had referred to her date several times as Geoffrey—not Leonard, the name Stone had been given—although Cyril had stated it was quite possible that the target was now going by a different name. But Stone hadn't been hired to wonder about these details. Just do the job and make the money, he reminded himself. Thirty years in this "industry" and he was tired—of the people he had to deal with, of this city. This last project would cover Charlie's ridiculously high college tuition, leaving enough for him to take a long sabbatical to an island with a stack a novels, a pack of Moleskins, and a case of brand-new ballpoint pens. Plus Anna, of course.

Get the job done. And eat faster. He hadn't had a reservation for the popular, upscale steakhouse that the couple had chosen; there'd been a delay in getting a table. He'd stood at the establishment's entrance, its lobby lush with palms and leather benches, listening to their conversation via a device Isabella had managed to place in Gayle's purse at the school. There hadn't been much to listen to so far, and now they were ordering dessert. He had a lot to do and very little time to do it.

But the gods were with him tonight. The man was excusing himself to go to the restroom. Stone let the man get halfway across the room, then got up himself and moved in the same direction. He mentally reviewed the evening's instructions and the lecture Cyril had given him about discretion. The accident involving the weird punk rock teacher had received too much media attention, and the target woman, Gayle, had rebuffed Isabella. Stone guessed Gayle was either suspicious or simply put off. Isabella might have come on too strong with the friend act. The operation was falling apart before it even got started, so Stone had been told to take it slow, take it easy, and most of all, be absolutely sure before he did anything. "I don't want a bunch of bodies, blood and gore, nightly coverage on KTLA," Cyril had fussed. "I want certainty. Get me what I need so I can have *certainty.*"

Frustrated, Stone had gone to Angus to get to the heart of the project. Angus rolled his eyes when Stone repeated Cyril's whiny tirade, but it had triggered a plan.

"Blood and gore." Angus looked at his desk and nodded, then looked up. The pupils of his eyes were sharp little black points. "Well, not the gore part. But get us a vial of his blood. We can compare it with our samples from when he was a baby. Then we'll know whether it's him or if we're wasting our time and need to move on to some other dipstick."

The men's room was without its attendant this evening, another thing in Stone's favor. He'd never understood the need for an employee whose sole purpose was to hand patrons a high-end paper towel or a little bottle containing a swallow of mouthwash. He couldn't imagine having to report in to work, shift after shift, for a day of exposure to pungent smells and coarse sounds. No wonder the poor fellow had called in sick.

Stone's target was in the only closed stall, again more convenient than he could have hoped for. He used a small metal clip to swiftly open the bathroom stall from the outside.

"Hey, buddy, I'm in here—" The man started to stand, attempting to pull up his pants with one hand.

Stone silently covered the man's mouth with a thin beige cloth and held it there until the man's body turned limp and he fell back onto the toilet. He quickly used a syringe to draw blood from the man's right arm. After the vial was filled, Stone capped it and placed it in his pocket along with the syringe and the cloth. He glanced at the unconscious wretch as he backed out of the stall, then used the metal clip to lock the door. He lathered his hands with creamy, patchouli-scented hand soap, rinsed and dried them with a solemn thoroughness, and exited the restroom.

Stone reentered the dining room and strolled back to his seat. His steak was cold, but he forced himself to eat politely, in a matter-of-fact way, as if he hadn't just assaulted a man. About ten minutes passed, and he could see Gayle over at her table, fiddling with her dessert spoon and looking toward the back of the restaurant. Stone watched her take out her phone and busy herself with it. At one point, she got up and started toward the restrooms but then slowly pivoted and retraced her steps back to her table. She motioned for the waiter, who promptly retrieved her check and brought it over. In a series of quick movements, Gayle stood up, threw some cash down, took a final gulp of red wine, and exited the restaurant, her head held high. A few minutes later, Stone laid a hundred-dollar bill on the table and left, patting his coat, his bounty secure.

FOURTEEN

Alejandro slowed as he exited the I-10. Cops who were behind on their monthly quota for moving violations often hid behind the foliage, waiting to catch some defenseless sucker as he flew by. He wasn't in the mood; this wasn't the day.

At the bottom of the off-ramp, a figure paced back and forth across the path of traffic. Alejandro brought his car to a stop within inches of the man. He did a quick analysis, surveying the man's shoes. *Homeless or hustler?* The dude's sign, written neatly in bold black marker, read "Hit Me—I Need the Money." *Hustler.* He started to drive on, then thought better of it and reached out his window to hand the man a five-dollar bill. You had to reward creativity when you saw it.

He continued south on La Cienega Boulevard, passing a mishmash of businesses as he crossed Venice and Washington. LA was adding a line to its Metro Rail, and as he crossed Jefferson, he looked up and saw they were testing the system in preparation for the ribbon cutting next week. The new train had shiny placards on its side that read "Look left, look right, trains run day and night. Hear bells? See lights? The train must be in sight!" Which overpaid administrative official had come up with that idea? It belonged in a Dr. Seuss book, not on the side of a train.

He'd replayed the conversation between Angus and Cyril at least five times. Any idiot who'd ever watched a prime-time cop show could read between the lines. These people were going to get to this Gayle Holland woman, and they didn't care if they did harm to some innocent teacher or anyone else who got in the way. And the only reason they were after Gayle Holland was because Alejandro had alerted the powers that be about the hit to the web page on the Goodwin man. He had just been doing his job for all of two minutes, and in that short time he'd put something in motion that might result in someone's death.

As much as he wanted to bail on this thing, just turn around, go home, and pretend it had all never happened, he couldn't. He had to help this Gayle woman and the people surrounding her. He couldn't sit idly by and let another woman come to harm on his watch. It was both a mandate and an opportunity. He couldn't travel back in time to prevent what had happened to Shelly; she was gone and the laws of nature wouldn't allow him to change that. But maybe if he helped Gayle Holland, he could somehow redeem himself—with the universe, with Shelly, wherever she was—and with himself.

———

SPM Inc. *Sic Parvis Magna*. The company's initials and full name were listed fourth on the business complex's marquee, despite the fact that it occupied the largest building and took up the most space. Alejandro hadn't bothered to look up what the Greek words—or was it Latin?—actually meant. Hell, he'd barely googled the company before accepting the position. He could kick himself for not asking more questions about the nature of the business before signing on. He'd just foolishly gone for it, riding on some misguided hope that the job would help him kill time and cure his feelings of worthlessness.

He parked his car near the back entrance and engaged in some brief self-talk. He half expected someone to accost him as he came through the security door. When this didn't happen, he crossed the threshold and proceeded to the staircase. No one looked up as he passed the rows of desks that filled the ground floor.

He started up the stairs in the direction of his workspace, then thought better of it. If Angus was in, he'd see Alejandro and notice every move he made from then on. No, it would be better for Angus to think Alejandro hadn't yet checked in for the day. Besides, if he was truly going to help Gayle, he'd need access to an actual computer. As colossal as the monitoring screens were, they weren't going to help him do jack.

He needed to find a place where his presence wouldn't seem out of order, somewhere a new guy might be expected to find himself. Human Resources. The woman had said she'd get him a benefits manual at a later date, from another administrative office. This was the perfect time for her to take a little walk.

He began his approach, challenging himself to remember the woman's first name by the time he got to her office.

Alli. That was it. Short for Alexandra. She'd made some comment in the interview about how both of their names were variations on Alexander, which she claimed meant *defender*. She hadn't hidden her attraction to Alejandro, and he'd played along—he needed the job. He'd even acted like he might take her up on an offer to grab lunch one day, knowing he'd beg off when the time came. He wasn't attracted to women who insisted on attaching all that false stuff— nails, eyelashes, hair, etc. They were trying too hard.

Back to business. Alejandro would need Alli's office, without her in it. She was a coffee drinker—maybe he could use that. He ducked into the tiny break room and looked around for the machine. A man and woman were talking, but as Alejandro came toward them, they abruptly ended their conversation, checking him out with narrowed eyes. Day two and he was already sick of this company and its clandestine bullshit.

He slowly pressed his palm to the side of the coffee pot. It was cool. *Perfect.* He filled a disposable cup with the lukewarm liquid and carelessly topped it with a lid, then left the couple to resume their top secret tête-à-tête. He turned the corner and headed toward Alli's office. It was one of the smaller units, made even tighter because of the many file cabinets it housed. She and her desk were amidst them, stuffed in as an afterthought.

Showtime. He knocked lightly on the glass window and she glanced in his direction, a look of irritation on her face. The annoyed expression melted when she saw Alejandro, her face transforming to sweetness and light. Now was the time to work it.

"Hey, I was thinking about you, thought you might want some coffee." Alejandro felt bad as he uttered this lie, but he quickly shrugged off the feeling. Guilt was out of the question; he had a job to do.

Alli came toward him, an overeager smile on her face. "Wow, uh, thanks."

"It might be cold, though, so I'm not sure—"

"I'll take caffeine at any temp. I'm a fiend." She laughed and reached for the cup. Alejandro thrust it toward her and the lid flew off. Coffee sloshed onto Alli's pale-blue top and continued down her gray skirt. She looked up sharply, pissed, but then seemed to remember that the source was someone she wanted to bed. Alejandro leaped into action, grabbing tissues from the box on her desk, playing the role of the apologetic klutz.

"You know, just stop, it's no use." Alli held up her hand and shook her head, laughing. "I'm just gonna have to change into something else." Her attempt to downplay the whole thing made Alejandro feel like even more of a schmuck.

"Sorry. Just . . . ugh, so sorry."

"It's alright." She pointed a finger at him. "But you definitely owe me lunch now."

"Hell, yeah, I do." He tried to sound authentic. "You know it."

"Alright, well, I'll grab something from my locker and come right back, with more coffee for both of us." She smiled and scrunched up her nose as if the two of them now shared some inside joke.

"Okay. And again, damn. I'm really sorry." He paused, because this next part required delicate handling. "And, um, on your way back, would you mind picking up one of those benefit manuals for me? You know, from the other office?"

Alli nodded, eyes downturned. "Yeah, I'll get it for you." She left the office silently, looking back once, her face full of disappointment. Alejandro closed his eyes and bowed his head, a silent prayer for forgiveness. One day on this job and he'd become a monster.

He bent down and pretended to dab at the mess on the carpet, looking up periodically to watch the woman as she walked off. Once she was gone, he moved swiftly to her computer. Access was thankfully easy; she had already logged in. He started typing, pulling up the file on Leonard Goodwin first and then the one for Gayle Holland. As expected, the information on both of them was lengthy and convoluted; he didn't have time to delve into it. Working quickly, he downloaded the files onto the flash drive he'd brought with him, then keyed Gayle's number into his phone. To finish, he went into the program's settings and cleared the cache, erasing his search history.

The final step was to return to the home screen, but something was tugging at him. He found himself typing in his own name to see what, if anything, these people had on him. His file came up quickly, and although it wasn't as long as the other two files, it was troubling. They had basic information, most of which he had given to them during the application process, but directly under his picture were a few notes. Notes indicating he, too, was under scrutiny. "Stone to determine why subject left school. Says he needed a break, what is real reason." Then a couple of lines down, a lone phrase: "Woman missing." Alejandro's throat contracted. *Shit, shit, and shit.* They didn't believe what he'd said. And somehow, someway, they knew about Shelly. They and who else?

Alejandro stood up and headed toward the door. He opened it and stepped out into the small walkway, then flinched when he saw Angus there, looking directly at him, his head cocked, his face scrunched up in a frown. Alejandro initially felt locked into place but was prompted into action when the tall man took a step forward. Time to go. Alejandro turned and walked in the other direction, then broke into a run. He plowed through the emergency exit on his left and stumbled down a bank of stairs and through the door on the next landing. He scooted through a labyrinth of corridors, turning left and right, then took the first exit he could. He flew down another staircase and went through a door at the bottom, realizing he was now underground and deeper into the company's underbelly than he'd anticipated. *This is not the plan.*

He stopped to regroup. Looking down the hall, he saw a group of people in blue hazmat suits gathered in front of a glass door. The man in charge faced the group with a clipboard, conducting what appeared to be roll call. Alejandro watched the workers raise their arms one by one in response, their suits emitting sounds of rubbery friction.

"James Laurent." Silence. Alejandro drew closer. "I said, James Laurent." The foreman was irritated.

In his peripheral vision, Alejandro saw a blue figure coming out of a door behind the group and, thinking quickly, moved to the door and pushed the person-slash-suit back into the room from which he had emerged. As the door swung shut behind him, Alejandro kicked the man in his knees, disabling him, then fiddled with the clasps on the blue helmet until they released. He roughly pulled the helmet off the man's head and punched him directly in the face before the man could give so much as a yelp. After this, it was unlikely James Laurent would ever be tardy to roll call again.

Alejandro peeled the suit off the man and jammed his body into one of the large compartments where the suits were stored. He slammed the door shut, donned the helmet and the suit, then headed back into the hall. He stuffed the ID badge Alli had given him the day before into an outside pocket.

"Laurent here." Alejandro raised a rubbery arm. The foreman grunted and marked something on his clipboard without looking Alejandro's way. The group was just starting to file into a room marked "Biohazard." Alejandro seamlessly fell in step behind the last suit.

The room was a huge lab, with at least thirty workers stationed at tables throughout it, manipulating vials of blood and other substances. The picture he'd flagged the day before, the one of the Goodwin man, was displayed on flatscreens positioned at each station. The room, silent and sterile, made Alejandro wary of breathing, twitching, or simply existing, as if the slightest movement might cause great destruction.

Alejandro's group had stopped at one of the stations. The foreman spoke to them in low tones through the microphone in his helmet.

"You will continue your experimentation on the blood sample we have in the archives. The sample obtained by the agent in the field was not a match. The male dining with the targeted female was not our subject. But we know he's out there, and we're going to find him. Once we get him, we'll be able to harvest organ, nerve, and skin samples, the tissue we need to complete the study. Keep working with the old samples we have, see what they can do. Then, when we get him, we'll be ready."

Alejandro tried to digest this information. It was a lot to make sense of, and even tougher in this strange environment. He looked to the side and saw Angus's face peering into the room through the glass door. *Shit.* Alejandro moved deeper into the group and retrieved his own badge from his pocket. Without detection, he clipped the badge onto one of the workers in his group, then eased to the other end of the room, where he had seen some of the other suits exit.

Once out of the lab, Alejandro peeled off the hazmat suit and headed for the exterior door, which led to more corridors. He eventually found a stairwell and ran up several flights until he came to a steel door that was clamped shut. He stepped back and, using every bit of strength he had, rammed himself against it. The door clicked open, and Alejandro ran into the street and continued running for several blocks. When he felt he had gotten far enough, he turned a corner and stopped, panting. Once he caught his breath, he took out his phone, rubbed his damp palm on his pants, tapped Gayle's number, and prayed she'd pick up.

FIFTEEN

The principal would place a well-deserved reprimand in Gayle's file for this. Leaving the children alone in class without notice, leaving the school's premises without warning—she'd committed a litany of no-no's. But according to Alejandro—the man who'd called, sounding frantic—she couldn't tell anybody anything. He'd also told her not to let anyone see her leave. And in very few words, he'd intimated it was paramount that she follow his instructions, otherwise she wouldn't live long enough to care about things like her employment record. Why she was listening to a complete stranger, actually following his directions, was a big, looming question. She wouldn't know this man if he hit her over the head. And it was possible he'd do just that, then drag her off to his lair for who knows what. But when she thought about it, the reason she was abiding by his commands, to the exact letter, was clear: He knew an eerie number of details about both her and David, all of it too accurate to have been guessed or fabricated. And there was something else she detected—patent fear behind his words.

Gayle had told her class that she was going to the library to get a few books, then slipped downstairs to where Mr. Woods hung out when he wasn't cleaning this or fixing that. If anyone knew a discreet, alternate route out of the school, it would be Mr. Woods, its custodian for the past forty-two years. His easy, joking manner brought back memories of her own dad; his heavy ring of keys reminded her of her little brother. At eight, James had decided that the number of keys a man had was directly proportionate to his importance in society. Her brother had ultimately become a Realtor, so he now carried a multitude of keys, along with an overblown sense of self-worth. To remind her—or anyone who happened to be around—of his status, he'd take the large silver ring out of his pocket from time to time, rotate the keys around in his hand, fondling them, then return them to their home, next to his loins.

"Mr. Woods, hi, I need to get out of here—real fast." The weathered man looked up from his ad hoc desk—two big barrels pushed together with a folding chair between them—and smiled. *Bingo.* She'd be able to count on him for help. Gayle had always been nice to him, unlike some of the other teachers. To them, he was a faceless worker whose sole purpose was to fulfill the requests and demands they barked out.

"Well, you know I'm always happy to help you out, baby girl. What can I do for you? Said you need to get out of the building?"

"Y-yes. I need out of here. Fast." Gayle clawed the strap of her purse, lifted it slightly off of her shoulder, then left her thumb underneath. *Wrong day to try out a new handbag.* She imagined an angry, deep-red imprint on her skin.

"Well, I don't know why you wouldn't just walk on out the front door like most folks. It still works, doesn't it? The front's the closest to your classroom, if I recall, right?" Mr. Woods was nothing if not efficient. And he'd never been one to simply follow commands, bowing his head like a well-trained dog. If a request didn't make sense, he'd ask questions until it did.

"Uh, Mr. Woods, it has to do with . . . well, nobody can see me leave. I have to get out of here without anybody seeing me." Gayle sighed, already exhausted from explaining this little bit. She knew it sounded ridiculous, so of course there'd be more interrogation.

"And why is that? What's going on?"

Gayle took a deep breath and started in again, editing her words as she spoke. "It has to do with my boyfriend. David. I think you met him at the Christmas party?"

Mr. Woods gave a long nod, his eyes suspicious. "Yeah, the big-time lawyer, right?" Mr. Woods didn't like attorneys; his dealings with one on his workers' comp case years ago had solidified that. The whole lot of them were overly educated, fast-talking crooks, unleashed into the world with the sole purpose of making a dollar off of somebody else's pain.

"Yeah, well, he's not necessarily 'big-time.' I mean, he's good at what he does, he's successful, but he works for the government so he's not one of the real slick ones. I mean, he's smart, but h-h-he's a good guy a good guy, Mr. Woods."

Gayle realized she needed to step it up. At this rate, they'd still be here at sundown, discussing David's career arc. "He's in trouble," she went on, "and because of that, I'm in trouble, too. Well, not trouble, but maybe danger. And I have to get out of here to meet him to figure this whole thing out."

There. Gayle felt a mild sense of relief. It was all out.

Mr. Woods had bowed his head during all of this, and now he looked up at her from under his eyelids, disappointment coloring his face, a grimace placed squarely on his lips. Gayle prepared for a mini-sermon.

"Well, I don't see why you'd get involved with somebody like that, baby girl. You seem smarter than that. Letting some fool drag you up into his mess. A mess he made for himself. Now *he* has to lay in it, of course, but you sure don't have to lay in it with him." His frown softened to a knowing, fatherly look.

"Mr. Woods, it's really not what you think, it's not his fault at all, any of this, and I just... I need you to help me if you will, sir, because if I stay here, they're gonna get him, and maybe me, too, and I have to go. Now." Gayle was shaking at this point, her eyes reddening and filling with tears.

Mr. Woods softened. "Look, baby girl, if there's one thing I know for sure, it's that I don't want anything to happen to you. And I do mean that, trust me, I do. There's never been any quarrel about that." He picked up the purse she'd dropped during the conversation. "Here, let's get your things and we'll get you out of here. Lickety split. Follow me."

SIXTEEN

David's drive to the Juvenile Justice Division required four left turns, three right turns, an illegal U, and an eternity on two traffic-laden freeways. For the last leg of the trip, he had to navigate an ill-designed intersection, infamous for hosting, on average, 3.2 fatal accidents each month. Despite all this, David arrived unscathed at the juvenile facility, barely conscious of the twists and turns of his journey. Most people, upon realizing they had engaged in such a mindless trek, would embark on a backtracking wild ride to make sure they hadn't left the garage door open, or run over some soul's furry companion. For David, it was par for the course; routines tended to take care of themselves.

He was glad for a reprieve from the courthouse. David had slunk back to court the day after the humiliating incident. Thankfully, no one had talked about it, they'd even gone so far as to act like it had never occurred. He could move beyond that, bury it in the past. His mind had too much to process; he didn't have the bandwidth to be pulled in a ton of different directions. His thoughts turned to his adopted mom, Regina, who would have been a great help. She was a firm believer in the notion that events, whether good or bad, always came in threes. She thought it was a proven theorem, but Hersh dismissed it as country. Either way, it would certainly pass muster today. Three pressing issues sat aching at his temples, like little screws burrowing into his consciousness: (1) The missing-child ad with him in it. (2) Gayle. (3) His job.

Harlow Temple, the head deputy of the public defender's juvenile department, had called David downtown last week for an annual performance evaluation. Harlow was a curious character; his rise in the office was just as perplexing. After working his way through training and a few short-term stints at various courthouses in the county, Harlow had moved swiftly into administration. Despite this dubious experience, most of the younger lawyers had great reverence for him. David couldn't understand it. *Must be the look*, he thought. Harlow's stark white hair, worn in a long ponytail tied back with a navy grosgrain bow, made him a perfect fit for the dusty room where folks had drafted the preamble to the US Constitution, quill pen in hand.

Harlow had spoken to David in the low, passive tones of a psychotherapist. "So you've been in juvenile for roughly five years. That's a pretty long time." Harlow paused and gently bobbed his head up and down, waiting for David to respond. When David didn't oblige, he took a deep breath and continued, "And you've worked up to deputy-in-charge, managing the newer lawyers. Reports say you've been a good D-I-C. Been doing that for two years." Harlow blinked. Still no comment from David. "So at this point, we really want to see our more experienced attorneys moving on to felonies, you know, adult cases. It would be the best use of your skills, not to mention a higher pay grade."

David had heard all of this before. This time last year, same place, same man, same lecture. And he'd made it clear then that he preferred working with the kids. There was no point in repeating it. This man was his superior, and David wasn't a fool. Keeping silent was the way to play it. If he started talking, he knew his voice would have a negative tone.

Harlow went on, "So the problem is, it doesn't look too great when a person is refusing to move up the ranks to handle the tougher cases. It makes management start to wonder."

The tougher cases. As if he currently spent the day handling nothing but truancies and petty thefts. In the past four months, David had defended a fifteen-year-old who'd shot half the face off his victim, part of a gang initiation. Then there'd been the mentally disturbed kid who'd killed his sleeping uncle with an ice pick. The images from the coroner's photos in both cases had taken up residence in the nightmare-producing part of his brain. He'd attempted, in vain, to keep both kids from being tried as adults.

"So we need to work this through—come up with a solution that works for the Office."

Of course. That was what this was ultimately all about. Workplace politics. The bottom line. They probably wanted to put a lower-paid, less-experienced attorney in David's spot as deputy-in-charge and make him earn his keep in the felony courts. Despite Harlow's talk about pay grades, David knew you didn't get an increase, just like that, the day you started handling adult felony cases. You had to work in a felony assignment for at least six to nine months to prove you were worth your salt. Then you had to take an extensive written test, offered sporadically. Finally, you had to undergo an intense performance evaluation in front of a panel of two supervisors. After all that, you might see the pay increase if the county's budget could accommodate it, which it usually couldn't. David knew excellent lawyers who had been handling felony matters for several years and weren't making a penny more.

But it wasn't the hoops you had to jump through that kept David from wanting to move out of the juvenile division. He'd encountered plenty of obstacles on his way through law school and the state bar. There was hope for the kids, even the violent ones. They were lost, like he had been as a child at that airport twenty-five years ago. Each kid was like a red rubber dodgeball bouncing down a street with a sharp incline. If you ran after it fast enough, put forth the right amount of effort, you just might be able to save it, the way Hersh and Regina had saved him.

But what, or who, had they saved him from? David's mind shifted from the conversation with Harlow back to the missing-person ad that bore his face. Hersh's calm reaction to the ad had thrown David off; he was convinced Hersh was withholding something. David would have to circle back to him, sooner than later, to discuss this whole thing. He wasn't going to be shut down on this issue as if he were a child.

Although some part of David wished he *could* return to childlike ignorance, when he'd known nothing about the ad. Prior to seeing it, he'd at least been able to operate from a place of stability. Now everything was opened up—old wounds that were scarred over and old wounds that had not yet healed. And then there was his newest, greatest fear—unnamed wounds, yet to be inflicted.

He wanted to talk to Gayle again. He had gone to dinner the other night assuming she would make him see reason, reassure him that the missing-person ad was a big misunderstanding, easily explained. But instead of brushing it off, she'd taken it seriously, looking off into the distance, befuddled.

David knew she was exasperated by the state of their relationship. Maybe if he'd picked her up at the airport, she wouldn't have gone out with that Geoffrey dude from the school district. David had heard about it from a coworker who'd seen them at a hoity-toity steakhouse the night before. He couldn't be sure it was a betrayal per se; it might have been work related, a platonic meeting over a meal. He'd asked a bunch of questions about any noticeable elements of romance—hand-holding, sultry looks, a kiss across the table—but the colleague didn't have any details. Regardless, David knew Gayle's evening with the man hadn't been centered around an in-depth discussion of the plight of LA's schools. For the better part of their relationship, David had failed to be the man Gayle deserved. She was tired of serving as his guidance counselor, surrogate mother, and disaster relief service.

David approached the youth authority entrance and looked over at the deputy staffing the booth.

"Family member or attorney?" His disdain for both groups was clear.

"Attorney." David knew most of the day guards but didn't recognize this deputy, his voice a low grunt. He may have been new, but he'd already been schooled in the trade. His priority was to gatekeep, not to get chummy.

"Number of wards you're visiting?"

"Four."

"ID?"

David handed the uniformed man his driver's license and public defender's badge.

The guard glanced at it then practically threw it back at him. "Okay. Entry at 10:17 a.m." The deputy scribbled on his clipboard. "Allowing thirty minutes per ward plus thirty minutes for entry and exit protocol. We'll expect you to exit by—"

David cut the deputy off and inserted the answer. "12:47 p.m." He knew the drill and lacked the patience to wait for this guy to do the math. He held out his hand as the deputy passed him a green placard.

"Place this—"

"On my dashboard, I know. Return it as I exit." David looked into the rearview mirror as he drove forward. The deputy was already onto the next car.

David parked in the vast lot and walked toward the building. As he drew closer, the air seemed to thicken, similar to the vehicles in the parking lot—thin and sparse on the outskirts, dense and compact nearer to the facility. He passed five deputies on post at the entry. Brief eye contact and a nod at each sufficed—they were on familiar, if not friendly, terms with him. He continued on to the metal detector and the next deputy he encountered waved him through. Off to the side, he saw an additional deputy patting down some kid's curvaceous mom. The machine had beeped as she'd gone through, and another deputy had stepped over to "help." David smirked.

He came to the final stop of the entry passage, something a colleague referred to as the "point of no return." An older, grim-faced deputy handed David his briefcase along with the greasy bags of fast food he'd brought for his clients—the one treat from the outside he was allowed to bring in. The deputy reached toward a box of masks, then looked at David and withdrew his arm, placing it back at his side. "There's something going around in the population so we're all wearing these. They're checking to make sure it's not TB. I'd offer you one, but in all these years, I've never seen you wear one. Even with all the germs floating around, you never seem to need it." David nodded and moved forward, his hands full, his time evaporating.

He headed down a grubby hall to a door on the right that led to a small enclosure, where he knew his clients would be waiting. He pulled the door open with some effort, and the scent of musty adolescent bodies assaulted him. He tried to look optimistic, in case the boys were watching his face as he entered. He'd filed appeals on behalf of the four youth, a last-ditch effort to get them another chance at childhood.

About two dozen kids milled around in the cramped holding room, boys of different shapes, sizes, colors, and demeanors, united by their blue jumpsuits. David took a seat at the table that ran the length of the cage, the mean metal stool pressing into his butt.

"Martin Richmond," he called out, in his tough "I take no shit so don't even try me" voice. A thin boy with petite features stepped forward. The boy went over his side of the story. The facts of the case and this boy's involvement had been clearly established at trial, but David listened intently anyway. His task was to convince the court that the kid's sentence—or disposition, as it was called in juvenile court—was unfair because it hadn't fully considered the circumstances and environment that had led to the minor's involvement. If he could present facts surrounding the failure of the school system and other social structures to address his client's needs, he might be able to obtain a result that would afford the child an education, training, maybe a bit of hope. He'd explained this to Martin, and to all of his clients on appeal, but they insisted on focusing on their innocence. "That may be all they have to hold on to," Gayle had once offered. "We both know justice isn't blind and the process doesn't excavate the truth." She could get on a roll about the two systems of justice and disparate sentencing; sometimes David thought she had attended law school on the sly.

David's phone buzzed and he turned away from the kid. Gayle's name came up as he pulled the device out of his pocket. *Speak of the devil and the devil appears*, he thought. It was a phrase Regina had hated. "It's like you're saying somebody's the devil," she'd cry. And Gayle was hardly that. She was the steadfast angel in his life, sticking with him despite it all, the Velcro to his thinning, loose fibers. There were things he needed to say to her, words he should have spoken long ago.

David punched in the code and unlocked his phone, his thumbs ready to translate his emotions into text. He read Gayle's message and his stomach turned. *On the way to ur office right now. With friend to help. Meet us there. Don't call me. Don't tell anyone. We're in danger. IT'S ABOUT U.*

PART II

SEVENTEEN

Stone listened to his messages, then returned to the home screen. Above the phone icon, the circle containing the number "2" vanished, something he wished he had the power to do. Now it would start. And he knew how it would end, the same way it always did—a dozen or so people dead, numerous others maimed. Destruction of public property, private property, and everything in between. As always, he would make it out by a slim margin, physically unscathed, but with plenty of emotional residue, buried deep within.

Isabella had reported that Gayle was gone. She'd simply disappeared from the school, leaving her class without supervision. To add to it, Angus had reported that some kid they'd hired, a college dropout, was also gone. They'd caught him in someone else's office and chased him through the building. They'd also discovered that Angus's phone had made a pocket call to the kid, so the kid had probably heard something not meant for his ears. The end result was that Stone now had two targets—well, actually three, because you had to include the Goodwin guy, the man at the center of this whole thing.

Why did people always feel they had to run? Running inevitably led to an undesirable outcome for those doing the running. Didn't they get that? Hadn't they watched the same TV cop shows he'd watched? People never escaped what they were running from, unless the grave could be considered a safe haven. But he knew the inevitable answer; he'd heard it in a sci-fi film once: "Everybody runs."

He slipped his feet into a pair of black loafers and instantly became several inches taller. Yes, he was one of those men who wore elevator shoes. Many schmucks thought the height of a man was commensurate with his skill level, especially in this line of work. On one of his first private gigs, back in '94, he'd dealt with a woman whose scrappy personality had won her the top position at a corporate management firm. She'd called herself the "directress"—it had actually been written on her business card—such a ridiculous word that Stone had worked to suppress an outright laugh. Standing at nearly six feet, she'd lorded her height over him, smugly looking down at the top of his bald head. After the interview, he'd gone straight from her office to a shop aptly named Napoleon and bought four pairs of what was truly the miracle of footwear. Now most folks thought he was 5'10". He'd never had to work barefoot—or in socks—and didn't know how he'd deal with that, but he'd find a way if and when the time came.

As he started toward the desk that held his lockbox, he heard Anna tapping on the door. She always tapped five or six times before entering. It might have been paranoia on his part, but it seemed that the tapping was a warning of sorts, giving him a three-second window to hide whatever untoward business he was engaged in. It was as if she knew his occupation was not what he said, but was willing to keep up the pretense.

"You ready to go?" Anna's head, her hair freshly cut in a precise bob, filled the space between the door and its frame. Now that Charlie was away at school, they were making a point to officially go on date nights.

"Yeah, babe, I was just coming out."

Anna nodded. "Good," she said, turning to go back down the hall. "Just give me a chance to pee."

Stone chuckled. Growing up, his mother had forbidden the use of the word *pee*, dismissing anyone who used it as crass and uncouth. She liked *urinate* even less and was irrationally offended by *bathroom*, preferring *restroom*.

Stone had explained this linguistic rubric to Anna early on, as part and parcel of a compilation of funny stories about his childhood. They'd both laughed, called it prudish silliness, but he still assumed she would subsequently refrain from using the word in the presence of his mother.

Anna had done no such thing, and in fact, she'd said "I have to pee" to his mother on their first visit, back when they were dating. It was this type of tenacity, these defiant risks she insisted on taking, that attracted him to her. He had finally met his match, someone as gutsy as he was, and he'd found that aspect of her incredibly sexy. Her sassy haircut, with a swath of heavy bangs temptingly swept over one eye, had also been alluring and different, at a time when most women her age were expending their efforts copying Farrah Fawcett's poster-ready feathered look. They'd sailed through the first years of their marriage, each a ballsy counterpart to the other, and both, without any real evidence, believing themselves to be hipper and more aware than the rest of the geeky, brainwashed world.

Stone's phone beeped, returning him to the less humorous present day. He sighed and glanced at the screen, knowing what to expect before he even read the text.

He found Anna in the foyer, ready to go. "I'm gonna have to miss the movie. That was work. They need me right now on something. I'm sorry. We'll go tomorrow." He quickly kissed her on the cheek, then brushed past and headed out the door, avoiding her face and the disappointment splayed across it.

EIGHTEEN

David glared at the man who'd arrived with Gayle. They looked all chummy and conspiratorial, the right side of her body seemingly glued to the left side of his. He quickly assessed that this Alejandro person was a good ten to fifteen years younger than he was, in better shape, and, on a broad scale, might be deemed better looking. He sniffed, both at the situation and at himself. He had never been one to compare himself to other men. But this was the second time, in a matter of days, that Gayle was gallivanting around with a man other than himself.

"Good to meet you, man." Alejandro extended his hand.

David ignored the gesture and maintained a steady, unfriendly gaze.

Alejandro frowned slightly. "Look, I've only had this job for a day or two, but if I've judged these people right, we don't have a lot of time. So, cool, we can forget the niceties, if you want to play it like that."

David's neck tightened. "If I want to play it like that? Look, I don't know you, don't know who you are. You call my girl, get her all upset, have her running from her job all undercover and shit, and then the two of you dance in here like soulmates. So yes, based on all the above, yes, I'm going to play it like that." He glanced at Gayle, including her in the condemnation.

The attempted rebuke was lost on her. Upon arrival at David's office, Gayle had collapsed into one of the worn government-issued chairs that were usually occupied by David's clients, then closed her eyes in relief. Now, hearing the ego in both men's voices, she stood. Her eyes darted back and forth, but she remained silent.

Despite having felt so single-minded in purpose earlier in the day, Alejandro now wondered why the hell he had gotten enmeshed with these people and their plight. Missing Man Goodwin had the nerve to be pissed off, challenging him about coming in here with his woman. And this chick was just going to stand there and leave his ass out to dry. That's what guilt would do for you. Have you hurling yourself forward under some self-imposed directive, thinking you could gain redemption for some act or omission from the past.

"Look, man, I'm gonna take the reins here, okay, otherwise we'll all be dead by the time you decide whether I'm friend or foe. Yes, I called your girl. Yes, I told her she was in danger, and you can bet your ass she is. And so are you, by the way, more so than any of us. Okay? And now—because I wasn't smart enough to keep my head down and mind my own business—so am I."

David opened his mouth to speak, but Alejandro kept on. "Stop." He raised a hand. "I'm gonna finish. Lemme say something about your girl. She's beautiful, okay, I'll give you that. And really nice. But she doesn't have nearly enough ass for me."

Gayle appreciated Alejandro's attempt to smooth things over, but she didn't see why it had to be at the expense of her backside. She had a pretty nice one; its size was more than sufficient. She knew Alejandro thought so, too—he'd appraised her when they first met. So he was both shrewd and sexy.

"I contacted Gayle right after I got out of there." Alejandro recited the chain of events at SPM, including Violet's accident, then pivoted to Gayle. "You got out of the school without anyone seeing you." It was a command.

"I did." Gayle said, although she wasn't completely sure. Mr. Woods had gotten her off school premises, but she hadn't paid attention to peeking eyes and following footsteps. After quickly proceeding down a narrow staircase, they'd gone through an end-less sequence of locked doors and chambers, Mr. Woods deftly choosing the appropriate key as they approached each threshold. Another inordinately long set of stairs took them to a depth Gayle believed was inches from the core of the earth. The atmosphere changed abruptly from a dingy basement complex to catacombs—like something she'd only read about in books. Without break-ing stride, Mr. Woods looked back. "Don't worry, baby girl, we're almost there, just about halfway." Gayle had blinked. *Just halfway?*

"Have it your way. I'm outta here." Gayle's attention was brought abruptly back to David's office. Alejandro was stalking out, his hands pressed deep into his pockets.

"What's this?" Gayle gestured down the hall as Alejandro's figure got smaller and further away. "Where's he going? David?"

David looked at Gayle with disdain. "And if you'd like to leave, you're welcome to."

Gayle was incredulous. "What did you just say?"

"You heard me. I don't know him, and it's clear I don't know you, either. I thought we had something."

"Please tell me what you're talking about. I'm clueless. And you seem to have lost your mind. We came here to help you."

"I'm not gonna be the fool here. I know you went out with that guy from the school district the other night. You had steak tartare. He had a porterhouse. Now you come in here with this dude. I don't know who he's working for. I don't know who he is. It was a missing-child ad, probably some freakin' mistake. I've lived my life, safe and sound, without any sinister company so much as touching a hair on my head. If I'm in any real danger, I'll get to the bottom of it myself and I'll handle it on my own. As for you, you can now feel totally free to see anyone you choose. But just do me one favor."

Gayle looked at David, her face a mixture of fear and hope. "Yes?"

David moved closer, his face twitching with anger. "Hand over the key to my fucking apartment."

NINETEEN

Hersh collapsed into his brown leather recliner. David had proudly dragged it into the house on Hersh's last birthday. Hersh had spouted appreciative platitudes at the time, the "you shouldn't have's" and "exactly what I wanted's," though he would have preferred a no-frills, straight-backed chair with some lumbar support. He didn't sit in the leather monstrosity much; it wasn't broken in. It certainly didn't embrace his body the way he needed right now, but it would have to do. After his taxing day, Hersh didn't have the energy to get back up.

He'd arrived at the museum that morning, shortly after the tour group had convened. Scanning the lobby, he'd settled on an assemblage of gray-headed patrons, both hoping and fearing she would be among them.

And there she was, standing toward the front of the group, her chatty, irritating friend at her side. Well, the friend actually deserved gratitude instead of derision, Hersh thought. Overhearing her conversation at the walking park had led him here, and as a direct result, Margaret was now in sight.

Coming here had been a huge risk. Margaret might recognize him, even after all these years. People's hair grayed, sometimes they put on a few pounds, but overall they didn't change that much.

He'd recognized *her* immediately. The ill-fitting wig lost her some points, but overall she looked good; time had been kind. They'd worked together at the precinct for just a few weeks, decades ago and in different departments, but he'd passed by her desk countless times. Hopefully, to her, he'd been just another thick-armed body in uniform. For him, she'd been a stable presence in an unpredictable environment.

But now her presence threatened to destroy his whole little situation—really, his whole life, the life he'd hunkered down and created for himself after the manhunt had lost steam and the force's short attention span had turned to other matters. He'd been keeping tabs on her since he'd learned where she lived, in his very neighborhood, for goodness' sake. But simply watching her was no longer enough. He wasn't going to be caught by surprise, and he most certainly wasn't going to give up his life. He had to know whether she would recognize him and what she remembered and what she would do if she realized who he was.

The room had started to clear out, the attendees directed by the docent to explore the remaining exhibits on their own. Margaret's friend had wandered off with a group of women, leaving Margaret alone to look at one of the sculptures. Hersh took a full-footed, hearty step in her direction. *Here goes everything.*

TWENTY

Margaret lay awake, sniffing the air. Was she imagining the smell of decay? She'd been unsuccessful in locating its origin, and the odor continued to follow her as she got ready for bed. Her sense of smell was heightened in the dark, and the scent, along with other events of the day, was keeping her awake.

She got up and turned on the bedside lamp, then methodically eyeballed the room. The source was right in front of her: the tulips. The foam heads, in all their wigged glory, mocked her as if she should have known this all along. The tulips had wilted more than a week ago, but they hadn't looked sorry enough to prompt any action from Margaret. Since then, their leaves had fallen down into the vase to create mushy, swampy water that smelled like the contents of an unflushed toilet.

Margaret discarded the lifeless blooms, then poured the water into the bathroom sink and scoured the vase with Lysol. What a waste. She'd signed up for a floral arranging class at the flower mart downtown, thinking she'd learn how to select flowers like the experts, craft her own bouquets. She'd keep an abundance of fresh flowers in groupings throughout the house. That was the dream. The truth was, she simply wasn't that into it. Back to succulents.

Another one of her little schemes, quite literally down the drain. She was full of these bright ideas, and many of them, some way or another, turned out not to be so bright. Like signing up for the PLATO Society at the local university. Well, that wasn't accurate. Joining the Society—a group of retired folks who met weekly for lectures and day trips—had actually been a good idea. It was inviting her friend Georgia Barnett to come along that was the poor choice. Margaret had joined the Society for the purpose of meeting new people, so it made absolutely no sense to bring someone you already knew, especially when that someone was Georgia's gossipy self. But as the first event approached, she'd felt skittish. "Come with me to this thing tomorrow," she'd blurted during their last phone call. Georgia had been all for it.

Margaret had declined Georgia's offer to drive, but she hadn't spoken strongly enough. As a result, what should have been a twenty-minute trip had taken three quarters of an hour. Georgia drove as if her car was an uncooked egg, gingerly approaching each dip and driveway as if the vehicle was just one pothole away from shattering into a thousand pieces. Parking had taken an additional ten minutes, as Georgia pulled in and then backed out of her chosen spot four or five times at various angles, terrified of scraping up against one of the thick white pillars lining the underground structure.

But the rigamarole of getting to the exhibit had been worth it. A collection of actors, chosen apparently for their ability to stand inordinately still for long periods of time, had been painstakingly costumed and made up for the purpose of reproducing well-known works of art. Elaborate backdrops and complex lighting schematics had been employed, the docent explained, to give a feeling of authenticity to this "living art." When the docent's talk ended, Georgia inserted herself into a group of cackling women, sauntering off with them in search of the gift shop. Margaret secretly rejoiced. She'd had enough of Georgia's running commentary.

Margaret doubled back to the highlight of the exhibit, a human reproduction of Leonardo da Vinci's definitive work, *The Last Supper*. It was hardly her favorite painting, but it was the most familiar. She could remember a time when the dining room of pretty much every Black churchgoing household had a knockoff of the portrayal of Christ breaking bread with his disciples.

A gruff voice spoke from behind. "They did a good job of this one, huh?"

Margaret pivoted slowly and found herself within inches of the face of a very nice-looking man. He was probably five or six years her senior, but he had the confidence of a man in his prime. He stood so close, she could feel his breath on her face, a sensation that was not entirely unpleasant. It had been some time since she'd allowed anyone so deep into her personal space.

"Yes, it's quite nice. Very well done." She winced as she heard herself speak. "Quite nice." "Well done." What was she, from Great Britain now?

"Hersh," he said, holding out his hand. Margaret shook his hand but didn't offer her name. The man, or Hersh, as he called himself, wasn't fazed. "I kinda want to touch one of the people, see if they move," he said loudly, his finger outstretched, his voice full of mischief.

"I don't know, you probably shouldn't—" She turned back to the exhibit and was startled to see that all twelve disciples, an ominous-looking security guard, and Jesus Christ himself were looking straight at them. She glanced over at Hersh to see if he might be deterred by this extra attention. He wasn't.

Not wanting to be associated with this nut, Margaret started moving toward the exit. Hersh kept up. As they passed through the glass doors, the guard nodded. Hersh saluted. And then they were out of the museum, standing awkwardly at the top of the steps.

Across the street, a noisy playground was filled with young mothers and toddlers. Margaret pretended to be engrossed with the scene while trying to come up with a way to ease away from Hersh. He was amusing, and charming, too, but something about him made her uncomfortable.

"We should get together for lunch one day," he proposed.

Margaret ducked her chin, pulled her head and upper body back as if avoiding a punch. "Lunch? I don't even know you."

"Lunch is an easy way to solve that."

Talk about overconfidence. Margaret liked that in a man; it was sexy. Leonard Sr. had been full of it.

Hersh listed a number of trendy restaurants that had popped up in downtown Culver City over the past few months. Food, Lunch, Milk, Meet, Public School. There was even one called Eat, which seemed like some type of authoritative command, ordering you to fall in line and consume whatever gruel was placed in front of you. Hersh digressed into a mini-rant about how the new culinary school graduates thought it was hip to christen their establishments with these overly simplistic, mundane names. What happened to names that made sense, like Mel's and Norm's?

Margaret smiled and turned back to the playground. She watched one of the mothers throw a ball in the air and bounce it off of her head, her preschooler grinning in amazement. The boy retrieved the ball, then tried it several times himself. She realized her hang-up—she'd been out of the game too long. Hersh's overtures were not unwelcome, just unfamiliar. She returned his gaze and agreed to meet him the following day.

As she thought about it now, in the deep silence of night, the air still smelling of Lysol, Margaret questioned the wisdom of meeting this man, even if it was just lunch. Well, she'd be in broad daylight, amongst a bunch of folks who could rescue her, if need be. But rescue her from what? What about this man made her anxious? Margaret supposed the feeling she had was the same as a child's when getting into a kind stranger's car—enticed by the prospect of forbidden candy, but wary nonetheless.

TWENTY-ONE

"Peace, peace, much peace to you, my brother, peace. Spare change for your fellow man?"

A warm spray of spit landed in Alejandro's ear, and his eyes bolted open. He instinctively leaned to the left, his chin tucked, then stood up from the park bench where he'd been dozing. The guy looming over him seemed pretty harmless, *but still*. He sported a kufi hat, brown and dingy, worn to threads and losing its shape. While Alejandro, still drowsy, continued to get his bearings, the man launched into a monologue on society's ills, his voice monotone, his eyes melancholy.

"Because the Creator didn't mean for us to be here, stressed out with our maxed-out credit cards, rushing from here to there, sitting in traffic, honking our horns, yelling. This isn't life. Spend all your time trying to be the biggest and the baddest, and then at the end of it all, just when you think you've outdone everyone and everybody, you drop dead from the stress, nothing to show for it but your regrets."

The man turned to the various people who walked past, holding the gaze of anyone who hesitated for a moment. His words were rhetorical, addressed to no one in particular and all of creation in general. Alejandro half listened, his thoughts replaying the day's events. After being dismissed from David's office, he'd taken a cab to Hollenbeck Park in East LA and flopped down on a bench within a grouping of trees. SPM would have confiscated and searched his car by now; he couldn't go back to get it. He couldn't go home, either, and he'd called his mother and told her to pick up his dad from work and go straight to his aunt's house. Whether he helped David and Gayle or not, he—and more importantly, his flash drive of files—was a threat to SPM.

The day had exhausted him and he'd fallen asleep at the park, despite the uncomfortable bench he'd landed on. He dreamt of Shelly, and he thought of her now, the way her thick red hair flopped back and forth in a high ponytail when she jogged. Alejandro wished he'd met her before she accepted George's marriage proposal. She'd told Alejandro she felt trapped—the wedding train was on the tracks, full throttle, with a crowd of people on board and a shitload of money spent. She didn't have the first idea how to stop it.

"But He's coming soon, and He'll change all this. Get ready, He's coming." The man with the kufi hat and sad eyes continued his running commentary.

Alejandro dug into his right pocket, feeling his wallet and a smattering of change. He pulled a handful of loose coins out, planning to give the philosophizing brother all of them. As he opened his hand to pour the change into the man's stained plastic tub, something gold caught his eye and he looked at the coins. It was the peso he'd kept from a family trip to Cancún. His first trip to Mexico, at eight years old. He'd been fascinated by the colorful bills, the different coins. He'd carried one in his pocket since then, never daring to spend his lucky peso.

Alejandro picked the coin out of the group with his left hand and poured the rest into the man's bucket, prompting the man to nod his head, a silent blessing. Alejandro turned away, a soft smile on his face. He had exactly $254 in his wallet. More than enough for a one-way bus ticket to Tijuana.

TWENTY-TWO

"You have to admit it, we both know it. You weren't exactly setting her world on fire." Violet's glare was a challenge.

David took a few steps back. "Look, Gayle and I were fine, things were fine. You don't know what you're talking about." He hadn't come to the hospital for this conversation. In fact, he hadn't planned to mention Gayle at all. If Violet knew he'd kicked Gayle out of his office, he'd be the next one tossed out on his ass.

He'd found out where she was and called her room. "Hey, Violet, how're you doing? I heard about the accident. Can you have visitors?" David's voice was gruff; he sounded like he was out of breath.

"Yes . . . well, no . . . I mean, I'm not sure." If Violet's leg hadn't been tethered to a steel bar, she would have kicked herself. She had no interest in seeing Gayle's pathetic boyfriend.

"Good. I'll be there in two minutes."

David had hung up before Violet had a chance to fabricate a reason why he shouldn't come. In her rare, brief interactions with the man, he'd come off as mealymouthed. But those were the ones you had to be concerned about. They'd sit and stew, passively taking one slight after another, then suddenly and unpredictably blow. Everyone had a breaking point. And from the few words he'd said, she could tell he was pissed. Or scared.

Now he stood just inside the door and sniffed. The scent from the hospital's hallway had made its way into the room Violet shared with an elderly lady. A nurse entered and passed by the pair, a tray propped against her waist. The smell, an amalgamation of mushy microwaved foods, made David's stomach tighten.

"I don't want a goddamn chicken pot pie!" Violet's roommate summarily rejected her dinner, using all the might in her weak, wrinkled hand to push away both the tray and its bearer.

The nurse, used to this type of reaction, was unfazed. She set the tray down on a table and smoothed the blankets over the patient's legs. "Okay, Mrs. Barry, I'll see what else they might have for you."

"Good." The lady crossed her arms in an indignant huff.

David moved closer to Violet's bed. "I want to ask you something. Was there anything out of the ordinary about your accident?"

Violet frowned. "What?"

"Just wondering. I've heard some things."

Violet's expression was droll. "I would venture to say most accidents are out of the ordinary."

David fought the urge to go one-on-one with Violet in a battle of who could be the most sarcastic. On any other day it might have been fun.

"I guess what I'm trying to say is, was there anything strange about it? Was there anything that made it seem, I don't know, pre-planned, contrived—"

"You mean orchestrated? You think somebody did this on purpose?" In the second or two it took for her to utter the words, Violet somehow managed to look vulnerable, physically smaller.

Good, David thought. In one sentence, he had effectively dispensed with the bravado, the impenetrable shell Violet liked to present. Now for some progress.

"Yes, exactly, orchestrated. When you think back, was there a particular car, something that made it all happen? You were the one driving, right?"

"Well, there was a car that came out of nowhere, but I don't know. I really can't say. I don't even really remember the whole thing."

David went on, "And something else. Has anyone come in here, anybody you don't know, asking questions about your life, your friends?"

Violet was on edge. "Yes, a ton of people I don't know have been coming in here. Doctors. Nurses. Residents. Specialists. And they all ask me tons of questions. What is this about?"

"Alright." David told Violet about Alejandro and Gayle's visit to his office, omitting how the encounter had ended.

"So where are they now?"

"Where is who now?" David stalled as he tried to come up with a palatable explanation, one that wouldn't get his ass kicked, miraculously, by a hospital patient.

"Gayle. The other guy. Where'd they go? Why aren't they with you?"

"We kinda decided it would be better if we split up to figure this out. We all thought we might get a little further, get a better handle on it, if we went our separate ways. For everybody to do some, you know, independent research, see what we could find out." David had never been a good liar. He prayed for the trait to appear in him now.

"Independent research." Violet bent her head down and looked up at him from under her eyelids.

"Yes." He'd crack if he said anything else.

"So you just let Gayle go out there somewhere, all on her own, with these people after her and—"

"Authorities are looking for this man, who police suspect of having stolen highly classified files and materials from biomedical company SPM Inc." The miserable lady in the next bed had turned the TV up, causing both David and Violet to look up to the set in the overhead corner. Alejandro's employee photo filled the screen. The shadows floating across his face made him look menacing.

"Police say this person is armed and dangerous, and should be avoided at all costs."

"Is that him?" Violet was in disbelief. How could a day that had begun with applesauce and a temperature reading be ending with this madness?

David nodded gravely, then looked down at the floor. "That's him."

"Citizens who see this man are warned not to approach him, but to contact authorities immediately."

Alejandro's face flashed on the screen again, then the broadcast returned to a shot of well-coiffed newscasters at their desk. David took a moment to register it all. This Alejandro person had presented himself as some sort of Good Samaritan. In all actuality, he was a fugitive and a thief. Who knew what his angle was—to get David and Gayle mixed up in something, to use them for his own ends? Had they gone along with him, they'd have ended up as accessories to some scam, just as wanted as he was.

David was glad he'd sent the man away, but he was worried about Gayle. She'd been so gullible. What if they were together right now, unified because he'd rebuffed them?

"What do you think we should do? Call the police?" Violet cut into David's thoughts.

"I'm gonna tell you what we're gonna do. You're gonna stay here, stay put, focus on getting better. Don't think about any of this anymore."

"What? Just sit here?"

"Yes, just like I said, sit there. Rest. This Alejandro thing, it's some type of scam. We're not getting mixed up in whatever he's trying to draw us up into, okay? I'm going to SPM to tell them what I know. If somebody's looking for me, I'm gonna let them know they found me. I'll straighten this whole thing out, get us all cleared of this mess." David stalked out, walking directly into the trail of a patient who'd just sneezed. The nurse standing nearby winced and shook her head, her lips mouthing *Sorry*. David waved and kept moving. It wasn't the first time he'd been sneezed on; if he felt like it, he'd grab some orange juice and he'd be just fine.

He passed the nurse's stations and managed to catch the elevator just as its doors were closing. The steel box was a temporary cradle of comfort as it silently descended, returning David to the hospital's ground floor. He wished he could time travel back a day and throw all the mail directly into the recycling bin, without so much as a glance at some random missing-child ad. He felt like a baby in a backward-facing car seat, barreling forward yet oriented in the wrong direction, unable to see the calamities ahead. Like an infant, he wanted to cry out uncontrollably, thrash his arms and legs about, then place his hands over his eyes and make it all go away.

TWENTY-THREE

Margaret and Hersh arrived at the restaurant's entrance at the same time, fifteen minutes early. Hersh smiled at Margaret when he saw her. "Hey, beautiful."

Margaret wanted to believe the compliment and bask in it, but she wondered if it was something Hersh said, in his infinite smoothness, to every desperate woman who agreed to break bread with him. She silently reprimanded herself for this line of thought and cautioned herself against second-guessing every word that came out of the man's mouth. Margaret's meditation teacher had offered a suggestion for when she found herself ruminating over small matters instead of engaging in the present moment. "Notice it," the inordinately calm woman had advised, "then say to yourself: 'thinking, thinking.'" Apparently, reminding yourself that you were thinking was supposed to keep you from thinking. When she'd first heard this, Margaret felt like laughing out loud.

Hersh held the door for Margaret as she went in, then strode to the hostess and confidently asked for a table for two. Margaret appreciated this; her last date hadn't stridden anywhere, he'd schlepped. Margaret had felt like she was on the verge of giving up the ghost, walking hand in hand with that man toward the grave. Score one for Hersh—he knew how to take charge.

And that's what this was, wasn't it—a date? What else would it be? He hadn't invited her here to discuss the merits of that museum exhibit. *Thinking*, she told herself.

They'd agreed upon Chez Colette, a hidden bistro in West LA. A cottage set amidst glossy, multi-storied office buildings, it was a respite for lawyers, industry executives, and other self-important people. An art studio for kids was also nearby, so moms with small children often congregated at the restaurant in the late morning hours, along with leisurely retirees.

Hersh had requested the patio, so the hostess seated them at a pretty table situated against the outer wall of the cottage. The two of them were flanked by flower boxes on the left and a table of mothers on their right. One of the women held a baby who Margaret decided was about nine months old. The baby, a boy, was decked out in navy-blue shorts, a matching striped shirt, and a tiny blue baseball cap with "Daddy's Little Slugger" embroidered in white on the brim.

Margaret accepted a menu from the hostess and set it down immediately. A previous patron had spilled what looked like salad dressing on the upper right corner of the menu, and no one had seen fit to clean it off. It was clear the spill had occurred a while ago, because the substance had congealed before drying into a gross and permanent clump, partially obscuring the list of entrées. Margaret took a long, deep breath, another tip from the meditation guru. If she made a fuss about the menu, she'd risk seeming picky at best, anal retentive at worst. This might scare off Hersh and all of his niceties before this thing, whatever it was, got out of the starting gate. She would avoid looking at the menu and demurely grant Hersh the power to order for both of them.

While Margaret internally dealt with MenuGate, Hersh chatted with the waitress who'd brought their drinks, asking questions about the origin of the mussels they served and other banal, overly specific matters that Margaret could not have cared less about.

Their waitress's back was to the table with the baseball baby, and Margaret watched as the baby's tiny, fat hand reached for the strings hanging from the woman's apron. The baby missed and ended up grabbing a chunk of the waitress's derrière, causing her to stiffen and squeal. She whirled around, ready to light into someone, then realized the baby was the culprit. The mothers at the table roared with laughter, as did the waitress. Hersh chuckled a bit, and Margaret smiled. She thought about her own baby boy, who she felt would never have done such a thing. Or would he? She hadn't had him long enough to find out. *Thinking*, she said to herself.

"I do work for tips, but not that kind of work." The waitress had regained her composure and now spoke to the baby in a mock-stern voice. The moms laughed again but looked at each other knowingly. The waitress would expect a healthy tip.

"So what kind of work did you do before you retired?" Hersh had asked.

"I was a clerk-typist for years, and eventually I ran a temp outfit." This was an understatement. Margaret had worked at the police station and a number of other places before becoming a faithful employee at one of the largest temp agencies in the city. She'd worked her way into management, taking business classes along the way. When the kindly, childless owner had died, Margaret had surprisingly been called to a meeting at the man's stately home. The entire business had been left to her.

"Oh, okay. Wow, that's great. And do you have family—any kids?"

Margaret didn't want to get into that. "Well, we all have family, don't we? Somewhere." She was starting to feel interrogated. Time to change the subject, and time to ask a few questions of her own, specifically about something that had started to bother her.

She took a long look at him, then spoke. "You know, I didn't really see it when we met at the museum, but now that we're sitting here, you seem vaguely familiar. Were you—"

A huge crash of dishes cut Margaret off. The entire restaurant turned in the direction of the mêlée; a few people clapped. The waitstaff scrambled to clean up and set things right, and Margaret could see a woman, presumably Madame Colette herself, peering out of one of the cottage windows with a stern look.

Margaret turned back to Hersh and flinched. The displeased expression of Madame Colette was nothing compared to his now hardened, steely look. It was as if he'd put on an angry, masked version of himself while she'd been looking away.

What had they been talking about before the server's crash had happened? Margaret didn't remember, but it was clear that Hersh did. Meditation be damned—she needed to think.

TWENTY-FOUR

Being present at the moment his dad died had been easy. It was arguably the easiest thing Angus had ever done. He'd never tell anybody that; he'd be shunned, deemed a sociopath. And they would be right. He may not have been one at the time, but he was definitely one now.

The suffering had hardened him. Watching his father writhe and wince, hearing the undignified moans, the soundtrack of his teen years. But he never shied away from his father's room or the unpleasantness that went with it. He dug in his heels, helping his mother with bedpans, heating pads, the intravenous setup. It went on for months, and then one day it was over, finished. Peace relaxed his father's face, the features no longer contorted in pain.

The realization that his father no longer had to suffer gave Angus some level of solace. But knowing his dad was in a different, hopefully better place hadn't been enough to fully satisfy him. The pain could have been prevented; his father could have had more time, a longer life.

Angus picked up one of the rocks that held down the stacks of paper on his desk. Closing his eyes, he ran his thumb over the rock's textured surface, feeling its uneven ridges and indentations. His mother had scattered these stones all over the house, on counters, in corners and nooks, both before and after his father's death. She'd collected them, buying them on impulse from the point-of-sale displays at drugstores and Hallmark shops. Each had something carved into it, a word designed to uplift. Angus had kept the rocks, for some reason. After his mother passed away, his aunt had sold his parents' home, and as they'd done a final run-through, Angus grabbed the rocks one by one and buried them deep into the pockets of his corduroy pants.

Angus fingered the rock over and over, pressing his thumb deep into the crevices until it felt sore. He knew the word that was embedded on its surface before he opened his eyes. HOPE. He had to continue his work, in the name of his dead father and mother. He would not stop until he found Goodwin, the one who could have prevented all of this. When he succeeded, no other pimply-faced teenager would be left with polished urns and rapidly fading memories.

Angus swiveled his chair around to face the window. He threw the rock directly at the glass, with the force of a boy whose parents were needlessly gone, way too soon.

TWENTY-FIVE

"You're mysterious!" The bold letters jumped out from the page. *What crap.* Violet had taken several of these inane magazine quizzes over the past few days, every one of them a direct assault on women's intelligence. This latest one—"What Your Favorite Donut Says About You"—concluded that her choice, an apple fritter, meant she was secretive and unpredictable.

She'd been on edge since David left, resentful that he'd blown in and dropped a bomb, or at least fragments of one. Then he'd departed, abruptly, leaving her with growing paranoia and the impossible directive to do nothing. She already felt exposed enough; hospital doors didn't lock and anybody could just pop in at will. The feeling of vulnerability was especially unnerving at night. Violet was dependent on her evening dose of painkillers to ease the anxiety so she could get to sleep.

Now she had to wonder about some ominous conspiracy. It might be legitimate, or it might just be something borne in David's neurotic head.

"After the break, more on the missing man who authorities say is a violent threat and still at large in the city. Stay with us." A tinny instrumental riff designed to convey a sense of urgency and suspense cycled through three times, the camera frozen on the reporters.

Violet winced. She had started the process of forgetting all of this. Thanks to her roommate, the TV was always on at a low drone, as if it were just another of the silver monitors lined up beside each bed, checking vital statistics. After a string of commercials played through, the station returned to the broadcast and eventually got to Alejandro. All the pertinent details and images were repeated, an essential replay of the piece she'd seen earlier with David. Alejandro's full name, his face, and the allegation that he possessed weapons and classified files, all of which posed a grave threat. Violet couldn't help but believe this was vastly overblown, amped up for the station's ratings. Yet curiosity, and her possible connection to the story, kept her watching. She felt around for the remote that controlled the angle of her bed, the brightness of the lights—really, the whole of her life, for the time being—and increased the volume by a few clicks.

"Turn that back down—I was trying to sleep," barked the woman in the other bed. Violet ignored her. The woman had been on the phone just a moment earlier. "Did you hear me?" The bark turned into a high screech.

"No. I didn't hear you." Violet turned back to the screen while the woman, indignant, went into an angered frenzy, pawing at the buttons on her own keypad to summon a nurse.

Violet noticed this segment was a bit longer than the earlier one. The producer was going to run with this event, making it the ratings-winning scare of the week. As the anchor spoke, the camera panned across the front of SPM Inc.'s corporate offices, the site of the breach. It then cut to the interior of the complex, where unsmiling workers in lab coats and business suits strode purposefully through corridors or stood engaged in weighty conversation. The next scene was a close-up of a reporter standing with a man in a lab coat, while a voice announced, "Jessica Stranoff spoke with one of SPM's top executives earlier today."

"This is Dr. Kit Howe," the reporter said, turning toward the man standing next to her. "He heads up the research unit that was compromised by the individual police are looking for."

Dr. Howe looked straight into the camera and began droning on about the magnitude of the breach. Violet recognized him immediately as one of the doctors she'd seen around the hospital. His look was memorable enough; his closely clipped but full beard, along with his tall, solid build, made him seem like Santa Claus's muscular young nephew. Violet recalled that at one point he'd popped his head through the open wedge of her door, scrutinizing her without introduction. Hazy from medication, Violet had dismissed it.

"What now, Mrs. Barry?" A nurse Violet wasn't familiar with ambled into the room, distracted.

Dr. Howe's interview continued on screen. Violet glanced at the nurse's badge but could only make out the first name. "Hey, um, Miss, uh ... Ms. ... well ... Nurse Patti."

The woman looked her way. "Yes?"

"Doesn't that doctor work here?"

"Which doc—oh, yes, he's in internal medicine. And epidemiology, I think." Nurse Patti had initially glanced up to the TV, irritated, but once she saw who Violet was referring to, she turned completely away from the other patient. Now her attention was fully focused on the screen, her face open and angled up, as if she was marveling at the sun.

"So you know him?"

"No, well, no, I don't *know* him, I've just seen him and you know, you can see how handsome he is right there, so photogenic. You know, I had to give him a file once and he said the nicest 'thank you,' not like most of the doctors around here who just grab it from you. And I asked Marta if he was married and she doesn't think so and—"

Violet interrupted this nervous—yet useful—stream of consciousness. "But other than that, have you ever really talked to him?"

"Not really. I mean, he's *really*, really busy and I don't know if he'd even be interested in somebody like me. He didn't really seem to notice me when he gave me that file that day." Nurse Patti looked hurt as she recalled this.

"Well, you haven't really given him a chance to like you or not like you." Violet needed to know more about Dr. Howe before she started to believe any of what David had been rambling about. There were too many coincidences to ignore, but she needed to do some checking of her own. Nurse Patti and her sweetheart's crush had unwittingly supplied her with a plan to get the intel she needed. The chief task was getting the nurse on board.

"Yeah, but—"

"'Yeah, but what? If you're interested in somebody, you gotta at least give it a chance, let the person know you're interested."

Nurse Patti considered this. "I guess the next time I see him I could make more of an effort."

"Next time?!?" Violet blurted, her voice high and stringent. Her words came quickly. "You can't wait until some 'next time.' That could be days from now and I don't have time to wait for—" She stopped mid-rant and mentally slapped herself across the face. Nurse Patti was looking at her strangely. *Take it down a notch, Violet. Way down. Before you mess this up.*

"What I meant to say is, you know, time waits for no man, or no one, however it goes. I think you should go up to his floor, or down, or wherever, and just find him and talk to him. See what happens."

"He's upstairs. On eight. Marta's station is right outside his office." Nurse Patti's eyes roamed from left to right and back as she said this, while she pondered the wisdom of following the advice of some random patient she'd known less than ten minutes.

"Well, then, that's perfect. Let's go. I've *got* to get out of this room, get away from..." Violet nodded in the direction of Mrs. Barry and smirked, rolling her eyes as if she and Nurse Patti were the closest of confidantes. Time to take the reins or she'd never get up to that man's office. "I'll be your moral support. Is there a wheelchair?"

TWENTY-SIX

Some people were brighter than others. There was a range of intelligence, and everyone fell somewhere within it, from Einstein to the Three Stooges. When it came to the gelatinous stuff between the ears, a variety of theories and suppositions existed about how people differed, and the nature-versus-nurture discourse was wildly debated. Between PBS and NPR, there was no shortage of programming on the topic.

Despite all of this, Stone still couldn't believe how unbelievably dumb some people could be. *Wasn't this guy a lawyer?* It wasn't a complaint; Goodwin had actually gone to SPM's office, making Stone's mission that much easier. His job generally required the use of refined skill and ingenuity to find a target, to accomplish assigned tasks. He could have done this one blindfolded.

Stone reprimanded himself for this line of thinking. He was getting ahead of himself, a little cocky. An overconfident attitude was the preface to disaster. Even though he had come face to face with Goodwin, even wounded him, he hadn't actually brought him in.

Patting himself on the back was a bit premature.

Still, he'd learned a great deal in the past hour, knowledge that would surely have him toasting his own success in a matter of days.

He put his cup down and looked around the café. Several of the tables were filled with creative hipster types, tapping away feverishly at their keyboards, working on what they felt was the next big thing. Stone seemed stiff and overdressed in his black suit; he looked more like an undertaker than a hit man. He felt a bit conspicuous, noticed a couple of people glancing at him, but he didn't care. He'd come in here to figure out his next course of action; he'd sit here until he had a plan. He had a right to be here, even if he didn't have the requisite laptop, a need for free Wi-Fi, or a pair of skinny jeans.

Stone had gone to SPM's offices earlier in the day to get some information on Alejandro, the employee who'd skipped out with classified files in tow. Although Angus had emphasized the importance of apprehending Alejandro, he'd ordered Stone to focus on the main target, Goodwin.

"I have a team dealing with the riffraff who muddled up this project," Angus said in his stoic, measured manner. "The Gayle woman. Alejandro Kichido. Anyone else who gets in the way. What I want you to focus on is Leonard Goodwin."

As Stone returned to the reception area, he'd heard a man's loud, rambling voice. "Listen to what I'm trying to tell you. The man you're looking for was just in my office. The one who stole the files. It's been on TV everywhere, okay? I don't want to be mixed up in all of this. So just get me somebody I can talk to, alright? Just do it." The man's monologue became an emotional, anxious rant. The receptionist placed her hand on the man's forearm, a futile effort to calm him. From thirty feet away, Stone could see the man's profile. Something clicked. He pulled a photo out of his inside left breast pocket, glanced at it briefly.

Stone was incredulous. The target was right here, in front of his face.

"Goodwin!" Stone yelled, sharp and sudden. Every worker in the lobby slowed and turned toward his voice as if in a synchronized dance.

David did the same. Seeing the beefy, bald-headed man, his impeccably tailored suit, the piercing eyes, he knew to run. He bolted toward the revolving door as Stone pulled his gun. People screamed and dropped to the floor.

Stone fired just as David made it inside one of the door's moving sections, then ran toward the door as David grabbed his arm, hit. As Stone began to enter the next rotating section, David hit a red button on the door's center pole, slowing its movement. The door came to a complete halt and Stone cried out in pain, his arm caught between one of the doors and the building's frame. As guards worked to make the door operable again, David fled toward the parking lot and out of view.

The doors released and Stone stumbled out. He shook his head. *Slipped right through my fingers.* At least he hadn't killed the guy in his haste. Angus's directive had been specific: "Let me make one thing clear, in case you didn't get it. He's no good to us dead. This whole operation, everything you see here, it stops if he dies. We. Need. Him. Alive."

Stone dropped back into the present. A boisterous group of middle schoolers came into the café, jostling and teasing each other, almost tipping over a display of gift cards and mugs. None of them were of age for coffee, but their parents were probably too busy scrolling through Instagram to care. Charlie hadn't had his first cup of coffee until his junior year in high school, and he'd hated it, Stone remembered. He still preferred hot chocolate. Stone and Anna had brought Charlie up right, unlike most of the people out there who called themselves parents.

Stone got up and took his cup and napkins to the trash can. He didn't leave messes for others to clean up, whether on the job or in a coffeehouse. The barista smiled at him, and he wondered whether it was because he had tidied up his area or because she saw him as different from and thus sexier than the usual dipsticks who came in.

He left the café, clear on his strategy. Goodwin was close, well within reach. And he was injured. Stone would find him, finish this thing off, and get his money, so he and Anna could go see their son.

TWENTY-SEVEN

Gayle recalled only one other time, in all of her thirty-seven years, that she'd been kicked out of someone's office. And she'd been just as indignant then as she was now. She was five, spending the day with her father, a high school counselor. Taking Gayle's hand, the assistant principal had escorted her to an anteroom to work on a Hello Kitty activity book while her father met with a student. She hadn't understood then the brusque displacement from where she belonged, and she didn't get it now.

"Involuntarily. I-N-V-O-L-U-N-T-A-R-I-L-Y. Involuntarily." It had been one of the challenge words at the school's annual spelling bee, and Gayle's student, Nala, had spelled it correctly. Upon Nala's request, the judges had given the definition: "From the Latin. Done against someone's will; compulsory." Could someone use it in a sentence? Gayle sure as hell could.

Gayle had been involuntarily ousted from David's office. There was some redundancy there, she admitted; an ousting from someplace was, as a general rule, involuntary, but semantics weren't important right now. She would have never foreseen how swiftly he could put her out. David's office was on the nineteenth floor of the criminal courts building, and the long ride down to the lobby hadn't been enough to assuage the disbelief at his callous, wrathful tone. After all she'd done to get to him, to warn him—sneaking out and dragging herself through rotten passageways, as if this was 1850 and she a runaway slave on the underground railroad. Oh, and he had the nerve to want his key back?

She had thrown it at him, and it had hit him in the neck. The people could come after him and slice and dice his hairy ass. She was done.

But she hadn't known what to do when the elevator reached the ground floor. In some silly fantasy, Alejandro would've been waiting for her, arms open, a look of pity splayed across his sexy face, a plan of action at the ready. Gayle stepped out and looked around. *No such luck.* Not knowing who or what would be waiting for her at home, she took a taxi to a Korean day spa. No one would be able locate her there.

Gayle parked and walked into the spa's grand entrance. She expected the sage-green decor and the sound of the fountain to soothe her. No go. Her thoughts and heart were racing a hundred miles per minute. She was tempted to leave but pressed forward. She paid her fee at the cashier's desk and moved toward the women's lounge, avoiding eye contact with the other patrons. As she entered the lounge, an attendant wordlessly presented her with a shower cap, a towel, and slippers. Gayle was grateful; she didn't know if she had it in her to utter any niceties, even bland, meaningless ones.

One of the lockers had a sign on it that read "Out Off Service." The typo represented the way she felt. Stuck. Stagnant. Uncertain. *Out Off Service.* She stripped down to nothing, entered the wet room, and sunk down into the whirlpool bath, letting the warm, bubbling water come up to her chin. Two statues, a frog and a tortoise, flanked the steps that led down into the tub, offering good luck to all who entered. The stone eyes gazed at a point on the far wall, as if the answers to mysterious questions lay just ahead. Gayle followed their gaze; she could use both luck and answers.

Enveloped in the cocoon of whirling water, she revisited the events of the day. She and Alejandro had come to David, desperate, and he had kicked them to the curb, despite the possibility that they were all in danger. *Alright, then.* He no longer had a place in the equation for getting out of this mess. Her goal now was to simply stay way out of reach of the people that Alejandro had warned them of, the conglomerate that was after them.

An attendant came by and looked at Gayle with disdain, then pointed to a sign overhead. "Shower caps must be worn at all times while in the wet room." Gayle grabbed hers from within the folds of her towel and smoothed it on. *Goodness.*

The conglomerate that was after them. But were they really after *her*? Alejandro had said they were monitoring David's page on a website and were only following her to get to him. The way things stood, she wouldn't be seeing David anytime in the foreseeable future. She could deal with some goon following her for a few days. They'd soon realize she wasn't going to lead them to David, that they'd misappropriated their resources by focusing on her. And then they'd move on.

A woman entered the hot tub and slowly crouched down into the water, a comfortable distance away. They gave each other quick, polite smiles and nods. An attendant came through and reminded each of them to keep quiet. Gayle gave the other patron a droll look. *Really.*

She wondered what David was thinking now, what his take was on this thing. At no point during the threesome's conversation at the PD's office had he remotely entertained the proposition that a company was maiming and killing folks in order to get to him. Despite everything he'd heard, David hadn't seen fit to buy into any of it. *Why?*

As credible as Alejandro seemed, the scenario he'd painted *could* be viewed as irrational. In fact, there could be a reasonably benign explanation for the various facts and events Alejandro relayed. Isabella, for example. Which was more likely? That she was an alluring, military-trained Charlie's Angels–type operative, put in place by a sinister corporation to cozy up to Gayle and get the inside track? Or that she was simply one of the thousands of annoying, pushy, overly ambitious people that LA attracted by the bucket-loads? And Violet. Maybe she had simply been the victim of a few distracted drivers, another commodity the city had no shortage of. Finally, you couldn't blame a company for going a little bonkers to protect itself from some newbie who had accessed confidential files from someone else's computer.

Gayle jumped up, startling the other patron. She grabbed a towel from the stack at the edge of the bath and scampered out. David had been right. And she had been a fool, doing the bidding of a strange man who'd called her out of the blue. Of course this ridiculousness had upset David. She never should have brought this to him. And when he'd balked at the whole thing, clearly not giving an ounce of credence to Alejandro's claims, she should have stood by his side. He dealt with criminals on a daily basis; he could assess a person's integrity in a matter of minutes. It was his job.

And now her job was in jeopardy. Gayle had left school prem-ises without notice, had left her students without supervision. She needed to get home, settle down, and come up with some story, some exponentially powerful excuse, that would help her salvage her position. She thought to call the principal at home but decided against it. She'd get to school early and speak to her first thing. And then, hell, she might even invite Isabella to lunch.

Fully dressed, Gayle emerged from the women's lounge, grounded by this rational train of thought. She admired the elabo-rate orchid arrangement positioned on a pedestal near the cashier's desk. From a distance it looked unusually intricate, with many stems entwined around thicker branches and foliage. When she stood closer, its simplicity was revealed; it was composed of just three orchids, expertly placed.

Gayle hadn't quite decided what to do about David. It was com-plicated. But she had faith that if she stayed on course, a simple solution would emerge. She stepped out into the evening, and as the spa's heavy doors closed behind her, she took in the smell of incense drifting over from the Buddhist temple across the street. She felt grateful for the cool air, and even more for her prevailing cooler head.

And then something abruptly covered her head—something like a silk pillowcase, only smaller and tighter—and she was dragged forward on the pavement. She cried out for help, and the dragging stopped. A rough hand came up under her head covering and stuffed what felt like a balled-up washcloth into her mouth. Then she was moving forward again, an oversized hand pressed firmly on her back, pushing her along. The thick fingers of another hand tightly gripped her upper right arm. She struggled to break away but was kept in place.

She felt herself being lifted into a horizontal position, her feet dangling. One of her shoes fell off, and she heard it tap the ground as it landed. Now her body was being lowered, and then she was compressed into a tight space, her limbs awkwardly bent. She heard the muted sound of a closing door and felt a puff of air on her neck. She was in a car's trunk. She tried, with everything she had, to keep the panic at bay. It wouldn't help her now. She twisted her shoulders back and forth in small movements, an attempt to free her hands and arms. She'd seen a talk show piece on safety a few years back, in which savvy people had given tips on getting out of dangerous situations. She'd almost turned to another channel; how likely was it that she'd ever be locked in an underground basement or stuck in an elevator on the eighty-ninth floor? But she'd stayed with it, and a camera-friendly officer advised that if you were stuffed into the trunk of a car, your best bet for getting out would be to punch out the taillight from inside and stick your hand out and wiggle it. Drivers of trailing cars who saw this strange sight would promptly notify law enforcement, leading to your happy rescue.

The car's ignition started, and Gayle's body shifted a bit. They were moving. She pushed against the inside of the trunk's walls with her hands, searching for a surface that might be a taillight.

The car drove for a while, then stopped short. A door slammed and the noise from the outside got louder—the trunk had been opened. The same thick hands as before took hold of her wrists and bound them together. The trunk door closed gently and the car took off.

TWENTY-EIGHT

Hersh stepped off the newfangled digital scale in a huff. David had brought the contraption over as part of his self-assigned mission to help him "join the rest of the world in the twenty-first century." He now knew the exact percentages of water, muscle, and bone that made up his seventy-two-year-old form, as well as his body mass index and his weight in both pounds and kilograms. It took thirty seconds for the machine to compute and display these readings, but to Hersh they were thirty infinitely long seconds, an enormous waste of time. He made a note to rummage through the junk in the garage to find his old spring-loaded scale.

It was odd for Hersh to be so preoccupied with his weight. Someone else in his mental state would have already downed a triple cheeseburger and a large bag of onion rings, just for comfort, without a thought to an increase in girth. But Hersh needed something mundane to hold on to; parts of his life he thought had been put to bed long ago were stirring. Once they were fully awake, his entire existence would quickly unravel.

The lunch with Margaret had been relatively uneventful, but it had left Hersh in purgatory. The meal ended with his questions unanswered, and in actuality this was worse than if Margaret had simply looked at him and said "I know who you are, you bastard, and I know what you did." This would have been terrifying, of course, and would have called for some unmercifully harsh action on Hersh's part, once he got his bearings. But at least he would have a clear directive on how to proceed.

The reality was that Margaret had been cut off from saying those or any other words that might have released Hersh from the quandary he was in. Once the shards of porcelain had been picked up and the restaurant had returned to relative quiet, Hersh hadn't dared jog Margaret's memory. "Never ask a question you don't know the answer to," David liked to say. Hersh had followed that counsel, and here he was, right back where he'd started.

In the name of regrouping, Hersh holed himself up at the house. On his way there, a motorcycle cop had driven up alongside his car, beckoning him to pull over. Hersh had shifted in his seat, his brain buzzing. *Boy, that Margaret acted fast.* He relaxed when he realized the officer was escorting a funeral procession. There were only two reasons that LA traffic would cease for you, Hersh thought. If you were wanted, or if you were dead.

At home, Hersh busied himself with a host of garden-variety tasks—changing a couple of lightbulbs; folding a load of underwear he'd deserted in a black garbage bag; flossing his teeth. After a couple of hours, his stomach had started rumbling, reminding him he hadn't eaten enough at lunch. He opened the refrigerator, took out fixings for a sandwich, and scattered them over the full length of the counter. As he grabbed a head of iceberg lettuce, he heard the squeaky, grinding sound of his garage door.

Frozen by the sink, he listened to the faint motor of a car as it slowly made its way into the structure, then heard the garage door roll to a close.

So Margaret had known exactly who he was, and rather than reveal it at lunch, she'd gone straight to the authorities. She'd put in a performance worthy of a stroll down the red carpet, closing out their meeting with a sweet kiss on his right cheek. It had probably been some type of signal, Hersh thought, a Judas-like betrayal. Hell, the funeral procession he'd seen might have been a farce, some contrived way for the men in blue to keep tabs on him. He knew all about how they worked and the vast resources at their disposal.

Yep, they'd let him catch his breath and get comfortable, all the while planning to ultimately corner him in his own habitat, like hunted prey.

"You're either a man of action or a man in traction." Hersh's own words mocked him. He had admonished David to an irritating degree with that little chestnut, and now it was coming back on him. There was no time to ruminate on Margaret's art-of-war tactics. He was supposed to be in fight-or-flight mode, wasn't he, triggered by some auto-something aspect of the nervous system?

Instead, he adopted a useless stand-and-suffer strategy, until a rattling of the door that led in from the garage prompted him to act. Need my gun. In the lockbox. Get the key. Short phrases tumbled around in Hersh's head like the words of a first-grade reading primer. *See Hersh walk. See Hersh run. See Hersh go to jail for destroying a man's life.*

Cradling the head of lettuce like a football, he jogged to his bedroom and retrieved his 9mm Beretta. Hersh stood in shooter's stance, his arms outstretched and legs wide, on high alert. The old floorboards in the hallway emitted a creepy melody as the intruder moved closer, his gait uneven. Hersh clenched his teeth.

"Dad, where are you?" It was David, for heaven's sake. Hersh exhaled and fell back against the wall. He'd forgotten that David had started using Regina's garage door opener after she passed away. David called out again.

As his son approached the bedroom door, Hersh placed the gun back in its box and kicked the steel contraption deep into the dust balls under his bed. Realizing he still had the lettuce in his grip, he hastily scanned the room. David had once advised Hersh that consuming iceberg lettuce was a mistake; it had no real nutritional value. Kale was the order of the day. Not in the mood for a lecture on cruciferous vegetables, Hersh stashed the lettuce behind a pillow, then plopped down onto the bed and pretended to peruse the newspaper.

When David finally made it to the threshold, Hersh jumped up, unprepared for the sight in front of him. David collapsed into a chair, clutching his upper arm.

"What happened, son, who did this to you, what the—" The questions ran together, pouring out of Hersh's mouth like a spigot. His chest burned as his eyes registered the blood smeared on David's clothes.

"I went to the place to straighten it all out and they shot at me."

"Wait." Hersh put both his hands up in front of his chest, fingers splayed, as if they might somehow stop the situation altogether. He shook his head quickly back and forth. "What place? And wh-who shot at you?"

"It's that ad I showed you. Gayle brought a man to my office who said there's a company looking for me, and he was right. I didn't believe him, but he was right."

Hersh glanced away from David, then reached for the reading glasses on his nightstand. He bent down to take a look at David's arm. Using the hole the bullet had made, he ripped David's shirt open at the site of the wound and examined the bloody flesh with a finger. "I can do this; I can handle it. We won't even need a hospital."

"We don't need a hospital? Are you serious, Dad? My arm is on fire."

"If it was that serious, you'd have already bled to death, okay? You wouldn't have made it here. Try to calm down." Hersh switched into the mode he'd used as a combat medic in the infantry, back when he'd served in the war. It had been decades since he'd done this type of work; it seemed like a whole other life. "Looks like you got lucky. The bullet just grazed your medial deltoid. Thankfully, it missed the humeral circumflex artery as well as the axillary nerves. You'll be fine."

David looked up at Hersh, his expression a mix of intense pain and incredulity. "Dad. You still remember that stuff?"

"You never forget, son. As painful as it may be, there's no pulsating blood loss. Just soft-tissue damage. We can definitely do this here. I have some things in the garage I can treat this with. And I'm not worried about any infection—even with all the stuff kids get into, you've never had to take an antibiotic a day in your life, or at least since you came to live with us. But what we really need to think about is what do we do next. After we get you all set. What's gonna be our next move to keep you safe."

Hersh hurried out of the bedroom and returned a few minutes later with a small pink tub and a first aid kit. Soapy water splashed over the sides of the tub as he kneeled at David's side. He took the sponge from the tub and manipulated it under the water, squeezing it, releasing it, turning it this way and that.

Hersh looked at David's solemn face. This was actually working out perfectly. Going into hiding was in both Hersh's and David's best interests at this point. "Maybe we should get outta here. Just for a while. Find out what exactly is going on."

"So the big groundbreaking idea is to leave town? Just disappear? And go where? DAMMIT." David flinched and struggled to stay still as Hersh flushed and rinsed his arm.

"I don't know. Napa? You used to love the train, and horseback riding—"

"Dad. I'm not twelve years old and this isn't some fun family weekend we're talking about. I have a job. OU-U-CH." David winced and jerked his shoulder away as Hersh cleaned the wound with hydrogen peroxide, then followed up with a spray of Betadine. "Shit, Dad."

"That's right, you have a job. One you barely like. And if you get killed by the company that's after you, you can bet that job will scratch your name right off your office and have someone else's name put up before your body's cold in the ground." Keeping his eyes trained on the wound, he dressed it with sterile gauze and applied a pressure bandage.

"They're after Gayle, too. I can't just bust out of town and leave her here. She tried to warn me and I didn't listen."

Hersh shook his head back and forth. "We'll go get Gayle, then. She comes with us, if that's what you want."

David tried to stand, using his good arm to push himself up. Hersh inched his way behind his son and held him steady. It was a good thing Hersh had kept tabs on his weight. Being in shape was an asset to someone on the run.

TWENTY-NINE

"We got him, sir."

"You got him?" Stone reached for the control knob of his car radio and shut it off. He was enjoying one of LA's popular weekly podcasts, an erudite critique of new film releases hosted by a man whose voice reminded Stone of his father. "What do you mean, 'we got him?' You weren't supposed to get him. You were just supposed to follow him until I could get there. And who the hell is 'we'? You're supposed to be working alone."

"Well, uh, Mr. Stone, we don't really—"

"Never. Call. Me. Mr. Stone. Ever. As a matter of fact, don't even say my name out loud, dammit. At all."

"Forgive me, Mr.—well, just forgive me. What I meant to say is that we have him in our sights. And, I mean *me*, not we. *I* see him. I was saying 'we' in the sense of, you know, the company, the collective, those of us who are working together, our outfit, so to speak—"

"Alright, alright, calm down and just answer me this—are you on the bus? Yes or no, just yes or no. Are you on it."

"Yes, sir."

"Good." Stone sat back in his seat. SPM had easily determined Alejandro's location using his cell phone number. An obscure program available only upon special request to those with a certain level of clearance allowed one to input any cell phone number and retrieve the phone's path and current location.

The app revealed that after barreling through SPM, Alejandro had visited the criminal courts building downtown, then had inexplicably spent time at a local park in East LA. Now he was on a Greyhound bus, headed for the border. Stone and Angus had sent a guy to watch over Alejandro until they decided their next steps.

Stone marveled at the efficiency of all this. Everything was automated now. There was a time, he remembered fondly, when a seasoned operative like himself would have relied on an intricate system of human contacts, painstakingly cultivated over many years. People of discretion whom he could go to for leads when he needed to find someone. He'd make his rounds through this web of well-placed individuals, piece together the info he received, weed out the less credible sources, then use street smarts, and maybe a touch of strong-arming to smoke out the person. Advances in technology had made this type of know-how obsolete. No jobs were immune from downsizing. It wasn't just factory workers and cashiers being replaced. Not even the snitches had been spared.

"Okay. I'm gonna get off the phone now and head toward your location. You stay on the bus, keep an eye on him. And keep up the good work." Stone added the last bit as an afterthought. Positive reinforcement, even if it was disingenuous, never hurt.

He sighed as he entered the I-405 southbound. It was sluggish, as usual, the cars ambling along, just slightly above twenty miles per hour. Stone wondered if cars had ever flowed on this freeway at a good clip, or if it had been lousy from inception.

He glanced at the folks in the cars around him. People never seemed to really look at each other as they inched along. Instead, they stared straight ahead as if entranced by the horizon, resignation on their faces. It was a community of sorts, Stone theorized. The community—or "collective," to use his minion's word—of traffic. You reluctantly joined the alliance when you got on the freeway, and happily defected as you exited. Everyone accepted this as natural, part and parcel of living in LA, all operating under the mutual conclusion that the pros of the metropolis outweighed the cons.

And for the most part they did. The city itself wasn't the cause of Stone's malaise. It was what he was engaged in, *in* this city. His job. He'd grown beyond it; it was too limited for who he was becoming, or wanted to become: a thinker, a peaceful being, maybe even the author of a memoir. But leaving this life wouldn't be easy.

"Stone here." He always answered his phone on the first ring. Anything longer gave the impression that one was slothful, avoidant.

"Sir, um, hello. It's—"

Stone took the call off his car's Bluetooth system and spoke directly into the phone, as if someone in an adjacent car might hear him. "I know who it is. And before you give me the status, you gotta remember that when you're in a public place, it's never a good idea to identify yourself or anyone else you're workin' with. Got it?"

"Got it. Sorry, sir."

"No need for apologies, let's move on. What's the deal."

"Well, I've, uh . . . I've—"

"Come on, spit it out, man. I don't have time for this." Stone did have the desire, ultimately, to be a serene person of patience and peace, but not today.

"I've lost the target, Alejandro Kichido, he's gone."

"You've . . . lost . . . him. Meaning, you no longer know where he is." Stone could feel it, a slow burn starting, the fire heating, the smoke rising from the top of his bald head.

"Y-yes, sir, I don't know where he is."

"Okay. Look. Are you on the bus?"

"Yes."

"Did he get off the bus?"

"Yes."

"And you chose not to follow him."

"No, sir, I did follow him. It was a rest stop and everybody got off the bus. They stopped at this mom-and-pop place that sells cinnamon buns. The driver said it was established in the '40s and people would come from all over to get them. And they *were* pretty good, to be honest."

Stone put his hands up and covered his face, until he remembered he was behind the wheel. Had the world gone mad? SPM folks were always raving about the donuts from the place on the building's ground floor, and now this fool was talking up some damn cinnamon buns.

He tried to keep calm. "Okay. So you got a really good cinnamon bun, and I'm gonna assume Alejandro Kichido got a really good cinnamon bun, and then you and everybody moseyed back onto the bus, but not him."

"No, sir, he did get back on the bus."

"Okay. And you got back on the bus."

"Exactly."

"So if you're both on the bus, how is it that you've lost him?"

"Well, he went to use the bathroom in the back and he never came back."

"Have you checked the bathroom?" Stone asked, exasperated.

"Yes, and he's gone."

"Okay, I'm missing something. You saw him go to the bathroom. And then he didn't go back to his seat, so you checked the bathroom."

"Yes, well, some time passed, and I saw other people going to the bathroom and then coming back to their seats, but he never did, and there's only one bathroom, so I started wondering about him. And while all this was happening, there was a funny thing I saw outside, and I didn't think too much of it at the time, but now it's all coming together."

"You've lost me again, kid. Something outside, where? What are you talking about?"

"He got away on the motorcycle, sir."

"What?"

"It's like I said, I saw something outside, something strange. A motorcycle came up real close to the bus, real close. And there was just one rider, and then it looked like somebody else was getting on, kinda came out from nowhere, and this new guy swung his leg over the back and they took off."

"Wait, what?"

"So I went back to the bathroom to look for him, and dang, it smelled bad. Not enough ventilation. Guess that's a tall order on a bus. Anyway, I look around, trying to figure out where he went, and I see a panel all opened up. You could go through to where they keep the luggage. So I crawled in there, and there was another open panel, and it leads outside. So when I put it all together, you know, what I had seen with the motorcycle and all, I'm pretty sure that was him getting on the motorcycle."

Stone took a deep breath, seething. He'd given this guy one simple thing to do. One lousy, lazy task, for goodness' sake. *Ride on the bus with the boy.* Instead, the man had blithely watched Alejandro ride off into the sunset, in plain sight, on the back of a motorcycle. Apparently Alejandro was a descendant of Evel Knievel, but that was no matter. Thankfully they could refer back to the app that they'd used to locate Alejandro in the first place to easily obtain his new position. He scolded himself for bemoaning the use of all this gadgetry just moments ago. There was no place for that type of sentimentality. Technology was his friend.

"Alright, dude, hold tight. I'll call you back."

Stone called Angus, gave him the news. Angus placed Stone on a brief hold, then returned to the line, irritated. "The target is still on the bus."

"Excuse me?"

"Get your head out of your ass, Stone. Alejandro Kichido is still on the bus. We show him on the 405, traveling south. Sixty-eight miles per hour. In the carpool lane."

Stone hung up and called the field agent. This time he couldn't hold back. "He's still on the bus, you idiot!"

The man spoke, his mouth clearly full. Stone couldn't believe he had the nerve to eat under these circumstances, after such a tremendous foul-up. *Hadn't he just had a cinnamon bun?*

"Sir, he's not here. It doesn't matter what the computers say. He's gone."

"Look. I have his number. I'm going to call it. You're going to listen for a ringing phone. You're going to watch for someone picking up their phone. He's there." Stone grabbed a burner phone from his glove box and tapped in Alejandro's number.

"Okay. What do you hear? What do you see?"

Stone could hear belabored breathing, but no words.

"Do you read me? What do you hear? Come on, man, what's going on?"

Finally, a response. "Sir, uh . . . uh, the phone is ringing. And buzzing."

"Good. And who's it coming from?"

"From me. The target's phone is in my pocket. I have his phone. It's on me."

THIRTY

1. **Given:** SPM manufactured an accident that killed two innocent people and put a teacher in critical condition.

2. **Given:** SPM is conducting secretive underground experiments on human tissue.

3. **Given:** SPM is sinister and creepy.

4. **If** all of the above is true, **then** SPM will do absolutely anything to get the highly confidential, extremely valuable files I have in my possession, and destroy any other evidence.

5. **Definition:** I, Alejandro, am equal to and the same as "any other evidence."

6. **Conclusion:** SPM is going to kill me.

Geometry had been Alejandro's least favorite subject in ninth grade; it was puzzling that he was thinking in the language of proofs and theorems. Maybe this was what his brain thought it would take, framing his situation in the lingo of something he loathed, to make him fully appreciate the peril he was in.

He'd known he was in some danger, known it when he went barreling out of the company's building, but he hadn't realized the extent. He assumed he'd be in Tijuana by now, lost to them, a señorita on his lap. SPM would tighten its security measures and continue on with its horrible mission, whatever it was.

Alejandro sat on the ground, his back against the dingy exterior wall of a vacant building in downtown Long Beach. He picked up an abandoned, half-empty bottle of water and rolled the container over his cheeks and forehead, letting the condensation cool his skin. He examined the bottle, then looked around. Trash and other miscellaneous items were strewn about, flattened and dirty. In all likelihood, the bottle had a dodgy history—who knew what lips had recently touched it? Forget that, he was thirsty as hell. He opened the bottle and poured the water into his mouth and over his head, letting it find its way down his ears and chin.

A woman who looked lost sauntered by on the sidewalk in front of him, holding the hand of a preschooler. The little girl's hair was dark and curly, like Alejandro's. She gave him a half-smile and a high-voiced hello as she passed, her eyes open and curious. The mother looked back at Alejandro, frowned, then clutched the girl's hand and hurried on. Alejandro shook his head. In two short days, SPM had turned him into a techno-thief, a hunted fugitive, and a derelict not fit to speak to children.

He'd figured out on the bus that SPM had traced his location via his cell phone, most likely with some Big Brother regulation-busting privacy spyware that taxpayers were financing but didn't know existed. He'd started to suspect he was being followed when a man who looked a bit too slick, a little too crisp for a Greyhound bus trip, got on at the Hawthorne stop. Most of his fellow passengers seemed to be … well, transients, traveling with only a few dollars and a small allotment of hope. This guy was suited up for a char-tered jet.

The man kept looking back at Alejandro during the trip. Alejandro entertained the idea that the man was checking him out, planning some flirtatious approach. But then the guy leered as a woman coated in fuchsia spandex pants walked by.

They disembarked at a rest stop–slash–bakery in Carson. Alejandro went behind the structure to a newsstand. The man appeared back there, as well, feigning an interest in periodicals on yoga and meditation.

When the ragtag assemblage of riders filed back onto the bus at the designated time, the man faded to the back of the group, probably to make sure Alejandro got on first. Once in his seat, Alejandro made a quick call, then ambled to the front of the bus, ostensibly to get a copy of the route map. He brushed past the dude on his way back, dropping his phone into the guy's pocket. That he was capable of this level of stealth surprised him. Certain circumstances brought out certain skills.

Getting on Reece's bike at roughly seventy miles per hour on the open road had probably doubled Alejandro's blood pressure and tripled his heart rate, no doubt causing tangible, permanent damage to his organs. But the scene back at SPM—combined with the confrontation at David's office and this dude stalking him—had given Alejandro no choice but to go all James Bond, crawling through dark passages, leaping off moving buses.

Here's a conclusion to a proof, Alejandro thought: The adventurous life is vastly overrated. What he wouldn't give right now to sit in a gray cubicle and peck away at a computer keyboard, bored to tears. Or simply hold Shelly's hand. She'd told George, her betrothed, that she'd taken on an evening yoga class; the jerk hadn't bothered to ask where. She and Alejandro would meet at his parents' sprawling home in Thousand Oaks, away from LA's prying eyes. They'd have dinner at one of the posh restaurants in the area, then return to the Kichidos' guesthouse to satiate other appetites. If he could have just one more hour with her, one more chance to talk, he'd tell her there was another way out of her predicament. But they'd never discussed it.

And now here he was, in the grimy warehouse district of Long Beach, close enough to the docks to smell the sea air. Fantasies about the ordinary life would do him no good. He should have stayed his ass in college like his parents wanted. Maybe even continued on to med school. A cadaver would be a welcome sight. If he continued on this path, he'd soon be one.

"Hey, yo. A-Man. I'm back."

Alejandro had closed his eyes during the short reverie. He popped them open at the sound of Reece's voice. He'd expected to hear his friend's motorcycle as it approached, but now he understood why he hadn't. Reece and about a dozen associates were silently paddle-walking their bikes into the area, in a formation that reminded Alejandro of a flock of birds. He wasn't aware that motorcycle gangs—well, *groups*, he didn't want to label them prematurely—traveled like that. It was strange.

And it got stranger. Reece pressed a key card onto a metal panel. After a few beats, the heavy corrugated door of the warehouse lifted. Reece took his bike inside, followed by the rest of the men. Alejandro stood watching the quiet pageant. Vigorous movement at the center of the group caught his attention. A gloved, beefy hand flew up, and Alejandro heard the sound of someone punching a slab of meat. The movement stopped.

Alejandro craned his neck back and forth and around, and finally located Reece deep in the warehouse. Quickly edging along the side of the group, he moved to Reece's side.

"What's all this?" Alejandro waved his hand in the direction of the men, then pointed specifically toward the center.

"Aw, A-Man, don't worry about that. Not your concern. I told you I had some errands to run."

"Yeah, well, I thought you meant you had to drop by the bank or something. Mail a letter. What kinda business you running?"

Reece backed up a bit, his chin tucked to his chest. "Look. Everybody can't be all straight-laced and silver-spooned like you. You left juvie with your high-priced lawyer, and your mommy and daddy drove you back to your little gated enclave. They sent me back to the hood. I had to do whatever I could to make it on my own out here. And now you're gonna sit on your high horse in judgment? After I showed up to help your ass?"

"I-I'm sorry, Reece. Damn." Alejandro took a deep breath and noisily blew it out. He needed to back down. Reece had most likely saved his life. "I appreciate what you did for me back there. I really do. But then I see all this going on, your, uh … associates … you know, these big goons following you in here all quiet and whatnot. And I know for damn sure I saw somebody get clocked over there. And I don't know what this is, what kind of operation I'm in the middle of, what the hell's going on. I have enough to deal with, without gettin' all mixed up in this." Alejandro waved his hand around. "Whatever it is."

A man appeared as if he'd been summoned. He had a thick neck and biceps to match. "Tell me I didn't just hear this raggedy-ass boy call us fools. 'Cause I'll show you what a fool can do. I'll fix your mouth so you won't even be able to say the word 'fool' again." The man advanced toward Alejandro, but Reece pushed him away with one hand like he would a gnat.

"Get back, Big Slop. This is my boy. You don't touch him. And by the way, you *are* a fool. Let me count the ways. Today turned to shit because of you."

The man schlumped off, head bowed. Alejandro marveled at this. Big Slop was twice as big as Reece, but clearly five times lower in the pecking order. One of the cases where size really didn't matter. He looked at Reece and silently mouthed, *Big Slop?*

Reece raised his right hand, gave a soft smile. "Long story. Don't ask."

Alejandro took a breath. "We cool?" It was what they'd said to each other back when they were fourteen, the day Alejandro left juvie for good.

Reece looked squarely into Alejandro's eyes. He nodded. "We cool."

THIRTY-ONE

"So she was saying that some highlights would bring out my eyes, maybe shave a few years off, and then I could..."

Violet was trapped, held captive by Nurse Patti and her segueing chain of stories. She thought about the people in wheelchairs who were quite possibly subjected to this type of meaningless drivel on a daily basis. Having some company was undoubtedly nice at times, but the motorized version was probably optimal.

This was your own clever, crafty idea, Violet reminded herself as they journeyed to the hospital's upper wing. She'd urged Nurse Patti to approach Dr. Howe and somehow opened up the topic of past romantic failures. Barney had been an absolute dream (and he could cook!), but during a trip to the farmers market, Nurse Patti learned he was married. Tobias was tons of fun and very adventurous, but emotionally unavailable, allergic to intimacy. Garrett only used her to get to her former roommate. Violet listened sympathetically to all of it, silently begging for it to stop. She found herself longing for the serenity of fifth graders and state capitals.

Nurse Patti had gone silent as the elevator inched its way closer to the eighth floor. As the doors opened, she bent down and blurted nervously into Violet's ear, "So what am I supposed to do when we get there?"

Patti had a point. What did she want this woman to do? In her haste to get to Dr. Howe's office, she hadn't bothered to come up with a plan. Hell, she didn't even really know what she was hoping to find. But they didn't need a complex scheme. It was simple.

They'd say Nurse Patti was taking Violet to the radiology department for a final set of x-rays and just happened to be passing by the good doctor's office. "Just follow my lead, watch for my cues. I'll help you with—"

"Hey, Patti, what're you doing up here?" Patti's friend Marta stood sentry at the nurse's station, screening all who dared come into her little kingdom.

Nurse Patti gestured toward the office across the walkway. "Is he in?" she whispered, as if speaking about a deity.

"Naw, girl, he's out. He's in big demand right now, was on the news about something. You see it?"

"Oh yes, I saw it. Sure did." The two nurses laughed. Nurse Patti went over and leaned against Marta's desk, settling in to talk.

Violet realized she'd been abandoned. *Rude*, she thought. Then her eyes lit up. Maybe this was a blessing, one with a limited shelf life, beginning right now. She silently maneuvered her way across the hall and managed to angle her wheelchair over the threshold of Dr. Howe's office. As she entered, she glanced back at the nurse's station; the nurses were oblivious, caught up in gossip.

Violet rolled to the doctor's desk, getting as close as the wheelchair would allow. She looked through the patient files in his inbox, then rifled through the medical journals stacked neatly in piles, putting them down as quickly as she picked them up. *JAMA. NEJM.* A memo from the hospital president about changing protocols. A pamphlet from a pharmaceutical company, hawking its new drug. Violet rolled her wheels back and forth with the palms of her hands, silently asking for direction. Mindlessly, she tried to do a 360-degree turn in the wheelchair, something she had seen a man do effortlessly in the middle of Santa Monica's Third Street Promenade. Turned out the move actually did require some effort. As she clumsily spun the chair halfway around, its frame bumped into an armoire she hadn't noticed. A green binder labeled "SPM" sat on one of the shelves, behind glass panes. She pulled urgently on the cabinet's knobs several times before becoming aware of the lock. Damn. It was infuriating to see the thing and not be able to get it.

Violet rolled back to the doctor's desk and glanced expectantly over its surface, as if the key to the cabinet might be sitting there in plain sight. She quickly shook her head. *Come on, Violet.* A key giving access to confidential, highly volatile information wouldn't be just casually lying around on a desk.

She opened the drawers and pawed at the bric-a-brac within. A tiny pair of surgical scissors caught her attention. She plucked them up. She could use these, if she could remember what Rafael had taught her. Raffi was an ex-boyfriend, adored by her parents because of his clean, Academic Decathlon–winning image. An image was all it had been. In their short time together, he'd taught her how to roll joints and pick locks, plus a few sexual tricks that would've made her parents' faces turn red.

Maneuvering the surgical scissors with the attention and fine, deliberate movements of... well, a surgeon, Violet got the cabinet to open. She touched a few fingers to her lips and sent a silent kiss to Raffi, wherever he was.

Violet extended an arm toward the binder, strained to reach it. She looked down with disdain at her injured leg, as if it had launched this malicious effort to foil her plans. She considered calling out to Nurse Patti for help—that was her job, wasn't it?—but then she'd have to explain why she'd jimmied a lock, destroying hospital property in the process, and now needed help retrieving a confidential document belonging to Doctor Desirable.

She'd soldier on alone. And that's what this was becoming, wasn't it? A war of some undetermined sort, with Gayle, David, even her own damn self as potential casualties.

Gayle. The only teacher who'd befriended her without hesitation, unlike the others, who gossiped about her, their eyes narrowed and wary, as she passed by in the hall. One of those biddies—her grandmother's word, probably because it was as close to "bitch" as a 1950s Methodist upbringing would allow—had set loose a rumor that Violet was a coven-leading witch.

"So yeah, girl, he's talking about heading up to Tahoe, or Reno, someplace like that and—"

Violet looked up. The low hum of the nurses' conversation just outside the door had been a lullaby, making Violet feel safe and sound as she committed trespass. Now it had stopped, abruptly. What was going on out there?

Frustrated about the interruption, about having to maneuver her wheelchair in this infinitely small space, about this whole damn situation—she was an elementary school teacher, she belonged in a classroom—Violet managed to get to the office door. She wheeled out and saw Dr. Howe down the hall, heading straight toward his office.

Eyes closed, fists clenched, Violet called to the powers of the north, west, east, and south, imploring them to prompt Nurse Patti to intercept the doctor. She pleaded to any otherworldly beings who might be listening: *Make her talk to him.* She didn't know what else to do to invoke the spirits, but she needed them. Now.

THIRTY-TWO

"Okay, chefs, you've seasoned your chicken, you've trussed your chicken with twine, you've—" The Cordon Bleu instructor paused as he caught a glimpse of Margaret's unappealing lump of poultry. She'd trussed the hell out of the unfortunate bird, now tied up in an unrecognizable mass. The instructor tugged on the knot of his white cravat and drew in his breath. He turned his face to the rest of the participants, blocking her station from view. "So, uh, now you transfer them to your roasting racks for, uh, for roasting."

Okay, so she wasn't going to be the teacher's pet. Fine. It was no surprise; she didn't like to cook. But she hadn't expected her level of humiliation to be this high. And this obvious. The class had been Georgia's idea, of course, a two-for-one deal she'd found online. Remembering the museum trip, Margaret volunteered to drive. The culinary institute was in Pasadena; if Georgia had driven, they'd still be on the windy 110 freeway, slowly twisting and turning at forty-five miles per hour.

Margaret picked up the container of pre-measured white wine at her station and inhaled its aroma. They'd already used a small amount to season the chicken; the rest was for the salad dressing. She looked around to confirm no one was paying attention, then took a long sip. It went down smoothly, just as she'd anticipated. She tipped the cup up to her lips again and emptied it. *Yum.* The arugula would survive without it.

Margaret searched the room for Georgia. She was in a corner near the knives, conversing with a woman whose forehead was an immobile slab of flesh. Margaret sniffed. *Too much Botox.* She approached the pair and quickly learned that Georgia and the woman were alumnae of the same university. Georgia was making over the fact that the woman had been a "Gabby," the name given to the school's cheerleaders in a nod to the founder's wife.

"Wow. I tried out to be a Gabby two years in a row, but I didn't make it either time," Georgia was saying.

The woman looked Georgia up and down, then spoke, her voice nasal, constipated. "Yes, well, to be a Gabby, you had to be either drop-dead gorgeous, like a model, or just really, really bubbly, and really, really cute."

Margaret glared sharply at the woman. Had she heard that correctly?

Georgia didn't miss a beat. She looked directly into the woman's eyes, held her gaze. "Oh? Then how'd you manage to get chosen?"

Margaret suppressed a smirk. If it had been her, she would have stood there immobilized. A comeback like Georgia's would have occurred to Margaret hours later, in the shower, way too late to inflict pain. She looked at her friend with new appreciation. Georgia could be gossipy, and yes, she drove as slow as hell, but she was also pretty quick-witted.

They moved away from the woman. Margaret glanced at Georgia out of the corner of her eye. She hadn't bothered to confide in Georgia about her dealings with Hersh. She'd wanted to sort through it on her own, make sense of it without someone else's filter. Now Margaret found herself wanting to hear Georgia's take on the matter. Although it couldn't really be called a "matter," could it? It was just a strangely attractive man, an odd feeling, and, well . . . confusion on her part.

"So I saw you consorting with that gruff-looking man at the museum." Apparently Georgia was also clairvoyant. "Were you going to tell me about that, or were you trying to keep it your little secret?"

"Yes, I, um . . . well, he came up to me after the tour was over and just started talking to me, and we ended up going to lunch."

"Lunch? You've already been to lunch with the man? And didn't tell me about it?" Georgia was indignant.

"Yes, and it wasn't a secret or anything, just, you know, I hadn't gotten around to mentioning it. We really haven't had any time for a conversation about that."

"Oh, yes, no time. None at all. Like the forty-minute ride we just had to this place."

"Okay. So I didn't tell you right away. I'm telling you now. And now you can tell me your opinion of him. I'm sure you have one." Margaret held her breath.

"Bad news."

"What?"

"He's bad news. Stay away." Georgia was resolute.

"And this is based on what, your intuition?"

"This is based on the following. One. He shows up at the art tour and he's not even part of the class. I asked the guide. Okay? Two. He makes a beeline for you, and all of a sudden, he's your new lunch buddy, your new best friend. Alright? Something's amiss."

"And what's so amiss about a man finding me attractive and asking me to lunch?"

"Nothing, sweetie, you're cute as pie. I'd date you myself. But here's what else. I've seen him up at the walking park a couple of times, so I asked some of the fellas about him." Georgia paused.

"And?"

"And. As I said. Something's amiss. His wife died suddenly, two or so years ago. And he has this grown son who looks nothing like him and didn't look like his deceased wife, either." Georgia folded her arms.

"Well, he's over seventy, isn't he? And the wife probably was, too. Maybe she was sick."

"Okay, and what about the son? What do you have to say about that?"

"Sometimes people don't look like their parents, alright? We all have lots of genes up in our family tree and you never know what's going to appear. My Aunt Vanessa was blond and blue-eyed. Or maybe he wasn't their biological child—there is a little practice they call adoption." Margaret didn't know why she had taken on the role, almost fiercely, of defending Hersh.

"Alright, fine. The other thing is that some of the retired deputies up at the park, they think he's odd. I overheard the men talking about him, and they were saying how he averts his eyes and turns away when he passes by. As if he's trying to avoid contact."

Margaret gave a noncommittal nod, the most she could do. It had been a mistake to discuss this with Georgia. The deputies' comments were a bit disconcerting, but it was part of the trade. Margaret had worked at a police station for a short time. They saw everyone as a potential criminal. That was what probably had the old cops thinking the worst about this man. Or maybe they had seen the same thing in his eyes that she had seen. A glimpse of something dangerous, something malcontent that, a whole day after their lunch, still had her spooked.

THIRTY-THREE

Muted light filtered through the bag that covered Gayle's head. Someone removed the covering, making sure her earrings didn't catch. *Strange.* TV kidnappers were rough, pushing and grabbing. Manhandling. Apparently real life was different.

As the bag came off, she breathed in the airy spaciousness and realized she was in a church, a hundred or more candles burning, glowing in wait for some solemn event. They were everywhere—along the sides, under the paintings, at the altar. Rows and rows of frosted glass votives, each gently flickering. Here was another surprise. Kidnapping involved cold, dank basements, emptied-out warehouses, her body roughly plopped into a folding chair in the center. Marbled carcasses hanging around. What was this?

A small side door was cracked just enough for Gayle to see that it was daytime, around sunrise, she guessed, judging by the sky's pale hue. She glimpsed an expansive front lawn outside the edifice. Open space to make an escape—or be shot dead.

"Wouldn't try that if I were you." The words seemed to float down from above, like wisdom from on high. And good advice it was—her wrists were tied together, her feet were bound at the ankles. Unless she planned to simply drop and roll, she'd never make it.

"I'd like to have a little talk with you," the voice said, closer now. "Just a little talk. Relax, answer my questions, and nothing will happen to you."

Yeah, right. I've heard that before.

The owner of the gravelly voice came into view. He was tall and lanky, with sharp bones that pressed against his clothes at the joints. His head was bald and angular with a light covering of pale, close-cropped hair.

The man knelt in front of her on a pointy knee and took her hand. "My name is Angus," he said, the corners of his eyes crinkling.

Gayle started to let her guard down, then noticed his eyes lacked something—emotion, empathy, whatever quality it was that made a person seem alive. He'd missed the supermodel's reality-show lesson on how to "smize."

Angus's mood changed and he shoved a paper at Gayle. She'd been right about him—he couldn't keep up the act long enough to get halfway into the conversation. "This is your boyfriend."

Gayle stared at the page, then looked up. She'd seen it before, on the missing children's website. David at eleven, all bravado and invincibility, then to the right, David currently, the eyes just like those of the man in front of her, soulless.

Angus looked at Gayle, waiting. "Did you hear me?"

Gayle looked directly into the man's dull eyes. "I heard you perfectly."

"Then answer the question."

"It wasn't a question, it was a statement. Even my eleven-year-old fifth graders would know that much. Your friends abduct me from my lovely evening at the spa, and then they bring me to this church. And you've come all nice and prepared, with your little color printout. So I don't think you need me to reply to your statement. It seems like you already know." Gayle wasn't exactly sure where this confidence had come from, but one thing seemed clear. She knew something they didn't, and all she had to do was figure out what it was—then use it as leverage.

Angus looked at Gayle, one eyebrow raised, his mouth pursed into a half-amused grimace. He yanked Gayle's bench toward him.

"Cute speech. Unfortunately I don't have one second for cute. You're going to tell me where I can find Leonard."

Gayle struggled on the bench, twisting and turning, tilting it forward with the weight of her body. Angus stopped the bench from tipping, holding the ends down solidly, grinding it into the church floor even as it moved.

"I don't know anyone named Leonard!" she cried.

Angus frowned and took a deep breath. He turned, sat down on the bench beside Gayle, and started picking at a dark, textured scab that covered one of his knuckles. "I know you think I'm being unreasonable. We brought you here against your will and you have every right to be scared. And I don't want to hurt you, I really don't."

Gayle started to calm down, her breath matching the rhythm of Angus's. "Then what do you want with me? I said I don't know a Leonard."

Angus continued to worry the scab, causing a part of it to lift, revealing the new, untouched skin underneath. He started to talk, but stopped when a boy in his early teens entered the sanctuary from a hidden door behind the altar. Gayle expected Angus to yell at the boy, tell him to scram, but he didn't. Instead he was silent, patiently watching as the boy lit the candles that had blown out. She opened her mouth, but before she had the chance to get any words out, Angus took her wrists and, squeezing, held them down. He looked her in the eye with that face, those cold eyes. She closed her mouth.

The movement caught the boy's attention. He squinted out into the rows of benches but said nothing. Angus watched as the boy replaced a golden chalice, moved an assortment of things around on the altar, then left as quietly as he had entered.

Angus turned back to Gayle and continued speaking. "You saw that boy, didn't you. Innocent, unaware of what goes on in the world, the evil, the betrayal. You saw how he went about his tasks, setting up for communion, keeping the candles lit, following what he's been taught to believe." Angus squeezed Gayle's wrists even tighter. "That wasn't a statement, it was a question. You saw that, right?"

Gayle nodded. Anything to keep him calm. Anything to stay safe.

He continued, "That was me. Literally. I had that job at that age, right here in this church. And my father, too, he grew up going to this church, and he also had that job as a boy. He was here practically every Sunday, his whole life, until he got too sick to make it." Angus had removed his hand from Gayle's wrist and was back to fiddling with the scab. She winced as he appeared to pull more of it up from his knuckle.

"He loved *Star Trek*, my dad. Really anything with 'Star' in the title. *Star Wars*, of course."

"*A Star Is Born*?" Gayle said. Maybe if she kept the conversation going, made Angus feel that he had been heard, she could somehow soften him up enough to release her.

Angus gave a slight smile. "No, not really that one. He didn't go for romance. It was like he felt some connection with the stars, with space, constellations, things from other worlds. We'd sit and watch these shows, and he'd make predictions about what was going to happen, or what somebody was going to say. And he was always right. Always."

"Sounds like a cool dad," Gayle said. "I can tell you have special memories of that." She'd learned the concept of active listening at a district workshop. Parroting back the person's thoughts, in different terms, was affirming and formed trust.

"He was. If only he could have predicted his own fate." The scab was now two-thirds of the way off. Angus went back to toying with it. "They knew what was wrong with him, and they knew how to help him. They were coming up with something, researching a cure."

"What did he have?"

Angus ignored the question. "They weren't able to come up with the cure in time. Someone stole the resources that could have helped him. And he died. My aunt handled the details of the funeral, but when the day came, my mother wouldn't go. I stayed at home with her, and later we drove here and just sat. Sat for hours, watching the candles burn down."

"That must have been pretty tough. I'm sorry." Even as she finished speaking, Gayle knew those had been the wrong words to say.

"You're sorry?" Angus yanked the scab completely off his knuckle and clamped it tight in his hand. "You're so sorry," he mocked in a sickly tone, "but when I show you a picture of Leonard, you say you don't know him. Leonard could have saved my father. I know you looked him up on the website, I know you have a relationship with him, but all you've done, this whole time, is lie. But it doesn't really matter. He's out there, and we're going to get him. One of my operatives shot him, so he won't get far."

"Wait, the picture—are you talking about David? From the website? I thought you were looking for someone named Leonard. David's been shot? Where? Why? Is he okay?" Gayle was terrified.

The two broad-shouldered men who had been standing guard nearby raised their heads.

"Oh, so his name is David now," Angus said. "They changed it to David. David what?"

Gayle didn't respond.

Angus grabbed her wrists, pressed his fingernails into her skin. "David what?"

"Byrdsong," she replied, deflated.

Angus let go of her hands and backed up. "Turns out you've actually been very helpful, Gayle." He turned to the two men. "Get me Stone. The big mystery is over. We know exactly who he is. And it won't take us long to find him."

THIRTY-FOUR

Violet pored through SPM's binder from her hospital bed. She'd started by skimming the pages. Now she was reading whole reports, including the small print, drawn in by the experiments and conclusions. Revelations. She removed some of the material as she read it, spreading it out on the now-vacant bed that had belonged to her former roommate. Thankfully, the old woman had been discharged while Violet and Nurse Patti were away. The material was exhaustive, covering decades of studies, reports, and abstracts—all having to do with David and a woman named Margaret, his biological mother. In the files, David's name was Leonard. A photo of him as a toddler was attached; it was easy to match the mischievous little boy's features to David's mature face. The binder concluded with an age-progressed 8" × 10" of a man—David, for sure.

Extensive research had been conducted on Margaret and David—or Leonard, as he'd been named at birth. The battery of experiments had cost hundreds of thousands of dollars, involving top-notch equipment and scientists at the highest, most clandestine levels. No wonder it had been under lock and key. No wonder they were hunting down Alejandro. He'd been right, he'd played the Good Samaritan—something most people never did—and as a reward he'd been rebuked and placed on a wanted list. She hoped David hadn't gone to SPM as planned. He'd never make it out.

Getting the binder out of Dr. Howe's office had been a feat. When she saw him approaching, she wheeled back in and managed to snatch the book, then placed it on her lap and covered it with her blanket. She looked over at the desk, stopped there for a moment, then maneuvered toward the door.

"What are you doing in my office?" The doctor's voice was gruff. Violet flinched.

"I was just leaving you a little note," she said.

"A note." Dr. Howe frowned. "About what?"

"About Nurse Patti—I mean Patti, the nurse right out there." She gestured toward the nurse's station. The nurses were no longer talking. "You've worked with her, right?"

"I'm not in charge of raises. She needs to see her manager or talk to someone in administration. I'm an epidemiologist, she should know that. And she shouldn't have patients coming up here."

"No, no, it's not about raises or anything like that," Violet said. "She, uh . . . well, we were just talking and she said she wouldn't mind getting to know you a little better. She didn't want to come up here, but I forced her. I told her I wouldn't take my medication if we didn't stop by your office."

The doctor glanced toward the nurse's station, then turned back to Violet. "So the note, what, it has her number?"

Violet smiled. "Exactly. Just a little push from a meddling patient, in case you might want to give her a call, go out. Even if it's just coffee in the cafeteria."

The doctor looked back out at Nurse Patti one more time and smirked, as if what he saw confirmed what he was about to say. "Well, I'm afraid you've wasted your time."

Violet looked out into the hallway to see if anyone had heard this. The nurses were both silent. "You're right, I've wasted my time. You don't deserve someone that kind. Nurse Patti?" Violet beckoned for the nurse to take the handles of the chair. "Back to my room, please." She glanced at Dr. Howe one more time. "Doctor Howe."

Nurse Patti said goodbye to Marta and pushed Violet down the hall. When the elevator arrived, she turned Violet's wheelchair around and backed her in. As the doors closed, Dr. Howe came out of his office and stared directly at Violet, his eyes piercing lasers, his mouth a straight, ominous line.

———

Violet needed to get these files to David, before he trotted down to SPM like a cowboy out for justice and ended up a lab rat. She wondered if Margaret—the woman who'd been through her own battery of tests and procedures—was still alive. A happy scene of the two of them reuniting played on her mind's visual screen. He would introduce Margaret to Gayle. The woman would be over the moon about a future daughter-in-law and the possibility of grandchildren. It was all salvageable, but she had to get things in motion. She rotated her legs and used the bed's rails to pull herself to a sitting position, then inched her bottom down the side of the bed until her toes touched the ground. Holding on to the rails, she made her way around the bed to the pale green visitor's chair and bent over to get her phone out of her purse.

"Weren't you advised to stay in bed?"

Violet jumped. She turned toward the doorway. Dr. Howe's form filled up the whole space.

"Hello." Violet's voice was shaky. "I was just calling my job to give them an update on my condition. My class has a substitute—" Violet stopped talking as she followed the doctor's eyes to the bed and SPM's binder.

"I knew you were up to something. You have no business with this, it's hospital property. It's *my* property."

"I'm sorry. You're right. You can have it back. I never should have taken it."

"The problem is, you've read it."

"I won't say anything to anyone about it, I promise."

"Alright. If you promise." The doctor gathered the binder and pushed the loose papers back into it. He opened it and flipped through. "Everything looks to be in order. Now let's get you back in bed." He set the book down on the side table.

Violet started to protest, but she allowed the man to help her back into the hospital bed with his firm, dry hands. Once she was settled in, he pulled the sheets and blankets to her chin, as if tucking in a child.

"There you go. You'll be just fine, okay? Nothing to worry about. You'll be just fine."

Violet nodded.

"You'll be just fine."

Hearing him repeat the phrase had the opposite effect, making Violet feel less and less "just fine." She wished the doctor would just take the binder and leave.

"You'll be just fine." The doctor stared at her and pulled something out of the pocket of his lab coat. With an emotionless face, he came toward her and put a cloth over her mouth.

Violet tried to scream, but nothing came out. She tried to reach for the nurse's call button but couldn't get to it. She writhed and turned, but the doctor held her in place.

Then Violet heard a bang and a crash, and the doctor fell away. She looked over the bed rail and saw the man laid out on the floor, blood seeping from his skull. Next to his head was the telemetry monitor that normally showed vital signs, making the flatline sound. A few of its pieces had scattered to the corners of the room. Either the machine had broken open after it crashed to the floor, or Dr. Howe was truly, literally, hardheaded.

Violet looked toward the door. Nurse Patti was there, panting, her hands on her hips.

"Well," she said. "I'm afraid he's wasted *his* time."

THIRTY-FIVE

"The destination will be on your left." *That came up fast.* It seemed like the voice had just told Margaret she was a thousand feet away.

"You have arrived." She could listen to this man all day. She'd set her navigation app to a British dialect. It was like the King of England had taken a break from ruling—or not ruling, whatever it was he did—to personally direct Margaret's movement. She'd never been to Europe, hadn't traveled much. She had tons of unfulfilled dreams, wishes she hadn't acted on, regrets, yearnings. Her baby boy's face appeared before her. She tried to imagine where he was, if he was even still alive. He wouldn't be a little boy now, of course, he'd be thirty-six. Today. Did he remember her? She wondered if he had a family of his own, and children. She tried to visualize them—who they were, what they looked like.

The search for Leonard Jr. had been extensive. Margaret was grateful for the substantial resources that had gone into finding him. She'd only ever seen that much interest when the missing person was white. The police said a private company had also stepped up to lend a hand, adding considerable funds. But these efforts hadn't stopped her from doing her own work to find him. She'd put flyers on telephone poles, knocked on doors, even wrote to the newscaster who covered the area, asking for prime-time coverage. Instead of imagining the horrific, she kept her mind on the prospect of wrapping him in her arms at the end of this nightmare, and never letting go. She held on to the feeling of his tiny hand gripping hers, the way he would reach for her over any other adult in the room. She'd have given anything to sing "What a Wonderful World" for the third time as she tucked him in.

Margaret made a U-turn and pulled into the strip mall's parking lot. She got out and scanned the shops until she saw the one she wanted: "Sheldon Prescott, PI." After all these years, Margaret had thought she was done with detectives. She still didn't feel she needed one; this was all Georgia's idea. She'd insisted, even offered to pay for it.

"Just do me this favor. Find out who this Hersh really is, see if there's anything to be concerned about," Georgia had insisted. "LA is a big city, with lots of creeps." Georgia had given Margaret a crumpled card, fished out from the bottom of her purse. She and her husband had hired Sheldon Prescott a few years ago to check out her daughter's boyfriend, a man she'd met at LAX while waiting for a delayed flight. Georgia hadn't liked that. The appropriate places for couples to meet were church, institutions of higher learning, even the produce section in the grocery store, brought together by stolen glances over Bartlett pears. Not an airport.

After finding nothing on the man, Prescott told Georgia she could give her blessing to the upcoming nuptials. They hosted an elaborate wedding. Then, six months later, Georgia's husband went to the newlyweds' house, packed the daughter up, and brought her back to their home. The man had become violent one night and broken one of the daughter's ribs.

Margaret stood in front of the detective's door, peered through the glass. *Big help he was then.* She pushed the door open and stepped inside. The office was nondescript, with an ugly metal desk in the center and chairs on either side. Ivory paint peeled away from the walls in several spots, exposing white primer and holes filled with putty. Faded yellow lines on the ceiling told a tale of water damage. The walls were bare, not a bookcase or file cabinet in sight.

A man emerged through a grimy door. He was average height, average build, average everything. She'd been expecting someone a bit flashier, but his nondescript looks probably helped him blend in.

"Miss Margaret? Hi, I'm Prescott. Come on in—well, you're already in." He laughed. "Have a seat. Sorry for the wait. I fell into some traffic."

Margaret lowered her body into the chair, unimpressed. She perched herself at the edge of the seat. The man had nice manners, but his cleanliness wasn't up to snuff. And traffic was a lame excuse. He could have just checked one of the apps like everyone else in all of Los Angeles. Brush your teeth, comb your hair, check Waze—that was the way of it.

"So tell me about your problem."

"Well, it's not really a problem, not like what you're used to, but—"

"With all due respect, Miss Margaret, don't worry about what I'm used to. I'm here for you. There's information you need. I'm here to get it for you."

"With all due respect to you, Mr. Prescott—"

"Just Prescott."

"Excuse me, Prescott, I'm here because 'Miss Georgia' wanted me to try this, and although you come highly recommended, it was surprising because you weren't really able to help her. You know, with her daughter."

Prescott put his hands together in a prayerful pose, bowed his head. "Right you are. And that's a great segue into what I do, and what I don't do. I don't judge personalities, I don't predict the future. I get the information, give it to you, that's it. Now if Georgia's future son-in-law had domestic violence in his past—and by that, I mean an arrest, a complaint, a conviction, even a hint of gossip—I would have found it and saved her daughter the trouble, saved the parents a load of cash. The truth is, there wasn't anything to indicate what ended up happening. Other questions?"

"I guess that makes sense." She did have a few more questions, particularly about why his office looked so dingy. She figured that wasn't what he meant, though, so she spent the next twenty minutes recounting the sequence of events with Hersh.

In the end, she decided to hire the man. As he brought out a contract from one of the drawers, he put on a pair of dark sunglasses and started going through the various clauses and conditions on the form.

Prescott looked up and caught her frowning at the dark lenses. He laughed and said, "Don't mind these. I lost my clear reading glasses, so I have to use this pair. Anyway, I'll start checking out our Mr. Hershel Byrdsong. It's early enough. I can pull up some info and start tailing him today."

THIRTY-SIX

David surveyed the street before exiting his car. He did another panoramic glance-around as he headed up the path leading to Gayle's townhouse. Tall snapdragons and dahlias in various shades of pink lined the walkway on either side. He smiled. Gayle refused to give up her favorite color, despite a feminist philosopher's claim that pink represented the infantilization of women, a disgrace to the movement. "Pink is not political," Gayle had said. "If the *movement* really wants to do anything, then the *movement* needs to focus on issues like intersectionality, pay equity, maternity leave, a woman's right to choose. Colors? Really?"

He lifted the butterfly knocker he'd installed and tapped a few times, then rang the doorbell. Silence. He waited a few moments, then used his flattened palm to hit the door. "Gayle! Gayle! You in there?"

Calm down. Just because Gayle wasn't home didn't mean that something bad had happened. There were a thousand places she could be—getting her car washed, having her hair retwisted, shopping for random pink things.

Yes, calm down. It was his birthday, a day usually reserved for happy things. He thought of his cousin Stephanie, who called him every year on this day and played Earth, Wind & Fire's "September." They'd always been so close, sharing the same unspoken sense that they didn't truly belong. When they were kids and Stephanie had somehow gotten chicken pox, he'd snuck over to her house to visit, against Regina's stern directive. Afterward, he'd waited vigilantly for days, looking for the first itchy bumps and figuring out how he'd explain them. When no symptoms manifested, he'd gone back to Stephanie's, bringing her favorite candy and a tiny teddy bear, designed to make her smile despite her misery.

In better times, Stephanie would cue up the song on a CD, then hold her boom box up to the landline, blasting it the whole three minutes and thirty-five seconds. David would yell into the phone after a while, trying to get her to turn it down and talk, but he'd have to wait until the song played through. He envisioned Stephanie dancing it out, tearing it up with her choppy pre-adolescent moves.

"You looking for Gayle?" A harsh female voice came from behind.

David turned around. It was Florence, the ornery neighbor Gayle always complained about. "Kill 'em with kindness," Gayle's mother liked to say. "You catch more bees with honey." Gayle had followed these adages, to no avail.

David turned, deciding to take Gayle's approach. "Yes, ma'am, have you seen her?"

"Ma'am! Did you just call me 'ma'am'? I'm probably the same age as you, maybe younger."

Here we go. Gayle was right. Try to be polite and respectful, get accused of slinging an insult. "I'm sorry, ma'am, I mean, I'm sorry. I was raised in the South." *Right.* David had been raised in the middle of Los Angeles; his sole trip to the Southern states had taken place one spring, on a tour of historically Black universities. "My mama taught me to say that to any woman over eighteen."

Florence softened, then told David she hadn't seen Gayle in a couple of days. "There were some men here asking about her, though."

"What men? What did they want?"

"Well, I don't know. They asked where she was, said she left work without telling anybody. If you ask me, she was probably going on another date. She went on a date with another man a few days ago. At first, I thought it was you. He came over, picked her up in an Audi, and they went off, talking and laughing." Florence raised her eyebrow, tipped her head to the side.

This was expected. One of Gayle's chief complaints about Florence was that she constantly peeked out of her windows, watching everyone's comings and goings. Asking questions about things that weren't her business. Now she was trying to stir the pot, drum up some mess.

"I know all about that. She went to dinner with our good friend Geoffrey the other night," he lied. Well, most of it was the truth—Gayle had gone out with Geoffrey—just not the "our good friend" part.

Florence kept on. "Well, these other men, they were pretty nice-looking. Who knows what she was gonna get up to with them."

David ignored this. "What did the men want?"

"They asked about where she likes to go, where she hangs out. I told them I didn't know any of that. I take my behind to work and to church, come home, clean my house, cook for my husband. I don't know what single women do with their time. Although there is that male strip club over on Manchester called the Right—"

David cut her off. "So did they leave when you didn't have any information to give them?"

"They got ready to leave, but then they asked me for her license plate."

"And?"

"And I gave it to them. It seemed important."

"You gave it to them. You gave some men you don't know my girlfriend's license plate." David had just about had enough. "Why do you even know her license plate?"

"Well, I thought I was going to have to call the police on her. Last month she parked her car in front of my house for several days, and that's way beyond the time you're supposed to have a car out there, so—"

"So she lives here! Right next door to you. You were going to have her car towed?"

"Well, I need my space for my own guests and whoever wants to come see about me and—"

"Did the men identify themselves? Were they cops?"

"No, I don't know, they were somebody with some kinda company. But I wouldn't worry about it."

"I have to go. Gayle's in—" He thought better of telling this woman anything. "I have to get going." David turned and lumbered to his car. He got in and immediately locked the doors. He stared out the windshield, saw the pavement dip as the street inclined down the hill. He raised his gaze upward and stared at the horizon. What had happened to Gayle? He sifted it over and over in his mind, trying to find something to latch on to, something to make him believe he would find her, that things would be alright. But he had nothing to go on. This was all his fault. And just like he'd failed earlier that week, with his cowardly performance in the courtroom, he'd probably fail at this, too, with much more dire consequences.

Why had EWF chosen this specific date for the song? David took out his phone and looked the song up on Wikipedia, hoping to find the worldly significance of September 21. A short interview with the group's lead singer revealed there wasn't one, that they'd sung through the days of the month to find the one that sounded best.

Reading this was sobering. September 21, today's date, was his birthday, and it wasn't particularly special. To top it off, for the first time in decades, Stephanie hadn't sent the song to him. He realized that in all these years, he'd never once called her on her birthday. He barely knew when it was—somewhere in mid-July? How worthless could he be? And what a mess he was in. All evidence pointed to a certain set of immutable facts that had been true all his life. He wasn't particularly special, and on many levels, he was a big disappointment.

PART III

THIRTY-SEVEN

Hersh looked at the clock on his bedside table. He wondered if David had made any progress finding Gayle. David had asked Hersh to come along, but he'd begged off. He needed to run some errands before they left. He also wanted to withdraw a large amount of cash, enough to last them a while. Credit cards were a nonstarter. He also planned to head over to the gun shop on Washington for some ammunition, then stop at the grocery store for nonperishable snacks.

Retirement was supposed to be serene, each empty day laid out before you to fill as you pleased. This escape was not part of the vision. There were so many things he'd rather be doing, like visiting Vivian, his sister-in-law, who substituted vodka for root beer in ice cream floats. When Regina first told him about this, he'd shaken his head. "She ought to be ashamed," he'd said. Now his tune had changed. A vodka float would be right up his alley.

———

Hersh parked his car in a metered spot, then jaywalked across the street in a half run. He turned back and craned his neck toward the car. He hadn't put money in the meter, and he didn't know if any time was left on it. Looking back across the narrow street, he could see a tiny red light on the meter's display. Jaywalking and meter neglecting—two violations in less than two minutes. An inner voice asked, *Are you trying to get away, or are you purposefully sabotaging this thing?*

"Culver City Guns." The words across the top of the white building were spelled out in blue in a Wild West–era font, followed by an outline of a pistol and a cowboy hat.

Hersh hoped to get in and get out. He'd called ahead and placed his order with Jeff, the guy he usually dealt with, so it was just a matter of popping in, picking it up, and moving on. Jeff was at the counter, unoccupied. Hersh paid with the last of his cash, then exited and jogged back across the street. As he settled in behind the wheel, he looked back over to the store. A man was looking at him from a car in front of the shop. Hersh nodded in acknowledgement. The man dropped his head to his lap as if the fly on his pants had suddenly become fascinating. Hersh got in his car and drove off. One errand down, two to go.

––––––

Hersh circled the bank's parking lot four times before nabbing a spot. Nodding to the guard who stood on post by the machines, he went to the first available one, inserted his card, and began pushing buttons. He heard the tones that meant money was on its way, and he put his hand up to the slot. The bills came directly into his hand, and he folded the wad in half and shoved it deep into his pocket. Hersh turned to go back to his car and almost ran into a man who was standing in line, way too close. He brushed past the man, then paused. Had he seen that face before, the expressionless look, the nondescript brown shirt? He went on, his thoughts on his grocery list.

––––––

Hersh headed toward the entrance to Ralphs and grabbed a cart on the way in. He recoiled and pulled his hands away—the handle was sticky. Probably the doings of a clammy-handed toddler. That's what he got for rushing, for ignoring the disinfectant wipes at the entrance. The rule was clear: Never stray from routine, no matter the circumstances, no matter the pressure. He'd learned this in the military.

He backtracked, cleaned the cart's red handle with a wipe, then scrubbed at his hands with another. Satisfied, he headed to the canned-food aisle. He just needed a few things that he, David, and Gayle could easily heat up to eat. He moved his hands across the cans, put a few in his cart, then stopped in front of the potted meat. *This is what I'm talking about.* He grabbed several cans each of Spam and Vienna sausages, then moved on in search of nuts and dried fruit. Turning into the next aisle, he came face to face with the man from the bank and the gun shop. Startled, the man turned around and tried to move away.

"Hey!" Hersh yelled, loud enough to make a couple in the dairy section look in their direction.

The man kept going.

"I said, hey! Stop!"

The man continued on, picking up the pace and widening the distance. Hersh abandoned his cart and ran after the guy. A coincidence or two in one day was one thing, but this was ridiculous. This guy was following him, and he needed to know why. More than that, he needed to put a stop to it.

The guy made it through the exit and took off across the parking lot, looking back now and then to see where Hersh was. While he was glancing over his shoulder, a car drove in front of him, and when he turned forward again to run, he collided with the car. Once the driver realized the man was okay, he laid on the horn and drove off, leaving the guy keeled over, trying to catch his breath.

Hersh caught up to him and, for the sake of any onlookers, pretended to help the man up. The man tried to put up a struggle, but he was too weak. Hersh walked him over to a big laundry truck and pulled him behind it. He slammed the man against the side of the vacant truck and grabbed him by the neck.

"You're fine, stop playing."

"I-I think I might need to go to the hospital," the man gasped.

"No, you don't. You're fine. If you don't answer my questions, though, you may just have to."

"Wh-what do you want?" The man was up and alert. The threat had suddenly made him whole.

"You know exactly what I want," Hersh said. "To know why you've been following me all day. First, I see you at the gun shop, then at the bank, and now you're slinking around in the grocery store. Who are you and what do you want?"

"I don't know what you're talking about. I'm just doing the errands my wife asked me to do. I can't help it if we have the same errands. It's a small world." With this the man smiled, toggled his head back and forth.

Hersh didn't laugh. He wasn't buying the wife-and-errand routine. What wife sent her husband to the gun shop? "It's not a small world, it's a big world. And you weren't at the gun shop for a honey-do project. Did she send you to get Spam, too?"

The man sighed. His eyes scanned the parking lot.

"Stop thinking and talk," Hersh commanded, squeezing the man's neck even tighter. "What do you want with me? Who sent you?"

"Okay, okay," the man said. "I'm a PI. I was hired to check you out, do a background check, see what you're up to, find out who you are."

Hersh's heart sank. He'd actually hoped the man was telling the truth about the errands, unlikely as it was. His situation was more urgent than he had thought. He needed to find David and Gayle and get the hell out of the city. He could take a pass on dried apricots and nuts at this point.

"Who hired you?"

"I can't say. It's confidential."

"I'll break your neck, real nice and confidential, if you don't start talking." Hersh squeezed again for effect, pressing in on the man's Adam's apple.

"A woman, and that's all I can say."

"I think you can say more. In fact, the emergency room over on Centinela and I both think you can."

"Okay, sheesh. Her name is Margaret. She hired me earlier today. Said she was thinking about dating you and wanted the scoop."

Margaret. His suspicions were confirmed. "And what's your name? You're a piss-poor detective, giving it all up like that."

"C'mon, man."

"Your name." Hersh refused to budge.

"Prescott."

"Prescott, huh. You need to find another line of work. 'Cause you suck at this." He let Prescott go. "And stop following me. The contract's off."

Prescott gave a phony salute and disappeared.

Margaret. He couldn't believe she'd gone this far. He'd been right to follow her to the museum and take her to lunch. He'd been wrong to hesitate in dealing with her. He wouldn't let any more grass grow under his feet. He'd take care of it and then this would all be over. The time had come to deal, decisively, with his unfinished business.

THIRTY-EIGHT

"It appears we need to go over a few things." Angus glared at Stone from across his desk.

Stone scowled. He didn't need to go over anything, and he resented being called in like a delinquent student summoned to the principal's office. The operation wasn't going well. He didn't need a formal reprimand to understand that.

The two men he'd been hired to bring in—David and Alejandro—had been within reach but had slipped between his fingers. In prior years, handling them would have been child's play. He could have done it on break, while reading a good novel and getting a foot massage.

The problem was, his heart was no longer in it. He'd had his fill. It was like there were only so many targets one could deal with, and then the brain and the body shut down, no longer inclined to engage.

"So I wanted to see how I could help. Maybe if we talked about it, we could get this thing back on track." Angus's face relaxed. "We need these guys. I can't explain why, but they're vital. Without them, it's over. And if it ends, there'll be no more need—or money—for further gigs."

Forget further gigs. Stone barely wanted *this* gig. It was nothing but a headache, and all he'd gotten out of it so far was an under-cooked steak. He'd been shrewd with his money over the years; having adequate funds wasn't an issue.

"So I thought we'd go over your process, see where the holes are, how we can tighten things up."

This was patronizing as hell. Stone didn't want to talk about his process with Angus or anyone else. It reminded him of the instructor in his writing workshop. "All writers have a ritual, a process," the teacher had counseled. He'd given a litany of writers with various levels of fame from different time periods, detailing their habits and routines. This one got up at dawn and wrote by a pond. That one dropped her kids off at school, then checked into an empty hotel room. Another one couldn't get the pen moving until he drank twenty-five cups of coffee. It was mildly interesting, but it didn't help his motivation. His failure to accomplish SPM's simple mission was based on the same thing—the lack of motivation to use his considerable skills and talents to do someone else's bidding. So he wasn't going to talk about "where the holes were," and "how we can tighten things up." If process were a hammer, he'd hit Angus over the head with it and walk out.

"Look, I've been in the game for a good twenty years, maybe more. I'm not going to sit here and discuss how I do my job. You hired me to do something; stop wasting my time and let me do it."

"Okay, then," said Angus, "let's cut right to it. I wanted you to bring in Leonard–slash–David Goodwin alive. Were you successful at that? No. He was right here, in the lobby of this building, no less, and you"—Angus paused for dramatic effect—"shot. Him. And let him. Get away.

"Now let's revisit Alejandro Kichido." Angus was on a roll, setting forth his case as if it belonged in front of the Supreme Court. "You had your flunky tail him, get on a bus with him, travel with him, and politely lose him. So whether you've been in the game for twenty minutes, twenty years, or twenty decades, you and I both know this—you're slipping."

"Look—"

"No, you look." Angus stood. "I want this job done. Now. And this is what you're going to do. You're going to take out both of these men. I no longer care whether they live or die, as long as I get what I want, what this organization needs. I want the flash drive from Alejandro, and I want a workable amount of blood and tissue from Goodwin. Enough to last. Get those things and dispose of the bodies however you like."

Stone was confused. He'd known these people were serious about their research, but now they wanted him to murder the targets? They were doctors and scientists. Hadn't they taken an oath about doing no harm? There was much more to this than he'd thought when he'd taken the assignment. "Taking care of people," so to speak, was something he'd done in his younger years, but he'd moved away from that and hadn't planned on returning to it. It no longer felt good—well, it had never felt good, but it was no longer something he could tolerate. He'd taken jobs with lower stakes to ease his conscience and work toward his goals, which he could definitively state in three steps: (1) retire to Trinidad, (2) write his book, and (3) never have anything to do with this lifestyle again.

"Of course, this new directive warrants a higher level of compensation," Angus said. "And here it is, in advance." He handed Stone a crisp check. The center line held a number with a long string of zeros.

Well, maybe one last time. He pocketed the check and wondered whether the bank was still open. It wasn't the type of check you deposited at an ATM.

THIRTY-NINE

Angus had reneged on his promise to release Gayle as soon as he got the information he wanted. He'd left abruptly after learning David's name. She gathered these people had referred to him as Leonard Goodwin for years, decades even, leading to innumerable dead ends. Somehow they'd found David and shot at him, but he'd gotten away. Now that Angus had the correct name, thanks to her, he was off to the races. Gayle needed to warn him.

Angus had left his goons in charge of Gayle, and surprisingly they had the good sense to move her out of the main sanctuary into an attached building. The large room was bare. Banquet tables were folded and stacked against one wall. The matching folding chairs stood upright in rows, like soldiers heading to war, against another wall. The men sat her down in one of the chairs. They milled around, passing the time on their phones.

My phone. If she could get to it, she could contact David and tell him they knew his full name and might be closer than he thought. But she hadn't seen her phone—or her purse—in hours. She'd had it as she exited the spa but didn't remember what happened to it after she'd been taken. It had to be in one of two places—the trunk of the car or the spa's parking lot.

The only way to find out is to ask. But the cloth stuffed in her mouth prevented her from doing that. And her hands and feet were still bound. She rocked back and forth, hoping it would attract attention.

One of the men looked up from his device, Gayle's movement registering in his peripheral vision. "You're wasting your energy on that," he said. "You're not going anywhere."

Gayle kept moving around, and soon both men approached and stood over her like mountains.

"What do you want?" commanded one of the men, the more senior of the two.

Gayle jerked her head around, letting them know she needed to speak. They moved away to talk in low tones.

The men returned to face her. The older one spoke. "Look, we want to help you, or at least find out what you need." His eyes softened. "I know this has been a lot, and it must be scary. You're wondering if you're going to get out of here alive."

Gayle stared at him.

"The thing is," he said, "you're definitely not going to get out of here alive if you do anything stupid."

"Now I'm willing to take this off, but if you scream or yell, we'll have to handle that. And. You should understand, very deeply, that my boss has the information he needs. In a minute, he'll have your boy with the magic blood or whatever. So we don't really need you anymore. We're just holding on to you for safekeeping."

Gayle nodded to indicate she "deeply understood" all of this.

"So you got it? When I take this off, don't scream. Don't yell. If you do, it'll be the last sound that ever comes out of your mouth."

Gayle tried to make her eyes look both scared and obedient.

"Alright." Then, to the other one, he said, "Take it off."

Goon Jr. looked skeptical, but he complied.

"So what do you want?"

"I-I need my purse," Gayle said, feigning a weakened voice.

"Your purse," repeated the man.

"Yes, you know, the thing women hang over their shoulder, filled with things like keys, Kleenex, glasses, money."

"Didn't Angus tell you earlier about being cute? Don't do it. What do you need your purse for?"

Gayle took another breath. *Slow your roll. You need these men to help you.* "Medication," she said. "My medication is in there, and I haven't taken it in over twenty-four hours and I'm supposed to have it two times a day."

"Medication for what?"

"For my condition."

"Yeah, I get that. What condition?" He turned to the other goon. "Her purse is in the car, right? Can you get it?"

Wonderful. If I play this right, I can kill two birds with one stone. She winced as she heard the old saying in her head. Her philosophy professor preferred the nonviolent phrase "feed two birds with one seed." She'd loved that and had promptly adopted it. But this wasn't the time for a gentler approach.

"It's kind of personal. I don't really talk about it because it's—"

"If you want your purse, you'll start talking about it right now. I'll be the first to know."

The other man came back with the purse and started rummaging through it. Apparently no one had told him that going through a woman's purse was a no-no. She had to get her purse before they confiscated her phone. And then she'd need a private place to call David.

"Is your medication in a bottle in here?" The man continued fumbling through her bag.

"I have ulcerative proctitis," Gayle said quickly. Some years back, a fellow teacher had had this condition. He'd often brought it up at lunch while they ate; Gayle wished he would keep to himself. Now she was grateful he'd been so open.

"Ulcera-ulcer . . . what? You're saying you have an ulcer?"

"Ul-cer-a-tive proc-ti-tis." Gayle repeated the condition slowly, carefully sounding out each syllable, as if for a toddler.

The man looked up for a moment, then continued raking through the contents of her purse. She had to stop him before he got to her phone.

"I have to insert a suppository cream and I use an applicator to do it."

"Suppository? Isn't that for... your butt? Like when people have hemorrhoids?" The man's hand stopped moving but remained inside the purse.

"Yes, it's like that, and that's where it goes." Gayle pretended to blush. "The cream and applicator are in there."

The man grimaced and pulled his hand out of the purse as if it was on fire. "I'm gonna just... I'm gonna let you get it." He held the purse out from his body like it was a dirty diaper.

"Thank you. And can I use that little bathroom over there?"

The men hesitated. Angus had been very specific—don't let her out of your sight.

Seeing their hesitation, Gayle added another tidbit, something else she remembered. "If I don't do it at the required intervals, I can have intense, severe bleeding from the rectum and—"

"Okay, go ahead, just go in there and do your thing. And wash your hands good before you come back out." The man untied her hands and feet. "I probably need to wash my hands myself," he said.

Finally. Gayle's plan had paid off. She was alone, her hands and feet were free, and she was in possession of her purse. She locked herself in the social hall's tiny bathroom, knowing the goons wouldn't enter—she'd fixed it so they'd stay far away. She sent out a quick, silent thought of gratitude to the coworker who'd given too much information.

She placed her purse on the corner of the tiny sink, then took a moment to look in the mirror. The whites of her eyes were dim with fatigue, her lips were chapped from dehydration. When was the last time she'd had anything to drink? Or eat?

She opened the purse wide and went into the zippered compartment where she kept her phone. It wasn't there, but she wasn't alarmed. Sometimes she just threw it in the bag without putting it in its designated little sleeve. She rummaged through the bag and still couldn't find it, so she emptied everything into the sink. She picked through the items—keys, lip gloss, her wallet, random business cards of people she never planned to contact—but the phone wasn't there.

Several loud knocks rattled the door. "You about done in there?"

Gayle raked through the items one more time, then started placing everything back in the purse. She tried to think back to the last time she'd had her phone. Had she taken it out at the spa? Did Angus or his men already have it? Wherever it was, it couldn't help her. Or David.

FORTY

David watched a group of men board the black-and-white bus. When it pulled off toward the county jail, he slipped through the side gate. Going through the front of the courthouse would take too long, with the metal detectors and pat-downs he'd have to endure, and it would also be too risky. That company—PMS, PPS, PSP, whatever it was—had labeled Alejandro a criminal and plastered his face all over the news. They'd probably done the same with David's picture by now.

A quick elevator ride put him at the door of his office. The smell hit him as it did each morning, a mix of sour milk and disinfectant. "I'm going to have to talk to someone about this," Clara, David's secretary, had said, many times. But she never did. The scent had been irritating to him at first, and then ridiculously funny, until it began to represent more—the sourness of his feelings about his job, the decay that needed to be excised from his life.

Clara sat in the secretarial pool, typing a report and talking on the phone at the same time, the receiver cradled between her chin and shoulder. She looked up and smiled when David came in, then frowned and mouthed, *What are you doing here?*

"Uh, I work here?" David said. Then he took a step back. Had he been fired? His meeting with Harlow Temple hadn't gone particularly well, but it hadn't gone *that* badly.

Clara hung up the phone. "I thought you'd be at the in-service retreat with the rest of the attorneys, but I guess not."

"Oh, I forgot about that." David relaxed a bit. Most of the staff was gone—an extra stroke of luck. "I've just got a lot on my mind. My girlfriend's—"

"I know, we all saw her leave in a huff. Figured something was going on. She break up with you? I'm sorry."

Of course, everyone would assume *she'd* broken up with him. When they attended office functions, his colleagues smiled in his face, said what a beautiful couple they were. The truth was, they believed she was way out of his league, probably thought it was just a matter of time before she traded up. They probably knew about Steakhouse Geoffrey, too.

"Actually, I was the one who—" David cut himself off again. There was no point. They'd also seen her arrive with Alejandro, then leave right after him. "I need to see the IT guy. Did he go on the retreat?"

"No, Andrew's here. He's down there, probably watching porn."

David headed back to the elevator. Once on the building's ground floor, he walked down the hall and pressed his key card against the IT panel. The door clicked and David pushed it open. Andrew sat at a desk with his back to the door. He turned his head slightly, then made a quick movement. His screen changed to lines of code.

"Hey, man," Andrew said.

"Hey. What're you up to?"

"Same old, same old, you know."

"I was wondering if you could help my friend with something," David said.

Andrew smiled. "Sure, what does 'your friend' need?"

"He's trying to find someone, and I told him you might be able to do it if we use her cell phone to trace its location. I've heard there's a program like that, something that's not available to the general public. I thought we might have it for investigative purposes, you know, to help our clients."

Andrew nodded. "Yeah, we have the ability to do that—but it's as you said, to help our clients. Not for random bullshit from people who don't even work here. Somebody up on the nineteenth floor is probably tracking everything I do. So I can't just get on there and use this technology for anybody."

"Okay, man, you got me. It's for me. I'm 'the friend.' And I'm looking for Gayle."

"Oh, yeah, that cutie you brought to the summer picnic last year. I liked her. She wasn't all snobby like some of these dudes' wives. But I thought she broke up with you. Clara said—"

"Look, can you help me or not? I think somebody has her."

"Has her? You mean she's been kidnapped?" Andrew's eyes lit up at the chance to get involved in something real, a good intrigue. He spent most of his time making sure investigators had access to rap sheets and research engines.

"I think so. If I give you her number, would you be able to locate her?"

"We should be." Andrew's fingers flew across his keyboard. Indecipherable sequences ran up and down his screen. When a single cursor appeared, his hands paused. "What's her number?"

David recited the number, and Andrew typed it in, then waited. "Yep, we got her."

"You do? Already? You can tell exactly where she is?"

"Yep, she's . . . okay, wait. This can't be right. I thought you said she's been kidnapped."

"Yes, that's what I said," David replied, impatient. "Where is she?"

"Dude," Andrew said slowly, "she's in your office, right upstairs."

"She's here! She must've come back to find me." David looked around smiling, giddy. "Thank you, man, thank you." He patted Andrew on the back and started toward the door.

Andrew shrugged. "Okay, well, glad to have been of help. Next time, maybe just check your office first."

David waited at the elevator for a few moments, and when it didn't come, he sprinted up the stairs and practically ran through the office. Passing Clara's station on the way to his office, he yelled, "She's here!"

"Who's here?" Clara asked.

"Gayle, you let her in, right?"

Clara looked puzzled. "Uh, I don't—"

David moved swiftly through the labyrinth of offices and finally reached his own space. The office was empty. Except for Gayle's phone, lit up on the edge of his desk. A glaring beacon, reminding him that he'd sent her away.

———

David stared, frozen in place, his mouth open, at the phone on his desk. Of course, Gayle had forgotten her phone when she stormed out, stunned by his words. And he hadn't been able to see anything other than his own anger. He tried to think of a good next step to find her, the next right thing, after all the wrong things he'd done. He looked at her text messages, saw the frantic text she had sent him when she and Alejandro were on their way.

Okay, wait. Gayle had left school based on Alejandro's advice. How had he gotten in touch with her? He looked for a text, checking the entries that didn't have names. Seeing nothing, he looked at her most recent calls. And there it was, the last call she'd received—a number with an 805 area code. The call had lasted roughly fifteen minutes.

Alejandro wouldn't want to talk to David. But finding him was David's only option.

He tapped the number. The call was picked up immediately. "Gayle? Are you with Goodwin, uh, I mean, David?"

David inhaled, gathered his courage, and spoke. "Alejandro. It's not Gayle, it's David. Gayle's missing, I think someone has her. You were right. And I was wrong to kick you guys out."

"Kick us out? What?" The voice went silent. "I mean, yeah, you were wrong to do that."

"Can we meet up? I need your help."

"Uh, yeah. Let's meet. I'm in Long Beach. Can you come down here?"

"Long Beach? That's a ways away. Could we meet halfway or something?"

"Look, do you want my help or not? You called me. And I don't know if you've noticed, but the cops are after me, SPM is after me. The last place I need to be is right in the middle of Los Angeles."

"Okay, yeah, you're right. Long Beach. Whatever it takes. We just gotta find her before something bad happens. I'm on my way. Tell me where I can find you."

He got an address, somewhere near the port, and took off.

FORTY-ONE

The lights in the parking lot outside Violet's window popped on, signaling the end of the day. She'd spent the last few hours poring through the SPM binder. She'd managed to hold on to it during the police investigation following Dr. Howe's attempt to—silence her? Murder her?

The inspector assigned to the case had asked Violet about her connection to Howe, why he would've done this. She deflected, saying she had no idea, had never met Howe. None of it made sense to the man, but he didn't press her. He sauntered around the room, moved things around on the bedside table, peeked into the bathroom. At one point he laid a hand on the top of the SPM binder. The inspector probably decided it was a forgotten medical volume; he moved on without opening it.

Violet was still in shock over the contents of the binder. She had to get this information to David; there was so much he needed to know, information that might change the trajectory of his life.

"Had a chance to get some rest?" It was Nurse Patti, here to check on her as she'd been doing at the top of every hour.

I'm okay, Nurse Patti. But I've gotta get out of here. I'm in danger, clearly, and there's some important information I need to get to my friend. I can't just sit here."

"I get it. This support group I'm in? My leader would applaud that. You're refusing to be a victim. You're moving back into your sense of power. And now you're going to do something, take action out in the world, to prove it."

Violet smiled. "Exactly. So can you help me?"

"Help you. Get out of here? I don't know, hon, you're still recovering, you still need a certain level of care. I'd have to check your vitals, talk to the attending—"

"But like you said, I have to reclaim my power, or else I'll be stuck in this phase, wallowing, victimized."

Nurse Patti brightened. "Yeah, it's important to do that. And the sooner, the better, is what my group leader says. While you have the mind to do it, the momentum."

"So you'll help me."

"Gimme some time to think and I'll be back with a plan." Nurse Patti headed toward the door, then looked back. "You're sure you're gonna be okay out there? I mean—"

"I'll make it, Nurse Patti. I have to."

———

"Wake up, hon, wake up." Violet's eyes popped open. It was Nurse Patti, gently shaking her awake. "I've come up with a plan to get you out of here, but we have to act fast."

Violet looked around, disoriented. She took the glass of water from her bedside table and drank it, then poured a bit into her hands and splashed it onto her face, stray drops sliding between her fingers. Now fully awake, she focused her attention back on the nurse. "Okay. Tell me the plan. After that nightmare, I'm ready for anything—and I can't stay here one more minute."

———

Here she was again, being pushed in the wheelchair by Nurse Patti, the SPM binder safely tucked into her oversized bag. This time the nurse was silent. Violet had on navy-blue sweatpants and a loose cotton blouse with a hideous floral pattern. Nurse Patti had hurried Violet out of her hospital gown and helped her change into the baggy sweats and ugly blouse.

They rolled down one hall after another, making turns through the labyrinth of the hospital. They rode the elevator to the eighth floor, where Dr. Howe's office was. Violet tensed up.

"Don't worry, hon," Nurse Patti said. "He's on another floor, in police custody."

Marta, the nurse they'd seen earlier, walked over, took Violet's hand, and secured a hospital-issue bracelet to her wrist. She gave a similar bracelet to Nurse Patti, who placed it in the deep pockets of her scrubs. Marta nodded and waved them on.

"Now we just get the baby and some transportation, and you'll be set."

"Wait, Nurse Patti, a baby? Don't you think that's going a bit too far? I'm going to take some other woman's baby out of here?"

"It won't be a real baby, just a doll, one they use in the classes. To get you to the discharge dock. So you won't be noticeable to anybody who might have worked with Dr. Howe. Anybody who might have noticed your empty room, might be watching for a woman your age leaving the hospital. No one will pay any mind to a mother leaving with her baby."

Violet glanced around. Could they really pull this off?

Nurse Patti read Violet's mind. "I've got it all worked out. Don't worry about a thing."

They continued down the hall. It opened into a spacious lobby filled with several sitting areas; its large picture window looked out onto the Los Angeles skyline. The maternity ward was beyond this area, on the mezzanine level. Violet's chest tightened.

"Nurse Patti, I really don't—"

"Shhh," Nurse Patti said. "Just let me handle this." She wheeled Violet into an alcove that was tucked away from the main hallway. "Stay put until I get back." The nurse strode off, looking back and forth as she hurried away.

Violet listened to the cries of infants coming from various directions. In minutes, Nurse Patti was back with a surprisingly realistic-looking doll wrapped in blankets. Placing the bundle in Violet's arms, she took the handles of the wheelchair and headed for the closest elevator.

The whole thing still seemed risky to Violet. "What if someone stops us on the way out?"

"Nobody'll stop us. Nurses bring new mothers and their babies to the discharge dock all the time. We look official."

"Whoa, whoa, whoa." A woman in green scrubs with a ducky pattern stopped them. *Here it comes. I'm going to jail in dingy sweats, for shoplifting a creepy doll.* She thought about what her mug shot would look like, the collar of the horrible floral blouse floating below her face.

"Yes?" Nurse Patti answered.

"I don't remember this mother and baby." She bent down and addressed Violet. "Did you attend my workshop on breastfeeding? I give it every morning to the new moms."

Violet started to answer but Nurse Patti cut her off. "No, she didn't attend. Breastfeeding is going to prove impossible for her, for a variety of reasons." The nurse started to wheel Violet away.

Ducky Scrubs put her hand on Violet's shoulder, slowing their movement. "At Mother's Milk Lactation Services, we don't believe breastfeeding is impossible for anyone. It's best for baby, what nature intended. Why don't you come back in and we'll give it a try? There's a number of approaches; one of them is bound to work."

"Thank you for the offer, maybe I'll come back for that," Violet said. "Right now I'm tired and just want to get home."

"No better time than the present," the woman insisted. "Get your baby off on the right track."

Nurse Patti spoke up. "She said she'll come back. And that's it. There's a ward full of women who want your services; go see about them."

The woman drew back for a moment, stung. Then her eyes narrowed. "Alright, then. But it's my duty to check your bracelets. You know that, Nurse whatever-your-name-is."

"Yes, I know that." Nurse Patti held up Violet's hand. "Bracelet #110758, see?" She took the bracelet from her pocket and showed it to the woman. "This is his," she said. "It was creating a rash on his little wrist so we took it off. Also #110758. Satisfied?"

Ducky Scrubs nodded, resigned, and turned to walk away. Then she turned back. The women held their breath. "Well, be sure to come back for my workshop. I'll be looking for you."

Both women nodded, and they stayed stationary until the woman turned the corner. "We've gotta get you on your way," Nurse Patti said.

They approached the discharge dock, and the nurse helped Violet into a waiting shuttle. After settling her into a seat, the nurse took the doll and exited through the rear door. As the shuttle drove away, Violet waved to Nurse Patti. She nodded and quickly entered the hospital.

"Where to?" asked the driver.

Violet, exhausted, thought about it, then answered, "I have no idea."

FORTY-TWO

Margaritas. The sound of the surf. Grainy, crystallized sand under his feet. A vivid blue sky that continued into the horizon, no end in sight. Alejandro would be luxuriating in these things right now, had he followed his original plan. Getting the Hell Out of Dodge was generally a foolproof itinerary, especially when things got rough and your face was being splashed all over the news as a corporate thief.

But here he was, still in Dodge, or more accurately, Long Beach. He'd taken a break for a while at Reece's warehouse, figuring out his next move. Plus, he needed a new passport. Reece had people who could do that. He'd put Big Slop on the job, and the giant man had taken a quick photo of him with his phone, made a few taps, then looked up, nodding. "About an hour," he'd promised.

Alejandro collapsed on the sectional that ran along the left side of the warehouse. He closed his eyes, and the reel that played in his head—the one that kept him up at night—promptly began.

———

It had been Shelly's suggestion to take the thirty-minute drive to the lookout point to catch a glimpse of the sunset. Alejandro had known better; the sun would be long gone by the time they got to the top of Topanga. But it was difficult to turn down Shelly's ideas. There was something about her that made him long to grant her requests, to make all her wishes come true. He grabbed his keys and they took off. At the lookout, she got out and went straight to the safety rail, toasted the air with a glass of wine from the basket they'd brought along. Alejandro had stayed in the car, finishing an email to classmates in his study group.

After pressing Send, he looked up from his phone, ready to join her. She was gone. He looked back and forth, then got out and called her name. He did a 360-degree turn, stumbling over the rocks, disoriented. He took a deep breath and started toward the railing. He leaned over, scouring the rocky terrain below, but he didn't see her. He called out a few more times, and then just stood there as darkness filled the sky.

Alejandro woke up to Reece calling his name, shaking his shoulders. Big Slop stood nearby.

"Your passport is ready. They're waiting for you. You got the cash, right?"

"Uh, yeah. I have the cash. About how much do I need?"

"Nothing," Reece said. "Let me take care of this."

"Naw, man, after all you've done, I can't let you do that."

"I insist. We got it." Reece went into his coat pocket and peeled ten bills from a big wad of cash. He folded the bills and handed them to Alejandro.

The top bill was a hundred-dollar note. "A grand? Reece, I can't take this."

"You can and you will," Big Slop, still standing by, cut in. "And what do you say when someone offers to do something nice?"

"Thank you." Alejandro practically bowed to Big Slop. Reece had refused to share the story behind the man's name, but he gathered it wasn't anything nice.

"Not to me," Big Slop said. "To him." He gestured toward Reece.

Alejandro turned to Reece. Their lives had turned out so differently. It was unfair. But Reece was surviving. "Thank you, man," Alejandro said. He stepped forward to give Reece a hug.

Reece hugged him back. He patted Alejandro on the back and pulled away, smiling. He slipped him a piece of paper. "Now go. Get your passport there and head out. You'll make it."

————

The paper Reece had given Alejandro wasn't an address but a series of circuitous instructions that read more like a treasure map, designed to lead him to a spot where the underground passport maker would meet him for the exchange. The destination turned out to be the back room of a lamp shop.

He entered the room from an alley and headed in to the main floor of the shop. A worn-looking man at the counter waved him toward the back room. As Alejandro weaved his way through the showroom, he noticed the lampshades were yellowed and looked ancient, like the chains they hung from. A strong sneeze might make the whole thing come crashing down.

He stood at the closed door of the back room, not knowing what to do. He reached for the doorknob, and just as his fingers touched it, the door opened.

"Come in" said a gruff, disembodied voice.

Alejandro eased into the room. A man in a hooded sweatshirt came into view. "You have the money," the man said, more a statement than a question.

"Yeah, I have it." Alejandro pulled Reece's stack of bills from his pocket and held them out.

The man took the cash, counted it, then turned and went to a small desk toward the back of the dark room.

"You want something to drink?" he asked Alejandro.

"Uh . . ." Alejandro didn't know what to do. On the one hand, it went against everything he'd been taught about accepting drinks in strange places from strange people. On the other hand, it might be considered rude—as in, fatally rude—to turn down a drink, as if you were too good to break bread with the people you'd hired to perform some shady service.

He decided it would be best to accept the drink, and then avoid drinking it. "Sure, whatcha got?"

"All we have is ginger ale; it's what the boss likes."

"Ginger ale it is," Alejandro said. His mother would have liked this guy's boss, despite his line of work. She loved ginger ale so much, she might have even forgiven him that. She called it the champagne of soft drinks.

The man headed toward a small side room and emerged with the soda and a clear sandwich bag containing a passport.

"Here you go," the man said, holding out the bag and the soda.

Alejandro took both items and turned to go. "Thanks a lot, man."

"Don't you want to look at everything, make sure everything's in order?"

"Naw, man, I trust you. I gotta get going."

"Oh, okay. I was gonna grab a soda myself, thought we could sit and talk, have the drinks."

This sucker is lonely. Alejandro imagined the man's dreary life. He must sit back here all day, maybe into the night, exchanging passports for cash. Alejandro almost felt sorry for him until he remembered the grand he'd just handed over. It wasn't his job to babysit this guy.

"I wish I could," he told the man, "but I really gotta go. For the same reason I need the passport on the fly. You understand."

"Yeah, I get it. Alright, well, nice doing business with you." He held up a hand. Alejandro imitated the salutation, then made his way out through the forest of decrepit lamps.

———

Now to the border. Alejandro's original plan had taken a major detour—several detours, really—but he was back on track. He couldn't chance getting back on a bus at this point—SPM probably had someone watching for him. He thought of putting out his thumb and hitching a ride with the first person who stopped, but his mother's warnings when he was a child kept him from doing that. His best bet was to head toward the port, where he might be able to catch a ride on a shuttle.

Thankfully he was close enough to the docks to walk. If he was vigilant, watched his surroundings, he could make it without running into anyone from SPM. He was sure they were still in Long Beach, and they'd probably recruited more goons to comb the area for him.

He made it to the dock and stopped at a makeshift hot dog stand. A dingy red-and-white umbrella stood sentry over a set of molded chairs and a matching table. As he walked up to place his order, he saw a person walking pointedly toward him. *Oh, hell no.* Alejandro didn't know what David was doing down here, but he didn't want any part of it. Maybe he was trying to get out of the country, too. Whatever the case, he thought, I'm done. This wasn't *The Shawshank Redemption,* and they weren't buddies escaping to Mexico to build a boat.

David was apparently just as apprehensive. He shuffled past, then turned back. "Alejandro?"

"David," he said, his eyes blank. He wasn't going to make this easy.

"Hey, man."

Hey, man? Was this David's idea of an apology?

"I, uh, I need your help, man. Gayle's missing, you were right, and I just . . . I don't know what to do. I've been shot at, and—"

"And now you want to talk. You remember what you told me last time I was in your office? I was trying to help your ass—hell, *save your ass*—and you went all loco and accused me of messin' with your girl."

David stood silent.

"And you're trying to talk to me right now," Alejandro went on, "because now you *do* want my help."

Alejandro had never been more regretful about getting involved in a situation that had nothing to do with him. He'd heard a conversation he wasn't supposed to hear. So what? The appropriate reaction: Delete and move on. He couldn't figure out why he'd bothered. Yes, he could. Shelly. She'd disappeared, and he didn't know what had happened. The lookout was a popular spot. No body had been recovered from the area; he'd paid attention to the news. His calls to her phone had gone unanswered. He'd never met Shelly's family and didn't know if they'd even reported her missing. He couldn't risk calling to report it. If something *had* happened to her, he'd be the prime suspect. *This* was why he was here: It was about proving something to himself. If he succeeded, maybe he could forgive himself and feel whole once again.

David finally spoke. "Look, I understand you're upset. I treated you like shit. You didn't deserve it. But you work for SPM and you have information that can help me. I know that now. And if you've washed your hands of the whole thing and don't want to help me find Gayle, I don't know why you agreed to meet me down here."

Alejandro lit in. "You're damn right you treated me like shit. And see where it's gotten you. And not that you care, but because I got involved with your mess, now I'm a target. The police have me listed as wanted, as if I'm some kind of killer, and goons from SPM followed me all the way down here." He took a breath, then continued, "At first I was some freeloader off the street who posed some sort of threat, and now I'm the long lost oracle. If you'd listened in the first place, none of us would be in this mess; Gayle would be safe. My track coach always said some people don't believe fat meat's greasy. Well, it is. And because of your masculine bullshit, we don't know who has her and what they're doing with her. And—wait, did you say I agreed to meet you here?"

"On the phone, about an hour ago. You don't remember? I called and you told me to come here, to the docks." David blinked.

"That wasn't me, dude. I don't have my phone. I left it on the bus when I got away from SPM. I left it in the pocket of one of the guys who was after me. I don't know who you talked to, but it wasn't me and—"

"It might have been me." Stone turned around and took the last bite of a hot dog laden with mustard.

Alejandro and David stopped talking and looked at him, then at each other.

Stone wiped his mouth with a napkin. "Now, this can either go very smoothly, and by that I mean both of you live to tell your grandchildren about this adventure, or it can go very roughly, meaning you don't live." He dabbed at a drop of mustard that had landed on the lapel of his suit.

Alejandro pushed Stone back into the hot dog stand and the other customers, which toppled the umbrella and sent the condiment display flying. He grabbed David's shoulder and yelled, "Come on!"

David started running down the pier behind Alejandro. They'd put a nice distance between themselves and the hot dog stand when they heard gunshots. They darted away from the long walkway and toward the parking structure where cruise ship passengers left their cars. They ran between cars and up a ramp, barely missing getting wiped out by a car, then across the length of the parking lot and down the ramp on the other side. After exiting the structure, they continued toward an open-air parking lot and crouched down between some cars.

"We gotta get some place with guards and police and people like that, where he won't be so quick to shoot," Alejandro said.

David peeked out from behind the car and looked around. "The *Queen Mary*'s right there," he said. "They have a ton of guards and official people." He'd accompanied one of Gayle's classes on a field trip to the ship as part of a social studies lesson. "And there's always tons of tourists. Plenty of places to hide," he added.

"Let's do it," Alejandro said. They peeked around the cars, then tore out toward the ship.

A couple of motorcycles pulled in front of them and stopped, blocking their path. David made a move to go around them, but Alejandro stopped. Reece was on one of the bikes, Big Slop on the other.

Alejandro looked perplexed. "What are you guys doing here?"

Reece smiled. "You're in trouble. Somebody's after you. I wouldn't be your brother if I didn't keep tabs, make sure you got to wherever you're going."

"So—"

"So, get on. And your friend here, he rides with Big Slop."

David looked at Alejandro and said, "Big Slop?"

Reece, Alejandro, and Big Slop said, in unison, "Long story."

"You getting on or not, dude?" said Slop. "Otherwise, I got things to do."

"Oh, I'm definitely getting on. Thanks, man," David said. He and Alejandro clambered onto the bikes. Just as they got settled on, shots rang out. Reece looked back, gave Slop the okay, and they peeled off toward the *Queen Mary*.

FORTY-THREE

David slumped in the back seat as the car wound through downtown Long Beach. He'd fallen asleep less than a mile after getting in, jolted awake when his head dipped down abruptly as the car barreled over a bump. He studied the back of the driver's headrest, then stared out the window.

After he and Alejandro had jumped on the motorcycles, they'd tried to exit the *Queen Mary*'s parking area, a maze of closely spaced concrete-and-steel pillars. All paths led to the attendant's booth, where a long line of cars waited in queue. Reece and Slop had maneuvered fiercely, circling and spinning, doing wheelies, to dodge the bullets from Stone and his comrades. They'd even gone up on onto the roofs of a couple of cars and spent a few moments in the air.

They ducked the pursuit for a while, until Reece's and Slop's oversized helmets turned toward each other and they headed toward the on-ramp of the big ship. Alejandro looked back and mouthed something.

"What?" David still couldn't hear him. "What?"

The bikes stopped for a moment as a pedestrian passed, and Alejandro repeated his words. "Hold on!"

Reece and Big Slop revved their bikes, then rocketed forward. They passed the entrance kiosk and glided up the ramp. A group of tourists shouted and scattered. They turned onto an empty deck, occupied by construction signs and equipment. They slowed down to steer around the ladders and tables stacked with drills.

David looked back—Stone was on a Segway and a man was running behind him on foot; another man was on a bicycle. He tapped Slop to warn him.

They turned down a narrow flight of metal stairs and arrived at a restaurant with a grand lobby and a view of the harbor. The diners gasped as the bikes powered through; those in their direct path were knocked out of their chairs. A few tables turned over, spilling drinks and crab Louie. Glass shattered and people screamed. The maître d' ran after them, waving a linen napkin, the tails of his coat floating behind him.

They exited the dining room and entered an ornate ballroom. Like a magician, Stone appeared in front of them on a raised stage and fired several shots. They spun and sped toward the room's double doors.

As the bikes made it out onto another deck, the man on foot came from the right, shooting as he ran, and the man on the bike sped toward them from the left, firing as well. Reece and Big Slop drove straight off the deck and landed on the wider deck below. They made a sharp turn and headed toward a sign that read "Special Exhibit."

The motorcycles flew past the velvet rope, startling the docent. "Stop!" he yelled as the blur of bikes whizzed by. They barreled through the elaborate display, an array consisting of tall glass cases showcasing a British duke's tuxedos, capes, and walking sticks. A detail-oriented curator had hired an artist to paint the mannequins' faces to resemble the duke's, highlighting his dark, bushy eyebrows and handlebar mustache.

Stone and his men had found their way into the exhibit and were coming up fast. The bikes drove past a low table with a display of watches, and David reached back and pushed the table to block the men. The bikes sped forward and Alejandro looked over and gave David the thumbs-up. Reece and Slop steered out of the exhibit and back onto the main deck, then left the vessel via the down-ramp. As they moved away from the ship, David looked back one last time. No one was following them. The cyclists rode up onto the roofs of two cars, gaining enough momentum to jump over the parking kiosk. Trailing dust and fumes, they headed back toward Reece's warehouse.

The wild ride on the *Queen Mary* played like a short film in David's head. While it had probably been the most terrifying episode of his life—other than the day the Goodwins had left him at the airport—being at the center of it had been exhilarating. He'd felt the blood flowing through his veins, the electricity coursing through his body, his cells moving and expanding, awakening from stasis.

When they arrived at Reece's place, David and Alejandro had fallen onto the sofas and lain there for some time, their arms and legs limp, dangling over the edges. Reece brought them water, while Slop secured the huge metal doors and posted a couple of men on guard.

Alejandro sat up, prompting David to do the same.

David spoke first. "Can you explain something?" he asked. "What made you do all this? Why not just delete the voicemail and move on?"

"I've asked myself that a million times. I just couldn't let something happen to another woman, I had to help. I had to prove it to myself, that I'm a good person."

"Another woman? So there was someone else—"

"It's all in the past, let's leave it there. And there was nothing I could do about it. This time, there was."

"Well, thanks, man, I appreciate it. Really. Now, about Gayle, I'm thinking that we could try to—"

Alejandro cut him off. "That said, I'm gonna have to bail now. I gotta look out for myself."

Reece, sitting off to the side, nodded in agreement.

Alejandro looked at Reece. "You have somebody that can get us into these secure files, right?"

Reece nodded again.

"We can all take a look at everything here and then you can keep the flash drive, but I gotta move on from this. I've done my part."

David stood up. "What happened to your little speech? About helping, being a good person, making up for some other woman? You're going to bail after all that?"

Alejandro stood up, along with Reece. Big Slop started heading over to the group.

Reece spoke first. "You don't talk to my brother that way. After all we just did? If it wasn't for Alejandro, you'd be in somebody's morgue right now, cold and stiff."

Alejandro held his hand up. "I got this." He turned to David. "Yes. I'm going to bail. And I really don't give a shit what you think about what I said. Here's the download." He tossed the flash drive at David. "I don't even want to look at it with you. Find someone else. And this isn't my place, but *I'm* telling you to go. Now." He motioned to Big Slop. "Can you call him a car?"

David caught the flash drive, looked at it, then put it in his pocket. "I found my way down here, I can find my way back." He looked at Reece. "Can you open the door so I can get the hell out of here?"

Big Slop gestured to one of the men at the door. David stalked off, hearing the steel doors close behind him. He walked a few blocks in the dark, then called a service to take him back to LA. While he waited, he called Andrew—he'd need someone to help him look at these files.

FORTY-FOUR

avid was caught off guard when he arrived at Andrew's address. He'd imagined the tech guy resided in some basement apartment, the cheapest unit of a neglected triplex. The ultramodern abode in one of the most coveted areas of the city was unexpected. But then he thought about how much money IT whiz kids made, probably more than David made as a government attorney. Andrew presumably had a number of high-paid gigs he could do from home.

David walked up the manicured walkway, then pressed a sleek, illuminated rectangular panel. A minute later, Andrew opened the door. "Entrez-vous. Come on in."

David followed Andrew through the foyer and down a hall. A sculpture made of intertwined wire sat on a lone table; abstract art covered the walls. When they got to the kitchen, Andrew turned around. "Remember the Thai restaurant we went to? I picked up some takeout and ordered way too much. You're welcome to a plate."

Realizing how hungry he was, David tried to remember the last time he'd eaten. Yesterday? "That would be great, man, thanks."

"Help yourself. Plates are on the counter. So what do you need this time? Lost your phone in your office and need me to find what bookshelf it's on?"

"Funny," David said. "But not this time. I actually have a password-protected flash drive that I need to get into."

"Okay. What's it about? A case? Because that probably could have waited. You sounded desperate and I have a little break before

I go back, so I told you to come over. But I'm off the clock right now. And the county doesn't pay me to work from home."

"No, it's not about a case. It's about me."

"You? What about you? Forgot the code to your home security system? Or, let's see... can't deposit your check on your mobile banking app?"

David took a deep breath. "Okay, okay, you got jokes." He held his right hand up. "But I really do need your help, on something really important."

Andrew took a bite of shrimp fried rice and raised his eyebrows. "Alright, what is it?"

David sighed, then took off his jacket. He proceeded to unbutton his shirt and removed his right sleeve, revealing the sturdy bandage that Hersh had used to dress his wound. A small amount of blood had seeped through.

Andrew stood up, alarmed. "What's that, man? What happened to you?"

"I got shot. Somebody's after me. So, as I said, I need your help on something really important. Believe me now?"

"Somebody actually shot you? Yeah, man. Okay, what. What can I do?"

"I need to get into this secure file." He handed Andrew the flash drive.

"Where'd you get this, because—"

"Look, does it really matter? It's a long story. I'll tell you about it later, but can you just see what's on there?"

"Okay, yes." Andrew grabbed his laptop, along with a bunch of additional attachments, which he methodically plugged in. He inserted the flash drive into the machine, then began typing. Periodically he adjusted some of the attachments, turned dials, then continued his rapid tapping.

Lines of code floated vertically on Andrew's screen. At one point, the movement stopped. "Here we are," Andrew said. "One minute."

David moved forward to see.

Andrew sat back. "This is a tough little sucker," he said. "It's going to make me work for it." He left the kitchen and went back into the side room, where he retrieved additional equipment, strange apparatus David had never seen.

"What is all that?" he asked.

"Cutting edge, dude. Only the best. Alright, here we go," Andrew said confidently. "I've got it this time. I'll download what's on here and print it out."

As the document printed, David heard the front door open and close. He looked at Andrew for a sign to run, hide, arm themselves, but Andrew just shrugged like it wasn't a big deal. A much older man walked into the kitchen and smiled. He gave Andrew a pat on his shoulder.

"How's it going, son?" he said. "You have company. And you are—"

"David. We work together."

"Okay, David, nice to meet you, welcome." He took a glass out of one of the cupboards, then poured himself a cold drink from the refrigerator and left.

"So that was your dad," David said.

"Yeah, that's my dad," Andrew replied. David smiled. "He's an artist—he painted all of the artwork you see around here." Andrew waved toward the front hall. "And the sculpture."

"So it's just you and him here?"

"Yep."

"Your dad's art must have a pretty high price point," David continued. "I mean, I didn't say it before, but this house is amazing."

"No, actually he doesn't sell anything. He's tried, but no bites. I told him to just display it here for now. Be proud of himself for creating something. I like his stuff."

"You told *him* that he could display it here?"

"Exactly," Andrew said.

"Did he really need your permission? I mean, it's his house."

"No, actually, it's my house." Andrew waved his hand around the abode. "The perks of a tech career."

David smiled and nodded. It was as he had suspected. Andrew had his stuff together. It was time for David to do the same.

———

David sat stiffly in his car, eyeing the pages Andrew had given him. The neatly folded stack lay in the passenger seat, ominous. He didn't know whether to read through them right then, or take them to the hotel Hersh had checked into before poring through them, his father by his side. He wondered what mysteries the documents held. It could be a pleasant surprise, welcome news about himself. He doubted that, though. The stakes—involving kidnapping, gunshots, motorcycle chases—were too high.

Maybe if he skimmed it, took a little peek, the muscles of his shoulders might release back down to a natural angle. His lungs might feel they could resume their duties. David picked up the papers and turned past the cover page. An official-looking report contained information on various individuals. Each entry listed the subject's name, age of discovery, and current age if still alive. The names of the subject's parents were also included, with a notation as to whether they were living or deceased. Below each name was the individual's last known address. A paragraph about each subject followed this information. Many words had been electronically redacted.

David scrolled through the names, wondering if Alejandro had made a mistake. This didn't seem to have anything to do with him. He continued to sift through the pages until he came to a subject named Leonard Goodwin. *Here we go.*

SUBJECT ███████████████532

Leonard Goodwin (in active pursuit)
DOB: 09/21/1982
Hair: Black
Eyes: Brown
Ethnicity: African descent
Current Age: 36
Address: Unknown

Parents:
Father—Leonard Ellison (deceased)
Mother—Margaret Ellison (file inactive)
Address: 43521 Don Bernardi Drive,
Los Angeles, CA 90008

Abstract with Chronology:

March 1980: Subject Margaret Ellison, 33-year-old married Black female and patient of Newman Gaylord, MD, (internal medicine) referred ███████████████████ after initial intake questionnaire, physical examination, and interview revealed ██████████████ ████████████████████████ ████████████████████████ ████████████████████ ████████████████████. Full laboratory workup, tissue collection, and a variety of tests ████████████████████. Tests and examinations continued to determine ████████ ████████████████████████ ████.

February 1982: Subject Margaret Ellison presents to Gaylord for pregnancy confirmation and to initiate prenatal care. Gaylord █████████ ███████████████████ guide the pregnancy at the highest level of care. █████████████ ████████████ the fetus and █████████ ████████ contained therein.

September 1982: Subject Margaret Ellison gives birth to live male baby. Child, named Subject Leonard Ellison Jr., is immediately ████████ █████████ given full laboratory workup, tissue collection, and a variety of tests ████████ ████████████████████████████████ ████████████████████████████████ ████████████████████████████████ ████████████████████████████████ █████████████████████. Tests and examinations continued to ████████████ ████████████████████████████████ ████████████████████████████.

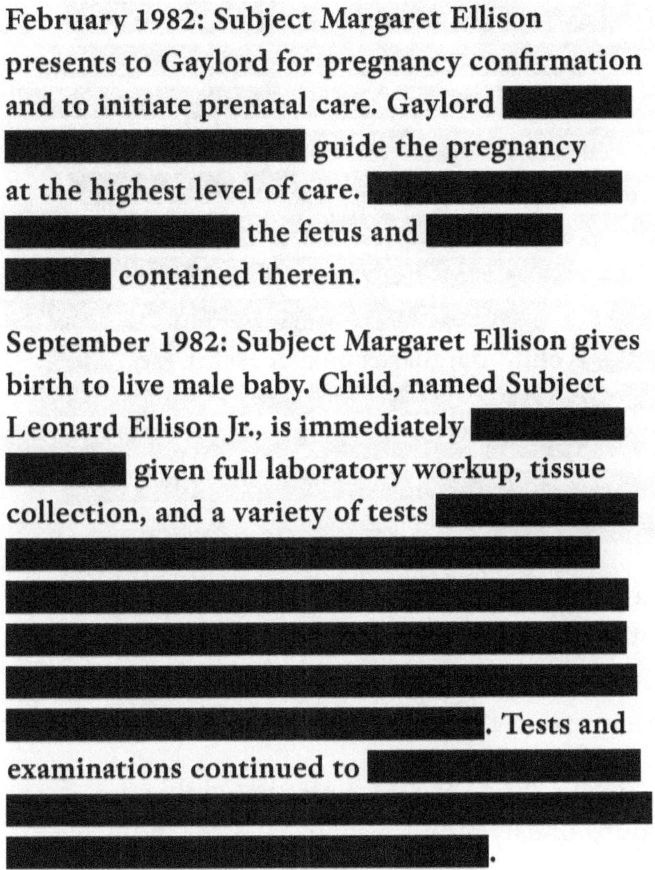

December 1982: Subject reports that her husband, Leonard Ellison, was killed on the job in his capacity as a construction worker.

July 1985: Subject reports that Child Subject Leonard Ellison Jr. is missing, wrongfully taken from childcare. Subject has contacted authorities and placed missing-child ads. SPM assists in efforts to locate the Child Subject and closely monitors all leads.

August 1993: Subject Leonard Ellison Jr. ████████████████████████████████

August 1993: Missing-child ad updated to current picture of Child Subject, obtained from the school he was attending at time of disappearance.

August 1993 to Present: Missing-child ad continuously monitored by SPM for inquiries. Computer progression technology employed to provide rendering of Subject at current age, updated every five years.

September 2018: Missing-child ad receives hit ███ ████████████ determined via IP address.

Current Status: SPM and associates actively seek Subject Leonard Goodwin. Full resources and capabilities to be placed behind this project for the apprehension of Goodwin and ████████ ████.

David scoured every letter of every word, every date in the chronology. Phrases jumped out at him: tissue collection, full laboratory workup, the fetus, continuously monitored. "The fetus"—that was him. "Full resources . . . for the apprehension of Goodwin." He stared at the document, trying to make sense of it. He was the biological child of Leonard and Margaret Ellison. Yet the Goodwins were the only family he'd ever known. And loved—at least until they'd left him alone at one of the busiest airports in the country, then cleared out their home and disappeared into the ether. How had he ended up with them, this family who made him feel as if he were their own? And why, after more than half his childhood, had they suddenly removed themselves from his life?

Then there was Margaret, the woman who had given birth to him. It was difficult to believe she lived right here in the city, just a short drive from Hersh and Regina's house. She'd placed the ad, been looking for him all these years, since he was a baby. She must have watched other children grow up while agonizing over what happened to him. He imagined the decades of searching—wishing, wondering, not knowing, feelings he knew all too well.

He scanned the page again. The notation beside Margaret's entry said "file inactive." Inactive with regards to what? She was alive, but SPM no longer bothered with her. Why? Beside his name were the words "in active pursuit." After the last couple of days, that didn't need further explanation. But what were they pursuing him for? SPM was following up on the responses to Margaret's ad—but not informing her. The redacted passages were cryptic, a puzzle. He scoured them with a close reading, his "thinking cap on," as an elementary school teacher used to say, and tried to fill in the blanks. A clandestine research study. Something that went beyond protocol, spawned by greed. Something operating under the radar, yet hidden in plain sight.

Despite all the emotion this stirred up, or maybe because of it, David's pragmatic side took over. There were two choices: He could sit here and try to figure all of this out in his head, or he could get moving. He thought about Hersh's "man of action" quote. The first person he wanted to see was Margaret, his ... mother. He wondered if he looked like her, if he'd see hints of his face in hers. He wondered if he would finally feel like he was home.

FORTY-FIVE

Margaret's Aunt Shirley had loved antique shops. Or junk shops, as she called them. As a child, Margaret had felt a kinship with her aunt, felt accepted by her in a way she hadn't at home. Aunt Shirley liked the same things Margaret liked—craft projects, vintage costumes, old movies, decadent desserts. When the older woman had a few days off, she'd invite Margaret to stay the night. They'd feast on fried catfish, collard greens, macaroni and cheese, and banana pudding from the soul food place that was a few blocks away, settling in to watch *Carmen Jones*, *Stormy Weather*, or anything starring Eartha Kitt. Margaret would sleep in the cozy loft and awaken to a breakfast of toast, bacon, and hominy grits, prepared at dawn. Later they'd walk to the shop and Margaret would follow her aunt inside, wide-eyed with wonder at the treasures bunched up inside the little store. Aunt Shirley would head toward the ceramic figurines, looking back at Margaret over her shoulder. "Find something you like and bring it to the front."

Other kids went straight to the toy section, but not Margaret. She'd learned from experience—no real finds could be unearthed in that department. The toys were generally broken and nonfunctional, carted over in a cardboard box by an ambitious mother hoping to clean her house and cash in. It was the book corner that would beckon to Margaret, calling, tempting. She'd lose herself while flipping through the old volumes, fingering the yellowed pages. She'd eventually emerge, her hair full of dust, a Nancy Drew set missing one volume in hand, as happy as if she'd hit the lottery.

Having this particular memory at this particular time was odd. The general thought was that as you prepared to meet your maker, a jumbled montage of seminal life events propelled you forward. The memory of Aunt Shirley and the junk shop didn't showcase any particular courage or inner strength on Margaret's part. Maybe what actually emerged was a sweet remembrance of the uncomplicated happy things, the little blessings and delights, the times when someone, through small acts and words, showed you love. A time when you didn't have to jump through any hoops for approval, but could just be. Maybe that was how it all ended.

Margaret felt herself drifting away, her thoughts harder to put together, the images before her blurring. She thought of the wallpaper that lined a wall of Aunt Shirley's favorite junk shop. It was a sepia-toned display of ancient queens, each featured in her own square, the sequence repeating across the length of the wall. Each queen appeared at least ten times—Margaret had counted—representing places from around the globe: sub-Saharan Africa, India, Europe, South America, Asia. Each proudly wore her native dress and gazed directly at the artist. After choosing a book or two, Margaret would stand in front of the wall, staring at the queens, wondering about their lives. She loved the wallpaper so much that she asked her aunt if they could buy it.

"What, off the walls?" She'd looked at Margaret in disbelief, then softened. "I don't think so, sweetie," she'd said.

Decades had passed and Margaret had forgotten about the wallpaper, until she'd seen it at her ophthalmologist's office. When the laser surgeon gave her at-home care instructions and asked if Margaret had any further questions, she'd asked about the wallpaper. The doctor shrugged and waved her to the office manager. "A vintage place—online," the woman had said.

Margaret had promptly found and ordered the paper and employed her handyman to install it in the sunroom next to the kitchen. She could see the eyes of several of the queens, their stately smiles oddly comforting, as she lay on the floor. Margaret smiled back, then closed her eyes for good.

FORTY-SIX

David made a right turn onto Don Bernardi Drive, his chest tight. He'd driven through town at a dizzying speed, slipping through stale yellow lights, barely pausing at stop signs. Now that he was moments away, he slowed. His mind ran through a thousand possible scenarios. He knew what he wanted: for Margaret to tearfully take him into her arms, hold him, tell him that this was where he truly belonged. To see her rejoice because her anguished, decades-long search was finally over. To let her look into his eyes and see the little boy she'd lost.

That was his fantasy. The reality could be that Margaret had forgotten about him, or at least gotten used to his absence over the years, numbing herself to the fact that he'd ever existed. There was no way to predict what the reunion scene would look like. Unless he called first, as Regina had always prompted. "Don't just drop in on folks," she'd say, when he was heading out to the home of a friend. "Let 'em know you're coming, give 'em a chance to straighten up, comb their hair, put on something decent."

David didn't want to call first. He had bucked against that rule from the first time he'd heard it. What was wrong with spontaneity? This was a situation, if there ever was one, that required an immediate face-to-face meeting. There. He'd convinced himself—he wasn't going to call. Speaking of calling, he wondered what he'd call Margaret when he saw her. Mother? Mom? He'd never referred to Regina by anything maternal, even though she'd mothered him for longer than any other woman. He'd begun by calling her simply

Regina, but Hersh had put a stop to it. "If you're going to call her by her first name, then you show some respect and call her Mrs. Regina."

The only person David had ever referred to as his mother was Ivy Goodwin. How did the Goodwins figure in, and why had he been with them for so many years? After he got separated from Margaret, the Goodwins must have taken him in, until they either tired of him or couldn't keep him. They'd left him at the airport and moved on, and Hersh and Regina had stepped in. He wondered what they knew of his past, what history they had kept from him. It was a lot to put together, and all he had was a few crumpled, incoherent puzzle pieces.

———

"So you think she took a fall? Or someone pushed her?"

"Hard to tell. Let's see what the coroner has to say."

David overheard the words as he approached Margaret's home. He'd parked a few doors down. Two police vehicles and an ambulance were situated at various angles in front of the house. He said a silent prayer, hoping they were referring to someone else—a housekeeper, a visitor, a cousin—anyone other than Margaret. Maybe she had a roommate?

He continued up the walkway and a uniformed officer stopped him. "Sir, I'm going to have to ask you to turn back around and leave the premises. Only authorized personnel."

"This is my mother's house," he said, unfazed by how easily the unfamiliar words formed.

The officer turned to someone inside and yelled, "The son is out here."

And there it was. He wasn't the son of someone he was about to be reunited with. He was "the son"—of someone he didn't remember and would never get to meet.

A response came from inside the house. "He can come in."

The officer turned back to David. "Go on in. And I'm sorry for your loss."

David pushed past the officer and followed the voices toward the kitchen. A shrouded form lay on the floor. The room of workers grew silent; a couple of the men bowed their heads as David passed.

"You might want to wait," a man in plain clothes offered.

"I want to see her now," David said.

"Alright." The man knelt down gingerly next to the body and lifted the sheet to reveal Margaret's face.

David inhaled and knelt on the other side of the body. He looked at her for a long moment, then touched her skin. It was still warm. He bent down and kissed her forehead, closing his eyes as he did so. Backing away, he took one more look at her peaceful visage. He wiped the tears from his eyes and stood.

David looked around, not knowing what to do. He'd just learned of Margaret hours ago, and now the years they might have spent getting to know each other had been stolen.

He didn't feel like leaving, so he stood around and watched the workers collect fingerprints. He leaned his back against the kitchen counter, then turned toward the sink for a glass of water.

A dark-blue planner on the counter caught his eye. David scanned the pages; they offered a view of Margaret's week. She'd had an appointment with someone named Sheldon Prescott earlier that morning. He saw a cooking class, somebody named Georgia. Then another entry caught his eye. He read it and reread it until his eyes blurred. He turned and ran out of the house, practically stumbling over the police equipment. Now it all made sense.

FORTY-SEVEN

After his errands—and the trouble with Prescott—Hersh checked into a small bed-and-breakfast on the north edge of the county, one with only five guest suites. They could pay cash, deal with just a handful of folks, stay under the radar.

The proprietor tried to strike up a conversation about the weather, but Hersh wasn't in the mood for small talk. David had been shot, Gayle had gone missing, and he'd been followed around town by a detective. All of this was a reminder of something else he'd done, an act he'd tried to shove to the outer edge of his consciousness.

Hersh sat on the bed, wondering where David was now. He'd been gone a long time and hadn't checked in as promised. He hated playing this waiting game. The selfish part of him urged him to just leave, self-protect, and help get David sorted out later. *Sorted out.* It was a term a British friend of his often used in reference to messy situations. When David returned, he'd tell him they needed to get moving, that they'd work on things from afar.

When he heard the key turn in the hotel room's lock, Hersh perked up. David was back and they could figure out—

"You've been lying to me this whole time," David spat.

"What? What are you talking about? And watch your tone. I'm still your father."

"Are you? Because if you were my father, if you really cared about me, you would've told me the truth."

"Son, look, I don't know—"

"Don't 'son' me. You knew this whole time that my biological mother was looking for me. And you knew exactly who she was. You kept that from me, and when I started getting close to the truth, you killed her."

"Your biological mother—"

"Yes. Her name is Margaret. *Was* Margaret. And you knew it. When I brought the ad over to your house, the one that said I was missing, you practically choked on your juice. You thought I didn't see that. You said you'd look into it. Well, you 'looked into it,' alright."

"Son, I didn't—"

"I said . . . Don't! 'Son!' Me!" David shook with rage. "I know you did it. And you know why? Because the calendar on her kitchen table, next to her dead body, was open to yesterday. '12:30 p.m. Lunch with Hersh.' You have lunch with my mother, conveniently forget to tell me, and twenty-four hours later, she's dead."

"She's . . . dead? I don't . . . I mean, I—"

"Dead. Somebody pushed her down and now she's gone."

"David, let me explain about Margaret. It's not as simple—" Sweat was rolling down Hersh's temple. His heartbeat sped out of control.

"Oh no, it's very simple. If the lunch was just you and her grabbing an innocent bite, why did you hide it from me?"

"I didn't hide anything, I—"

"You just forgot to tell me. Right. You killed my mother. You and Regina—I guess she was in on it, too, you lied to me all these years. All these years I knew something was wrong, I just didn't know what. I never fit in. I never felt right. And you took away the one person who could have helped me. You killed my mother."

"David, if you would calm down, I could try to explain. Everything I've done has been for you, for us. Margaret was—"

"She was my mother! And you kept me from her. Everything I've believed my whole life was a lie. Even down to my name, which apparently is Leonard—after my *real* father. The police—"

"You went to the police? Are they—"

"No, I didn't go to the police, although I should have. They'll find you soon enough. I'm outta here. I gotta get Gayle and deal with this mess we're in. Or are you involved in that, too?"

"David—" Hersh reached out for his son, who shrank away in disgust. David went to the luggage rack, slammed his bag shut, then headed for the door.

"It's not what you think, David. Please. Listen," Hersh cried.

"I'm tired of listening," David said. "All you do is lie. And apparently, kill." The door slammed shut behind him.

FORTY-EIGHT

"What do you want, a cookie? Some nice words to make you feel better? Well, I'm not your mommy."

Stone looked out at the Long Beach harbor. The two men stood on either side of him, waiting for a reprimand, his orders, some words to break the silence. He felt like throwing them both over the railing, watching them fall into the unknown. Or maybe he'd just take the leap himself.

They'd failed, once again, to apprehend both Leonard/David and that sneaky Alejandro, the college dropout with street smarts and damn good connections. It was hard to believe the two had gotten away, and if he hadn't witnessed it with his own eyes, hadn't actually been a part of the expedition, he would have assumed a mistake of gargantuan proportions on the operatives' part. The only other feasible explanation was an act of God, a higher power stepping in to save the targets, scooping them up in a huge, heavenly palm.

"Don't you have someplace else to be? Some other assignment waiting for you to fail miserably?" Stone snapped at the goons and gestured, shooing them out of sight. The two men sauntered away. They were helpless without instruction. And most likely out of a job.

And so was he, come to think of it. As soon as Angus got wind of the situation, he'd withdraw Stone's contract. And demand his money back. That was another thing Stone had to think about. He bent over and leaned onto the ship's railing, his head in his hands. He'd deposited the large check Angus had given him for the job, wiring the funds to an offshore account. Getting it back would be impossible. The money had to be dealt with, meaning laundered, so there would be no proof of its origin. Protocol had to be followed, and the funds wouldn't be available to him for at least thirty days. Angus would want the money back in less than two minutes, after he learned what had happened.

What he needed was—he wasn't sure what he needed. For some reason, this particular case had torn open a carefully tended wound and exposed him to the truth about himself. He had failed to accomplish his mission, not because he'd lost his considerable skills but because his heart wasn't in it. It was like being forced by a parent to play the oboe when you had absolutely no interest. You'd go through the motions, make it look like you were trying, but ultimately it was half-assed. Nothing other than your own intrinsic motivation could make you master that instrument, no matter how much you were chastised, grounded, or bribed.

He knew what he needed—a good strong drink. He'd go to the place where he and Anna had gone when they first met. A critic's pick, praised as a "hidden oasis where the cocktails were inventive and the ambience, sublime." It was out of the way, but Anna loved it.

Stone found his way off the boat, avoiding areas that had been damaged by the chase, the accusing eyes who recognized him from the mêlée. He got in his car and sat for a moment, then turned on the ignition. As he drove through the parking lot, he saw a car so distinct that it could only belong to one person. It was a Bentley, done up in an eye-catching deep-gold patina. Angus.

Stone tried to find a path that would keep him from passing by Angus's car, but a maze of cones and barriers prevented that. The exit route led him right past the spot where Angus was parked, their cars facing opposite directions. As Stone passed by, Angus looked directly at him through his car window. His face was deadpan, his eyes lacked expression. Several police cars and an ambulance had arrived, their lights flashing, along with a fire truck. Stone's car came to a stop as he waited for his turn at the parking attendant's booth. He watched Angus scan the scene. After taking a long, disgusted look, he turned his attention back to Stone and motioned for him to roll down his window.

Stone glanced over for a second and then drove on. He knew this insubordination would escalate things, but he was too tired to care. He'd lost his edge on this case, but he wasn't going to be intimidated by some corporate thug whose only skill was giving verbal orders while sitting behind a desk. Angus could throw his weight around at some other sucker.

But he knew this wouldn't be the end of it. In addition to the money issue, he was now a target. He'd been in the game long enough to know how these things worked. He hadn't accomplished the task at hand. He'd been given a large sum of money—money that, as far as Angus knew, might trace back to SPM. Stone knew too much. He and the goons had created a public spectacle. All of that meant there would soon be a bullet or three—the general routine was one to the head, one to the chest, and one to the abdomen—with his name on it.

Stone would have to figure out a plan, and quick. He'd drive back to LA, have the coldest, darkest beer possible, then get a fresh start, make his move. SPM stood for a Latin phrase, he'd told Anna a number of times. "What does it mean?" she'd asked. Something to do with science, he told her. Well, Stone knew a touch of Latin himself, a phrase that epitomized the way he was going to handle this situation. *Illegitimi non carborundum.* Don't let the bastards get you down.

FORTY-NINE

David wasn't a big drinker, but he loved good jazz music. After a long day in court, the warm notes of a baritone sax, coupled with percussion and tinkling piano keys, was the perfect comfort. A hot toddy spiked with whiskey would top it off. He'd passed by the Green Horse, its roof adorned with a life-sized, lime-green ceramic stallion, many times when he was a small boy. The horse had been a wonder to him, a toy of astronomic proportions that was out of his reach. He'd imagined the children of giants plucking it from the roof and playing with it by night, then returning it in time for sunrise.

After learning his new post would be the Inglewood courthouse, just a few miles away, the first thing David had done was head to the Green Horse for a self-congratulatory drink. It later became his ritual to land there, especially after a difficult, emotionally charged hearing. He'd also head there after a big win, like keeping a juvenile from being tried as an adult. He mostly went alone, but occasionally one of the other attorneys or a paralegal would join him.

Today he entered the bar from the back door and walked past the tiny kitchen where the owner's wife prepared tapas to accompany the cocktails. She looked up from her work, nodded and smiled at David, then went back to it. He continued on toward the sounds of the live music, the tones low and inviting. The bar was relatively empty, with a number of free stools at the counter.

"Let me guess—hot toddy? Or are you up for something else today?" The bartender, Maynard, was usually on shift at six when David came in after work.

"Something else," David said. "Surprise me."

"Oh, living wild today, huh?"

"You wouldn't believe it if I told you. I've been front and center, the main character in a verifiable shit show," David mumbled.

Maynard was busy pouring liquids into a highball, elbows bent, both arms working. "What was that?"

David shook his head and lifted his palm. "Never mind. Whatcha got for me?"

Maynard presented an iced drink with a golden-green hue. "Enjoy," he said, and moved away.

David drank his cocktail in peace, savoring the unusual mix of flavors. He'd definitely have to find out the name of the concoction so he could order it again. His eyes scanned the collection of bottles, lined up against the bar's back wall, noticing how they seemed to glow, a trick of the mirror behind him. He thought about Hersh. It still didn't register—Hersh had killed an innocent old woman. He couldn't believe that Hersh, and Regina, too, apparently, had kept a secret from him about his origins for so long and so well. He scoured his bank of memories for clues, for snippets of conversations he might have missed or misconstrued. But there was nothing, making it all the more horrific. If two seemingly upstanding, forthright people could behave this way, what was the world to expect from those who clearly lacked principles?

He sat there, mulling over his childhood, then remembered Gayle. He'd thought the flash drive might offer some insight into Gayle's whereabouts, but it hadn't. Going to the police was the logical next step, to report her as missing. But if SPM was as powerful as it appeared, the stink of it might reach to the highest levels of law enforcement. Contacting the police might place Gayle in even more danger.

He thought about going back to her house but decided against it. He'd gotten all he could from that meddling neighbor, Florence. Going to see Violet wasn't an option—she'd be pissed when he told her about the episode at his office. Maybe he should go to Gayle's school, see if the principal or other teachers had heard anything. Everyone would be gone by now, though, and he couldn't wait until morning to act. What if he—

A couple sat down on the two stools to David's left. David found this irritating; there was plenty of room to spread out. He debated whether to move further down the length of the bar or stay put.

"How's it going?" the man said. The woman was seated directly to David's left, and the man was on the other side of her. She looked at him and smiled.

Too late. To move now that they had acknowledged him would be rude. "Good. Doing good," David lied, nodding as if all was well with the world. What else was he going to say? *Things are actually pretty messed up, if you must know. My girl's missing, kidnapped by goons, and I could have prevented it. My dad killed my mother, and before that I got chased by thugs on a ship.*

He took a long gulp of his drink, finished it off.

Maynard appeared in front of him. "Another one? Judging by your empty glass, you liked that."

"I did, and yes, I'll take another, thanks, M."

"Okay. And you know, I'm closing out tabs right now, my shift is over in ten minutes. If you don't mind."

"Of course not. I got you." As David reached for his wallet, he inadvertently elbowed the woman sitting beside him.

"Owwww," she said, grasping her side.

"Oh, I'm so sorry," David said, "I didn't even—"

"You didn't even what, dude? Know how to keep your hands to yourself?" The woman's date got up and came around, putting his face within inches of his David's.

Normally David would have remained seated and tried to apologize and talk the man down. But this was not normal times, and David was on the edge. He stood up, chest puffed out. "If you know what's good for you," he said, "you'll take a step back and calm down."

"Is that right?" The man drew closer.

"That's right," David said, standing his ground.

"And what're you going to do about it if I don't?"

"Well—" David looked down, not knowing what to say. Maybe defusing the situation would have been the better idea.

Another customer approached and put his hand on the man's shoulder. "See the wood this bar is made of?" he said. "Beautiful, isn't it? I'll knock your head into it so hard, there'll be a mold of your face permanently imprinted in it. It'll be like an inverse Mount Rushmore."

David looked up to see who was responsible for this ominous yet oddly creative threat. He recognized the speaker, but from where? And then, as he came face to face with the voice's owner, his heart stopped. It was the man who'd shot him at SPM, the man who'd chased him through the decks of the *Queen Mary*, the man who apparently wanted to either capture him, or kill him, or both.

The man and the woman moved away quickly. David wished he could go with them. He'd rather take a couple of hearty punches from the woman's boyfriend than the beatdown—or worse—that this man would dole out.

"Look," David started, "I don't know what it is you want, but I don't have it."

Stone held up his hand. "Relax. Sit down, finish your drink."

"What, I get to have a last drink? So courteous of you." David didn't know where the sarcasm was coming from. It definitely wouldn't help matters. But maybe matters couldn't be helped—when it came to this matter, it wouldn't matter what he did. David didn't know if he'd ever, in his life, used the same word that many times in one thought. He was going nuts, for sure—and maybe this was what happened to you before you died an inordinately violent death. You lost your mind.

"How'd you find me here, by the way? Gold star for you—sleuth of the century."

"Ha-ha. I'm not going to kill you. I didn't even come in here looking for you. I came to get a drink." Stone sat down and motioned for the bartender.

"So this is pure coincidence? After everything that happened today? I didn't just dream all of that up."

"No, you didn't dream it. It's just . . . I'm done."

"You're done? Just like that?"

"First of all, I'm Stone. Okay. We should at least know each other's names. You're Leonard, or David, or—"

"David."

"Alright, David. And yes, I'm done. I was hired to do a job, I didn't do it, and I'm done."

"And the job was to kill me?"

"The job was to bring you in."

"Bring me in for what?"

"I don't know and I don't care. Something big."

"Something big? That's all you have."

"I was a hired gun. Literally. Like a bounty hunter. They don't tell us the details."

"So now you've just given up? You're going to let me go?"

"Let's just say I've had a change of heart." Stone pointed to David's glass. "Drink your drink. Chill."

"Well, that's all nice for you and everything, but I can't just chill," David said. "You may be done with me, but they have my girlfriend, and now that you've bailed on the job, who knows what that means for her?"

"Gayle." Stone raised his glass and took a sip. "I know where she is."

"You do?"

"Yeah, we could go there right now and get her."

"Right, and then they'll have both of us. They'd probably double your pay."

"I told you, I'm done. And I may not be a lot of things, but I *am* a man of my word."

David looked at Stone, dubious.

"And let me tell you something else. I quit. And they don't do well with insubordination. So now they'll be after me. Not to mention, they prepaid me, handsomely, for a job I'm not going to finish."

"So you're saying you'll help me find Gayle."

"Yeah, I'll help you." Stone picked up his glass and held it up for a toast.

David frowned, but then picked up his glass and clinked it against Stone's.

They sat in silence. After closing out their respective tabs, Stone and David headed toward the rear entrance. As they were about to exit, Alejandro appeared at the door. The three men stopped, each looking at the other, a triangle of confusion.

"What is this?" Alejandro asked David. "What're you doing with this guy? He was the one who was chasing us. Are you in on it? You must be in on it!"

"Calm down," Stone said. "He's not in on it. Nobody's in on it. It's me—I'm out of it. I'm no longer on the job. I quit."

"Then what are you both doing here together? It looks like—"

"It looks like a coincidence, which is exactly what it is. I needed a drink, I take it he needed a drink, and strange as it seems, we both ended up here." Stone put his hands in his pockets and looked around, impatient.

"Alright, then why are you leaving together?"

"We're going to get Gayle," David replied. "And he knows where she is. Now. My turn for questions. What are you doing here?"

"I was looking for you. I want to help you find Gayle."

"I thought you had to go your own way and whatnot. Mexico was calling."

"Let's just say I had a change of heart," Alejandro said.

David and Stone glanced at each other.

"Apparently there's a lot of that going around," David said. "Alright, then, let's go get my girl."

FIFTY

When she was a small child, Gayle's parents had told her the meaning of her name: *Gives joy.* Well, she was about to give those goons something, alright, and if she was successful, it wouldn't be anywhere in the ballpark of joy. Since she didn't have her phone, extracting herself from this situation was her responsibility alone. She'd gone over what she knew of the layout of the church and its grounds, trying to come up with a plan. If there had only been one of them, she might have been able to burst out of the room and get away. But between the two of them, one of them was bound to catch her.

"Are you about done in there?" one of the men said. The door-knob turned.

"Still applying my medicine," she called out. The knob stopped turning. Gayle almost laughed—her feigned bowel-related condition could put off even the toughest thug.

She looked around the bathroom. It wouldn't win any interior design awards, but it was clean. At the very least, a custodian did a regular, if cursory, run-through. A few supplies should be nearby.

She bent down and opened the small doors beneath the sink. They revealed a tight area, damp from a leaking pipe. Spray bottles, a few worn sponges, and a variety of cleaning and antiseptic solutions crowded the space. How could she use these? She recalled what she said to her students at the beginning of a new project. In addition to the basics, she wanted to instill in them the ability to think critically and be open to their own ideas. This was how inventions like the car, the airplane, and the internet got made, she'd explain, by being willing to accept the odd notions that showed up in your head. Once, she asked them to think of an object and come up with five unusual ways that it could be used, beyond its original purpose. "A book, for example," she'd said, holding up *A Tale of Desperaux*, one of their favorites, "is usually for reading. But books can also be used as a doorstop, a pillow, a tool to teach good posture, for pressing flowers, or making origami." She'd moved around the room, demonstrating each of these things in dramatic fashion. The kids had laughed. "This is how I want you to think about this project. Give me something different, something I haven't seen before. Wow me with your creativity. Catch me off guard."

The advice was applicable now. Gayle took a few of the cleaning items out of the cabinet and placed them on the counter. After unscrewing the tops of the solutions, she raked through her purse until she found what she was looking for. She continued to survey the little room, her eyes narrowed. A roll of paper towels sat upright next to the sink fixtures. Looking up, she noticed that the metal towel bar that was attached to the wall was hanging by a few loose screws. She pried it loose and stuck it in her purse for easy access.

"I'm coming out," she called, hoping the two men would step forward and face the door. She waited a few beats, then opened the door and stepped out into the hall. She kept her left hand concealed behind her back.

"What's in your hand?" one of the men asked.

"Oh, it's just my perfume," Gayle told him. She moved closer. As she got to within a foot of the men, she brought her hand out and held out the atomizer she kept in her purse. "Want to smell it?"

Without giving him a chance to respond, she pushed the perfume bottle in front of the man's face and sprayed him directly in the eyes. A stream of antiseptic mist took him by surprise. Without missing a beat, she sprayed the second man. Both men groaned and set off spinning, their hands cupped over their eyes in pain.

While they were bent over, she pulled out the towel bar and forcefully hit each of them in the head. She took off across the social hall toward the closest exit, but it was locked from the inside, a chain weaved through the handles. She ran toward a hallway with an exit sign, then heard a gunshot. She froze and looked back. Both men had recovered enough from the blows to stand; they had their weapons out.

As one of the men fired his weapon again, David appeared from the hallway. "Gayle!" he yelled, and tackled her, pushing her to the ground. The gunfire continued, and Alejandro entered, ducking, and ran over to the side of the room. He tackled the other man from behind, taking him down to the floor with a thud.

The first man was still firing randomly. David and Gayle tried to crawl their way to safety. Hearing the chain of her purse dragging on the ground, the man aimed in their direction. Stone walked in calmly and shot first, taking the man down with a sole bullet to the head.

Stone and Alejandro pulled the other man to his feet, and Stone gave him a few punches to the face. They secured him to a chair with rope. David and Gayle stood and looked at each other with relief. They came together in a long embrace, Gayle's head snuggled into David's chest. After a moment, he held her away from him and they looked into each other's eyes, then kissed.

"Are you alright?" David asked.

"I'm fine now. I can't believe you found me."

"I had some help," David said, gesturing toward Stone and Alejandro.

Gayle looked at Stone, puzzled. She'd never seen this man before, yet he had killed someone in order to save her. Then she looked at Alejandro, surprised that he and David were even speaking, let alone joining forces.

"This was all my fault," David said. "I should have listened to you guys but I was too stubborn. Too caught up in my own head, my own issues. I placed you in danger, and I'm sorry. I hope you can forgive me."

"I understand," Gayle replied. "It was weird how we came to you, out of nowhere. I might have had the same reaction. And there's no way you could have known they would do something like this."

David smiled. How could he ever have been ambivalent about this woman? "A lot has happened since the last time we saw each other," he said.

"That's obvious." Gayle's tone was droll.

"Let's get out of here, I'll tell you everything."

"Okay," Gayle said, "but there's another man still out there, looking for you. These guys worked for him." She waved at the two men. "I don't think we should go back to your house or mine. How about we go over to Hersh's, figure out what to do from there?"

"No," David said. "Absolutely not."

"Why not?"

"He killed my mother."

"Huh? What are you talking about? Regina died of a stroke, you know that."

"I'm not talking about Regina. I'm talking about the woman who gave birth to me. I told you, a lot has happened. I found out who she was."

"Okay. And how is Hersh involved?"

"He knew. He knew this whole time. He kept it from me. And she lived just over the way. When he saw that she was getting closer to me, and to him, he went over there and killed her."

Gayle was incredulous. "That doesn't make any sense."

"I was there, at the crime scene. She was dead, and Hersh had lunch with her the day before. Didn't even mention it. And that's exactly how you behave when you're guilty. Withholding facts. That's what liars do."

"David, stop. This doesn't make any sense." Gayle looked at Alejandro for support. He just shrugged. "I know Hersh, and I don't believe it. There's more to it than this, there has to be. Did you talk to him?"

"There was nothing to talk about. The facts were plain to see." David said, resigned.

"Let's go see him. We have to hear his side of it, give him a chance to explain. He's been the only father you've known for all these years," Gayle said. "You owe him that."

FIFTY-ONE

After being honorably discharged from the army, Hersh had returned to Southern California and joined the police force. Images of the battlefields—a silent, terrifying, endless reel—took up too much space in his brain. Training at the police academy was a welcome diversion; the level of attention it called for allowed him to turn off the constant barrage of images.

For his first assignment, he'd been partnered with Scott Gentry, one of the more seasoned officers, in a neighborhood not far from his own. The two men had gotten along well. He liked Scott, especially because he was one of the few officers who didn't refer to the residents of the all-Black neighborhood they patrolled in a derogatory way.

One night, there'd been a call directing all available officers to head downtown. A bank had been robbed; the force was in hot pursuit of the suspects. Hersh and Scott sped down there to help. The cars formed a blockade on one of the streets, and at one point, the suspects' car barreled toward them. Gunfire rang out from the fifteen or so officers on the scene, riddling the car with holes, disabling its tires. The car stopped close to Hersh and Scott's patrol car, and after a while had gone by without seeing any movement, Scott yelled "Cover me" to Hersh, and ran toward the vehicle.

The shots fired by the officers, as well as from his own weapon, continued to reverberate around Hersh's head, whisking him back to South Korea. For the first time in months, the images returned. Images of blown-off limbs landing next to him, images of children huddling in fear, their eyes wide and innocent, images of fire and burning and blood and death and misery that continued in an endless loop.

He froze, unable to move. He just stood there, the images trapping him in his head. As Scott approached, the assailant, still alive, got out of the car and fired. Scott's body fell to the ground, and the other officers shot and killed the assailant, then captured the suspect who had remained in the car. A couple of the officers had run past Hersh, looking at him with disgust. "What's wrong with you, man? Why didn't you cover him?"

Ashamed, Hersh had run from the scene, disappearing into the night. He'd run all the way to Northern California, hoping to avoid the inquest—and being branded as a coward. No one would want to work with him. He'd forever be known as that cop who froze and let one of the good ones die. And Scott had been so much more to him than another comrade on the force—he'd been a brother.

Hersh had found work as an orderly under an assumed name in a small hospital near a vineyard in the northern part of the state. After twenty or so years passed, he figured the case was cold and most of those involved would have moved on or passed away. Los Angeles had always been his home. And the city had changed in many ways. Government agencies had bigger fish to fry than an ancient event, no matter how tragic. He'd met Regina at church and they'd gotten married. Still, Hersh never let his guard down, always following the laws of the road to a T, avoiding even the smallest altercation. He didn't know if there was a warrant with his name on it, and he didn't want to find out.

"I don't understand," David said. "If this was about something way back in your past, why did you have lunch with Margaret the other day?"

"Margaret was one of the clerks at the precinct where I worked. I remembered her from those days. She still looks pretty much the same. I started seeing her at the walking park, and every time I passed her on the track, she'd look at me funny," Hersh said.

"She looked at you funny." David was impatient. "So—"

"So I started to think that she recognized me, that she might rat me out. At first, I decided to just wait and see. I mean, if nothing ever happened, if the black-and-whites never came for me, then I was in the clear. But then it started to bother me, the waiting and wondering. So I tried to get close to her, see if she actually did know who I was."

"And what were you going to do if she did?"

"Just talk to her, David. I wouldn't have done her any harm. I would've just asked her to keep my secret."

"Did you ask her at the lunch?"

"No. That was the point. If she did know, I would talk to her. But if she didn't, I wasn't exactly going to alert her to the fact."

"So you didn't go over to her house, then?"

"David, I don't even know where that woman lives." Hersh waved his arm around. "Somewhere in South LA, is all I know. But then she put a detective on me, and I planned to go talk to her once and for all, to clear the air so we could both go on with our lives."

"Then how did she end up dead?"

"I have no idea. The last time I saw her was at the restaurant—Picnic, or Chez Food, or whatever."

"Well, why—"

Gayle cut him off. "David, don't you think you're being a little disrespectful? This is your father. And he just told you something very painful."

David softened. "Okay. I just have one last question. You said you didn't know she was my mother?"

"I had absolutely no idea, son," Hersh said. "When Regina and I took you in, they told us you belonged to a family named Goodwin.

You were a Goodwin. A couple and their daughter, your sister, they said, had abandoned you. Got on a plane and just left without you. That's all we were told, that's all we knew. And I'll tell you something, if I'd known this woman was your birth mother, if we'd known that for sure, the way you do now, with the proof and all, I'd have taken you straight to her."

"Well, why did you act all nervous when I showed you the missing-child ad with my face on it?"

"To be honest, I was just tired of going through this. We'd gone over it many times. You'd see something on TV or in the newspaper about some people named Goodwin and we'd investigate it. Uncle Ricky would look into it. We'd put all this energy into it, you'd get your hopes up, and it would inevitably lead to a dead end. You'd be crushed. I saw you set yourself up like that too many times, then crash to the earth with disappointment. Those people are gone. They've been gone. And I just wanted you to move past it, get on with your life."

"And why—"

"You said one last question," Gayle said, taking David's shoulder.

"I just have to know—why were you so anxious to get out of here? It seems like you were running from something."

"You're my son, David. And you came to me with a gunshot wound to the arm, saying you were being hunted down. And while I may not be your father by blood, I'm your father. You came into our home and gave it new life. I froze back in the day, on the beat, and you don't know how much I regret that. The planet lost a good man. I wasn't going to freeze this time; I had to keep you safe. Even if you are grown.

"I wasn't running from anything, I was running for you. I love you, not *as if* you were my own, but because you most definitely are my own. All this time, you've been going through life as if you don't belong to anybody. And I hope after all of this, you see that you do. You're mine." Hersh gestured to Gayle. "You're hers. You belong.

And even if you didn't have either of us or anyone else in the world, you belong to yourself. You've got yourself."

Tears spilled from David's eyes. He went over to Hersh and embraced him. "I'm sorry I put you through all of that. I'm sorry. Sorry. Sorry."

Hersh rubbed David's back. "It's okay. No worries. It's okay. And I'm sorry that you never got to meet her. She really was a sweet lady."

After they moved apart, Hersh looked at David. "So, are we good?"

David nodded. "We're good. Dad."

FIFTY-TWO

Violet's father appeared at the door of the woodsy cottage in LA's north county as Gayle and David came up the walk. His expression was cordial, but unsmiling. His solemn face told Gayle he wasn't pleased. His daughter's life had been placed in jeopardy, even if it wasn't their fault.

He hugged Gayle as usual and nodded at David. He directed them to the living room, where Violet sat, eyes closed, both of her legs propped up on the sofa. She was wrapped in shawls and blankets, and an IV drip stood nearby.

"We had our family doctor set her up here since she didn't feel safe on hospital premises," Violet's dad told them. "He stabilized her and she's doing fine now. On the mend."

When Gayle had called Violet's phone, Violet's mother had picked up and told her what had happened. A shuttle had dropped Violet off at David's office, where she hoped to share the contents of the binder with him. When she couldn't find him there, she'd gone back down to the lobby of the courthouse and promptly passed out from dehydration as she got off the elevator. Security called an ambulance and notified her parents, who arrived and reluctantly withdrew her from the hospital, against medical advice. She refused to release the binder, holding it to her chest at all costs. It was only when she was safely at home that she let it go, insisting that it remain within view, no further than arm's length.

Gayle and David sat silently on matching chairs across from Violet, watching her nap. Violet's mother brought in tea and madeleine cookies. When Violet woke up and saw their concerned faces, she smiled.

"I'm pretty tough, guys," she said. "They can try, but nobody can keep me down."

"Are you alright?" Gayle went over and sat on the edge of the couch, as close to Violet as she could get. "I . . . we heard what happened. I'm so sorry you went through all that."

"You're not to blame, you didn't do it. Besides, I'm fine."

David leaned in, as well. "Yeah, Violet, but this was too much. You risked your life for me. You could have been killed."

"I could have been, but I wasn't. They did their best, and I'm still here. Not that I would want to run into that Dr. Howe again on a dark street, but I think they have him under control. "But what I want to get to is this." She pointed to the binder, gestured for Gayle to hand it to her. "Mom, Dad, could you give us a minute?" Her parents, who had been hovering in the room, left begrudgingly, looking back as they shuffled out.

"This book"—she tapped the volume's sturdy leather cover—"contains everything you need to know about . . . you." She looked directly at David. "And it's pretty captivating."

"I've seen part of a report," David said. "I was born to a woman named Margaret and then I went missing and was taken in by the Goodwins, and then, after they left me, I was adopted by Hersh and Regina. Margaret and I were part of a medical study and the research had to stop when I went missing. Apparently it was something pretty important, and they want me back."

Violet smirked. "Well, there's much, much more to the story," she said. "It's all in here. I'm pretty tired, so I'm going to head back to dreamland, but you can take it with you. I pulled the overview and placed it on top. Start with that."

David thanked Violet and stood to go, then leaned over and kissed her on the cheek. "I know you didn't always think I was the best person for your friend," he whispered in her ear. "And I wasn't. But thank you, anyway, for going the extra ten miles for me."

Violet pulled David's face close to hers and said, "You rescued our girl, brought her back safe and sound from the clutches of evil. You've proved you're worth it. More than that." She smiled at him and patted his cheek. "Now get going. It's time to learn how magnificent you really are."

As David retreated toward the front of the house, Gayle looked at the two of them, puzzled by the intimacy of the exchange. She wondered what words had been said to make them so chummy all of a sudden. She hugged Violet, made sure she was securely wrapped in the blankets, then turned and headed toward the door.

"Hey, one more thing," Violet yelled. "Tell my fifth graders they better know those state capitals when I get back. I'm not letting up. They've had plenty of time. No extensions!"

———

David handed the binder to Gayle and tucked her into her seat, then jogged around to the other side of the car and got in. He looked at the binder, untouched on Gayle's lap, a literal Pandora's box that he simultaneously wanted to open and leave shut.

"What did Violet say to you at the end?" Gayle asked. "It looked ... secretive."

"Something about me finally proving that I deserved you. And she said I was ... magnificent."

"Magnificent? She used that word?"

"Yeah, that's what she said."

They both looked at the binder. David took a deep breath and Gayle opened the hefty volume. Just as Violet had said, a report lay on top. Several lines were highlighted with light purple marker. *Violet.*

"I've seen this before," David said. "Andrew from the office printed this for me—it was a file Alejandro downloaded to a flash drive. Most of it was redacted so I couldn't figure it out. Violet got the whole thing."

"Here," Gayle said, handing him the report. "You read it yourself. Then you can decide whether you want to share it with me or not."

"No," David said firmly. "I know I want to share it with you. And whatever it is, we'll get through it—together. No more equivocations, no more holding back, no more half-assed-ness."

"Is that even a word?" Gayle asked, smiling.

"To me, it is," David said. "And what I'm saying to you right now is, I'm all in."

SUBJECT 1-022035069904-55532

Leonard Goodwin (in active pursuit)
DOB: 09/21/1982
Hair: Black
Eyes: Brown
Ethnicity: African descent
Current Age: 36
Address: Unknown

Parents:
Father—Leonard Ellison (deceased)
Mother—Margaret Ellison (file inactive)
Address: 43521 Don Bernardi Drive,
Los Angeles, CA 90008

Abstract with Chronology:

March 1980: Subject Margaret Ellison,
33-year-old married Black female and
patient of Newman Gaylord, MD, (internal
medicine) referred to SPM for research study
after initial intake questionnaire, physical
examination, and interview revealed possible

complement-enhanced immunity, which characteristically affords individuals a better response than the typical individual to the common cold and a number of the weaker viral strains. Full laboratory workup, tissue collection, and a variety of tests confirmed said immunity. Tests and examinations continued to determine extent of the condition and applications on a global scale.

February 1982: Subject Margaret Ellison presents to Gaylord for pregnancy confirmation and to initiate prenatal care. Gaylord and SPM work in partnership to guide the pregnancy at the highest level of care. Testing on subject ceases in order to protect the fetus and enhanced abilities contained therein.

September 1982: Subject Margaret Ellison gives birth to live male baby. Child, named Subject Leonard Ellison Jr., is immediately referred to SPM and given full laboratory workup, tissue collection, and a variety of tests which confirm both complement and enhanced killer T-cell immunity, rendering him not susceptible to all known pathogens and granting him enhanced and unprecedented ability to fight and clear all known viral and bacterial infections. Tests and examinations continued to determine extent of the condition and applications on a global scale. Profit potential deemed exponential.

December 1982: Subject reports that her husband, Leonard Ellison, was killed on the job in his capacity as a construction worker.

July 1985: Subject reports that Child Subject Leonard Ellison Jr. is missing, wrongfully taken from childcare. Subject has contacted authorities and placed missing-child ads. SPM assists in efforts to locate the Child Subject and closely monitors all leads.

August 1993: Subject Leonard Ellison determined to have been kidnapped by staff scientist Michael Goodwin, PhD. Goodwin's wife suffers from a newly discovered condition and is severely immunocompromised. Goodwin thought to have taken Child Subject in order to control and develop research for the benefit of his wife. Pursuit of Goodwin unsuccessful despite application of full resources and intel. Search for Leonard Ellison Jr. in school records and similar child databases unsuccessful. Assumed that Subject Leonard Ellison has been renamed Leonard Goodwin. Search for Leonard Goodwin in school records and similar child databases unsuccessful.

August 1993: Missing-child ad updated to current picture of Child Subject, obtained from the school he was attending at time of disappearance.

August 1993 to Present: Missing-child ad continuously monitored by SPM for inquiries. Computer progression technology employed to provide rendering of Subject at current age, updated every five years.

September 2018: Missing-child ad receives hit, from Gayle Holland, determined via IP address.

Current Status: SPM and associates actively seek Subject Leonard Goodwin. Full resources and capabilities to be placed behind this project for the apprehension of Goodwin and resumption of research.

FIFTY-THREE

"So you can't get sick?" Gayle leaned back and stared at David. She turned and looked out the car window, half expecting a doctor, a scientist, an alien—really, anybody—to pop up and make sense of all this.

David took Gayle's hand. "Of course I can get sick, I just—"

"Have never gotten sick. Have you?" Gayle cocked her head. "I can't remember one single time. All these years—not once. Think about it. Colds, the flu, conjunctivitis. That hand, foot, and mouth disease I got when I substituted kindergarten. You never came down with any of that."

David blinked a few times, mentally scanning both his life and his body, head to toe, looking for a rebuttal to both the report and Gayle's conclusion. After a long silence, he nodded, resigned to this new truth.

"I don't even know what I'm supposed to do now."

Gayle smiled. "You're a smart man, counselor. You'll figure it out. And stop acting like this is a death sentence, because it's just the opposite. It's about life and the very special one you happen to have been given."

"I never got to see my mother. Margaret. She died not knowing what happened to me."

"She's at peace now. And just maybe, wherever she is, she now knows everything and is sending you love, the same love she never let go of all these years."

"Well, should I—"

"Well, stop. Okay? You don't have to decide everything right this minute. Let it all sink in. Get used to the idea. You're a superhero. *My* superhero. And not just 'cause you're permanently germ- and virus-free. You came and got me after they stalked you and shot at you and threatened to cut you up in little pieces and sell your parts off to the highest bidder."

David frowned. "I don't think anybody said that, about little pieces—"

"My point is, you're in the control seat now. You have the power to decide how you want to use what you have, who you want to help, and to what extent."

"Well—"

Gayle pulled David close and kissed him, cutting off his words and his thoughts. For a moment he forgot about medical reports and motorcycle chases, kissing her back with a passion that used every perfectly immune cell of his body.

"Mmmm. What was all that about?"

"Just trying to get some of what you've got. Maybe it'll rub off." Gayle raised one eyebrow and shrugged her shoulders, smirking.

"Oh, that's it?"

"That's it." She pulled him in again for more.

FIFTY-FOUR

Deanna rolled over and pulled an arm from under the covers to silence her phone. She opened one eye and tapped the snooze button. *Just five more minutes.* Lying on her back, she inhaled the cool air, then blew it out. She took another breath and examined the ceiling. Her thoughts seemed to be written across it in 50-point font, all caps, calling for action, obsession. *Shit.* She snatched her phone from the nightstand and started scrolling through email.

She zipped past the *Monterey Herald*'s morning missive, even though it would contain the information most relevant to her, as a resident of California's first city. Instead, she opened the newsletter from the *Los Angeles Times* and glanced at the headlines. Then she began her daily ritual, swiping through electronic pages, scanning for articles containing the name Margaret Ellison. Seeing none, she turned to the obituaries. Deanna had begun reading the section a few years ago, when, according to the file, Margaret would have turned sixty-five. When the idea had first taken seed, she'd recoiled against it. Sixty-five was still very young; most people lived well past that, and there was no reason to believe Margaret wouldn't be one of them. But death notices were good sources of information.

Besides, after watching her parents leave this earth, she was on intimate terms with the grim reaper. She'd barely missed being snatched by the curved sickle herself.

Her father had explained the situation one night, while David slept. Deanna was sixteen. "I made a huge mistake," he said. "It was out of love, but it was wrong. And I have to try to make it right."

While at a conference in Los Angeles, Dr. Goodwin had been one of a few select scientists invited to tour a private, little-known research operation. Physicians had discovered Margaret Ellison's enhanced immunity during routine tests, and when she'd given birth, they tested the baby for these properties. The child—with his unparalleled immunity to all known viral and bacterial illnesses—was nothing short of a miracle. If they could harness his immune system and bottle it, so to speak, it would change the course of all human life. Dr. Goodwin had seen the child's biological gift as the key to changing his sick wife's life. Waiting around while the research was done, or for the discovery to go public—these weren't viable options if he truly wanted to save her. He'd attempted to get a position on staff, to no avail; those in charge had tightly closed fists.

He'd decided to take the little boy and bring him back to Monterey, where he could conduct his own research, on his own terms. But he'd underestimated the opposition. He'd deprived extremely powerful entities of their cash cow; they would stop at nothing to find him.

He didn't remember when he'd known they were on to him and were getting close. Since that point, he'd awakened each morning with a lump in his stomach, a lump that told him he couldn't let David—whom he'd grown to love as a son—fall into these people's hands. The Goodwins would leave him somewhere safe, in a manner that would allow him the possibility of a normal life. He couldn't erase what he'd put Margaret Ellison through, but he could do this for David.

Deanna had protested, wriggled away from her father's grip. "He's my brother! We can't just leave him!" She stalked to her room; he didn't follow. She lay in bed, tears running down her eyes as she considered the terrible possibility of never seeing her brother again. She'd eventually fallen asleep, and when she woke up, David's file was on her bed. She'd pored through it and had come to realize what was at stake.

———

After her parents were killed at the bank, Deanna had been placed under the care of an aunt and uncle in New Jersey. She finished her education on the East Coast and took a position as an adjunct professor, but eventually followed her yearnings back to California. She settled in Monterey, dreaming that David would somehow find his way back home.

It hadn't been difficult to locate Margaret. She'd stayed put, probably for the same reason Deanna had returned to Monterey. On the few occasions when Deanna was in LA, she'd drive by Margaret's house, looking for signs of a grown man with her little brother's face. Back at home, she scoured the newspaper. If mother and son were reunited, it would be a big story. If something unfortunate happened to David—a result of the violent people whose behavior had no bounds—that would get coverage, too.

Deanna quickly looked over the names of the deceased, ready to move on. Then she saw it. She sat up in bed and enlarged the page.

> **Margaret Ellison (1947–2018) now joins in glory her husband, Leonard Ellison Sr. She is survived by the son of this union, David Byrdsong, her longtime friend Georgia Barnett, and a host of beloved family and friends.**

She'd found him. And Margaret and David had found each other. She tried to imagine their reunion. Her heart felt thick in her chest; her throat closed up with emotion. She looked around her bedroom, unblinking.

She swiped to her home screen and started pressing the numbers of colleagues in LA. She did a Google search. When she had what she needed, she tapped eleven numbers—and held her breath.

FIFTY-FIVE

"**S**o tell me again why this place is called the Green Horse." Alejandro took a sip of his drink, a Long Island. "Other than that big green horse on top of the building."

"I don't know, man," David replied, laughing. "I never asked."

"I mean, you'd think they would have portraits of various horses on the walls, or riding gear, green leather seats, something."

David waved toward the waiters and bartenders roaming from table to table. "Ask one of them about it, if it's that big a deal."

Alejandro looked around the dark room. One of the waiters was staring at him. They locked eyes for a moment, and Alejandro frowned. The waiter turned away and busied himself with a pitcher of water.

"So I never figured out how you found me here," David said. "Of all the places in LA."

"Went to your office. I decided I wouldn't be able to live with myself if I didn't help find Gayle."

"And they just told you I might be here?"

"No, dude. They wouldn't give me anything. That secretary of yours acted like she was your mother. I told them how important it was, but I still got nothing."

"So—"

"So I rode down in the elevator with a guy who worked there," Alejandro said. "He'd overheard and asked me what it was about. Said his name was Andrew. He seemed to know something was going on with you. He told me you might be here, said you come here on either really good or really bad days. And this was both." He took another sip of his drink, motioned to the bartender to refill a bowl of nuts. "So what're you going to do now? Now that you know the truth, now that you know your . . . gifts?"

"I'm still digesting the whole thing. But when I look back on my health, and my life, it makes sense. And I want to do something. There's a lot of people out there suffering. I could help them."

"Yeah, it's amazing what you could do. The possibilities."

"But I want to do it on my terms, not as some lab rat for the government or some corporation who'll decide who gets what. People who look like us have always been the first to be experimented on. And the last to benefit. That stops now."

Alejandro raised his glass. "Amen to that."

"Andrew, the guy you met, he's some kind of whiz kid. I'm gonna ask him to hook me up with some biotech experts."

"Cool. And you know, I was a student—I *will be* a student at UCLA. I could work with you to find some of the top people in the field, people with the same vision, to come on board."

"That would be great."

"And what about Stone? Is he gonna be involved?"

David looked at Alejandro and cocked his head. "The man responsible for the hole in my arm?"

"The man who let you live," Alejandro reminded him. "And who led you straight to Gayle. Didn't he say he was paid to kill us? He took the money but reneged on the task—remember? He might want to invest some of that money. Think about it."

David glanced around the bar, surveyed the other patrons, then turned to Alejandro. "We should find the other people."

"What other people?"

"The ones on the list, in the binder. SPM wasn't just looking for me. There was a list of people, other files, other reports."

Alejandro nodded. "Right. When I worked there—for all of three minutes—a dozen other missing faces scrolled through the screen.

I wonder what extraordinary things they can do. Whatever it is, SPM wants them, too."

"Your tacos, gentlemen. Let me know if you need anything else." The tall waiter who'd eyed Alejandro moments before arrived with a plate of the Tuesday special. He busied himself moving things around on the bar's surface to make room, avoiding both the men's eyes. Alejandro watched him walk back into the kitchen. The man had an eerie similarity to Angus, but that didn't seem right. What would a corporate monster be doing here in uniform, waiting tables? Alejandro thought about it. He hadn't really spent that much time with Angus, not enough time to memorize his features. This was probably just another tall, bony man. The past few days had been traumatic, and it was dark inside the Green Horse. He was seeing things.

"You should definitely contact Stone," Alejandro told David.

"For an investment?"

"For security," Alejandro said. "You're going to need it."

FIFTY-SIX

"The concert's starting, we should go in," Deanna said. "Groove *is* in the heart."

David laughed at his sister's deep-voiced imitation. He should have known he'd recognize her. She was still the same goofy creature she'd been as a teen. He heard a whistle and looked back. Stone was standing guard in an alcove off to the side. He saluted David, then nodded and mouthed a few words. David caught the sentiment: *Have a good time.*

The ticket line snaked forward. Deanna turned to David. A solemn look had replaced her smile. "You got a new family, right? They loved you, didn't they? You turned out good."

David thought about Hersh and Regina. They had done their best for him. Hersh was still doing that. "Yeah, they did," he replied. "But what about you? Where'd you go after they died?"

"Boarding school back east. I only had a couple of years left in high school. The couple they appointed as my guardians weren't in the mood for a teen."

"So you were alone, too."

"The good news is, we both made it. We both survived. And we have the rest of our lives to—well, for me to be irritated by my little brother." Deanna gave David's shoulder a light punch. "And I want to meet Gayle. Make sure she's good enough."

"I think she'll meet your approval," David said. "Anybody who stuck with me through all of this deserves six gold stars."

He looked at the photo of the Goodwins that Deanna had brought, remembered the warmth of their last Christmas together. He'd been loved by three different families. His childhood had been far from conventional, but he'd had a home in all their hearts.

"Hey, bro, you still with me?" Deanna tapped David's forehead. They looked at each other for a moment, then embraced.

"I'm glad I brought that picture. All of us together," Deanna said. "I didn't know if you'd want to see it, after . . . everything."

David looked down, frowning, holding back tears. Deanna took his arm. "They worried about you every minute after we left the airport," she said. "Right up until their last breath at the bank, they were thinking about you."

"Couldn't they have done something else? I mean, to just . . . leave me?"

"That was exactly what I said when they told me the plan. And they really did try to come up with another way. There wasn't any other solution. They didn't want you to end up a guinea pig. They wanted you to be free. Especially Mom, even though it meant she might die. I know it's hard to understand, but it was an act of love."

"STAPLES CENTER PRESENTS: DEEE-LITE." They were under the marquee, almost at the entrance. Deee-Lite's hit tune had been David's victory song, the one he played when he hit a home run for his Little League team; the day he won the spelling bee. He'd blast it, his portable CD player on repeat. Unlike some self-absorbed big sisters, Deanna had never complained. One evening when the video came on, the singers dressed in retro outfits, colorful swirls moving in the background, they'd danced around the living room together. Deanna sang the song's hook while David occasionally inserted the bass line with the deepest voice he could muster. "Groove *is* in the heart."

It had been Deanna's idea to meet at the concert. She'd offered to get the tickets, said she'd get good seats. She'd kept the name of the headliner a secret, only telling David the date and location. David had resisted the temptation to look it up, a small exercise in trust.

The vendor scanned their tickets and waved them through. David put his arm around Deanna's shoulder and they stepped forward, together.

FIFTY-SEVEN

David delved deep into his pocket, feeling for the key Margaret's executor had given him. Her death had been ruled an accident—a fatal fall. As next of kin, David had inherited her estate. He'd spent hours wandering through her home, smelling her perfumes, looking at his baby pictures. Trying to learn who she was, finding the proper way to honor her. He remembered how the man had tossed the house key to him, casually, as if it was inconsequential, like a complimentary bottle of water. He felt around inside the pocket, the key escaping his grasp, and just when his fingers grazed the cool tip of a ragged edge, it descended deeper, beyond his reach.

He touched something damp and flimsy. He rolled it around in his hand and played an unnecessary guessing game. He managed to unfurl it, flattening the item, then rubbed the substance between his fingers. Paper.

He pulled the slip out of his pocket. It was the missing-child ad, the thing that had started it all. The first time he'd seen the ad, he'd only glanced at the childhood photo. He'd focused on the computer-progressed adult picture on the right, the mirror image. He remembered thinking the photo had no energy, just soulless eyes. This time, he focused on the left side of the ad, the young boy full of confidence, ready to go wherever his life would lead. The boy looked out at David from his stationary place, the mischief in his eyes reaching through time. As if the two shared an inside joke, and David had finally gotten the punch line.

ACKNOWLEDGMENTS

There were many moments when I thought this book would never be finished. Once it was complete, there were many moments when I thought I'd never see it in print. The following people made those feelings dissipate, resulting in this book. I am truly grateful.

To my beautiful crew, Timothy, T.J., Maya, and Elias, I love each of you so much and am deeply thankful for your support. In some ways, this book has been like another member of our household, one you fully accepted, nourished, and helped grow to maturity.

To my parents, Carolyn and Rudy Jackson, for instilling in me a love of learning and providing an endless supply of books. Those early readers planted a seed that blossomed into the call to write.

To my grandfather, Noel Glover. You taught me I could do anything. No limits.

To Tiffany Anderson, Colette Simmons, and Lolita Pierce. You cheered me on when this story was just a few paragraphs long, reading the first few passages way back when and urging me to complete it. Thank you for the solid, unending belief you had in me to see this dream through.

Much gratitude to my family, friends, and neighbors, including Robin Bennett, Kimberley Williams, Vanessa Hoppe, Elisabeth Keneally, Anita Holzhauzen, and David & Rekha Kuenstle, who, over innumerable years, never tired of hearing about "the book" (or at least pretended not to) and continually lifted me up with encouraging words.

Many thanks to beta readers Don Bush, Cristina Trujillo, Noelle Allison, Victoria Clayton, Claire Sheridan, Steve Haskell, Robin Yang, Elizabeth Perlman, and Sibylla Nash. You slogged through the first drafts and your thorough notes helped this story evolve into the best version of itself.

To teachers and mentors Giulietta Nardone at writers.com, Heather Lazare of Northern California Writers' Retreat, and my Amherst Writers & Artists colleagues. Thank you for your honest feedback and balanced critique. Command of the craft is your superpower.

To Mrs. Elizabeth Nunes, my high school English teacher from Stratford-on-Avon (the home of Shakespeare, as you reminded us weekly), for loving every word in every paper I wrote in your class.

To Akiko Tamano, also known to me as "editor extraordinaire." Your attention to detail—right down to the accuracy of the flowers on a walkway and whether they'd be in bloom at a certain time— offered the ultimate in clarity and polish.

To David Wogahn, Manon Wogahn, and the entire team at AuthorImprints—your guidance and expertise has been invaluable. Thank you for walking me through this process, every step of the way, from my initial manuscript in a Word doc to the book I now hold in my hands.

And finally, to the man whose photo inspired this story—may you be at peace, wherever you are.

AUTHOR'S NOTE

The school where Gayle teaches is named Spikes Elementary, in honor of Richard Spikes (1878–1965). Spikes was a Black inventor and a Californian who held more than a dozen patents, including the automatic gear shift and automatic safety brakes. His creations deeply impacted the transportation industry and his influence continues to this day.

ABOUT THE AUTHOR

KIMBERLY LEE, JD, is a versatile writer, workshop facilitator, editor, and creativity coach with a passion for nurturing the imaginative spirit and helping others reveal their own inner wisdom. She left the practice of law some years ago to focus on motherhood, community work, and creative pursuits. A graduate of Stanford University and UC Davis School of Law, Kimberly holds numerous creative arts certifications. She's a teaching artist with several writing centers and leads workshops for retreats, conferences, nonprofit organizations, private groups, and corporate events. Kimberly is a former editor at Literary Mama and her writing has appeared in a variety of publications and anthologies. She trusts in the magic and mystery of miracles and synchronicity, and believes that everyone is creative and has unique gifts to share. She lives in Southern California with her husband and three children.

Learn more at www.KimberlyLee.me